THE
GLASS
WORD

D0720712

Other books by Kai Meyer

The Flowing Queen

The Stone Light

The Wave Runners

KAI MEYER

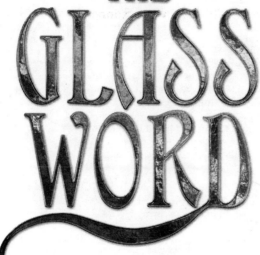

THE GLASS WORD

Translated by Anthea Bell

EGMONT

EGMONT

We bring stories to life

First published in Great Britain 2007
by Egmont UK Limited
239 Kensington High Street, London W8 6SA

First published in Germany 2002
under the title *Die Gläserne Wort*
by Loewe Verlag GmbH, Bindlach, Germany

ISBN 978 1 4052 1639 5
ISBN 1 4052 1639 5

1 3 5 7 9 10 8 6 4 2

A CIP catalogue record for this title is available from the British Library

Typeset by Avon DataSet Ltd, Bidford on Avon, Warwickshire B50 4JH
Printed and bound in Great Britain by the CPI Group

CONTENTS

ICE AND TEARS

The pyramid rose above deep snow.

All around them, the Egyptian desert lay buried under the cloak of a new Ice Age. Its sandhills were frozen rigid, its dunes had become towering snowdrifts. The dust-devils of the old days rose from the plain as ice crystals, circling whirlwinds that danced round themselves once or twice and then collapsed again.

Merle was crouching in the snow on one of the top steps of the pyramid, with Junipa's head resting in her lap. The girl with the mirror-glass eyes had closed her lids. They quivered as if a pair of beetles behind them were trying to get out into the open. Her white skin and pale, ash-blonde hair made her look like a china doll, even without the hoarfrost that was gradually covering both girls. She seemed frail and rather sad, as if her mind were always dwelling on some tragic loss in the past.

Merle was miserably cold, her limbs were trembling, her

fingers shook, and every breath she took felt as if she were drawing ground glass into her lungs. Her head hurt, but she didn't know if that was because of the cold or what they had endured in their flight from Hell.

A flight that had brought them straight here.

To Egypt. Into the desert. With its sand and dunes buried under a covering of snow a metre deep for the first time since the last Ice Age.

Junipa murmured something. She was frowning, but she still didn't open her mirror-glass eyes. Merle was not sure what would happen when Junipa finally woke. Her friend had not been herself since a fragment of the Stone Light was implanted in her in Hell, replacing her old heart. In the end Junipa had tried to hand Merle over to her enemies. The Stone Light, that mysterious power at the centre of Hell, had cast its spell on her.

She was still unconscious, but when she woke . . . Merle didn't want to think about it. She had fought her friend once, and she wasn't going to do it again. Her strength was exhausted. She didn't *want* to fight any more, not against Junipa, or the Lilim down in Hell, or even the henchmen of the Egyptian Empire up here. Merle was at the end of her tether, her courage and determination all gone, and she just wanted to sleep. Lean back, rest, and wait for the freezing wind to lull her into icy slumbers.

'*No!*'

The Flowing Queen woke Merle abruptly from her drowsy state. The voice in her head was familiar by now, yet at the same time infinitely strange. As strange as its owner, the spirit who had taken up residence in her and now accompanied every thought that crossed her mind and every step she took.

Merle shook herself and summoned up her last reserves of strength. She *must* survive!

She quickly raised her head and looked up at the sky, where a bitter struggle was still raging.

Her companion Vermithrax the winged stone lion was fighting a desperate air battle against one of the Egyptian Barques of the Sun. After his immersion in the Stone Light, Vermithrax's black obsidian body had shone as if it were cast in lava. Now the lion was tracing luminous trails across the sky like a falling star.

Merle watched Vermithrax ramming the Barque of the Sun from above yet again as it spun out of control. Clinging to the crescent-shaped vessel, he settled on top of it and folded his wings around both sides of the hull, which was about three times as long as a Venetian gondola. Under the lion's immense weight the Barque rapidly lost height, dropping to the ground, to the pyramid –

– and to Merle and Junipa!

Merle finally emerged from her stupor. It was as if the cold had wrapped her in icy armour, and she now broke it with a single swift movement. She sprang up, took the unconscious Junipa under her armpits and dragged her through the snow.

They were on the level of the top third of the pyramid. If the Barque of the Sun shattered the masonry as it crashed, they didn't have a chance. An avalanche of stone blocks would sweep them down into the interior cavity with it.

For the first time Vermithrax looked up and saw where the reeling flight of the Barque was taking them. There was a sharp crack of air resistance as he spread his wings wide, trying to correct the fall of the Barque. But the ship was too heavy for him to brake it in the air by himself. It went on falling steeply to the depths, making straight for the side of the stepped pyramid.

Vermithrax roared Merle's name, but she couldn't spare the time to look up. She was dragging Junipa backwards along the stone step, always having to pull her own feet out of the deep snow, an arduous task, and she was in danger of stumbling the whole time. She realised that if she fell she wouldn't get up again. Her reserves of strength were almost exhausted.

A shrill howl reached Merle's ears as the Barque of the Sun shot closer, like an arrow aimed at her by Fate. There wasn't much doubt that it would hit its target.

'Junipa,' she managed to gasp, 'you must help me . . .'

Junipa didn't move. There was only that quivering of her closed eyelids, and a faint murmur of sound. But for those signs of life, Merle thought, she might just as well have been dragging a dead body through the snow: Junipa's breast did not rise and fall, for no heart beat there now. It held only a sliver of stone.

'Merle!' roared Vermithrax again. 'Stop!'

She heard him but did not react. She took two more steps before his words registered with her.

Stop? What on earth . . .?

She looked back, saw the Barque – so close! – saw Vermithrax on the hull with his wings spread wide and threatening to veer back again as he faced the wind, and realised what the lion had seen a moment before her.

The Barque of the Sun was spinning more than ever,

swerving away from its original downward trajectory, and was now racing towards the opposite flank of the pyramid, the very place that Merle had been making for as she tried to get herself and Junipa to safety.

It was no use turning back now. Instead, Merle let go of Junipa, flung herself on top of her and buried her face in her arms. She waited like that for the moment of impact.

It was two or three seconds in coming – but when the ship did hit the stone it sounded like a mighty gong struck right beside Merle's ears. The ground vibrated so violently that she was sure the pyramid would collapse.

The stones shook again when Vermithrax came down beside them, falling rather than landing, snatched both girls up from the step with his great paws and lifted them into the air. In spite of the shining glow of his body, it felt cool.

But his precaution proved unnecessary. The pyramid stood firm. Only a few huge clumps of snow broke away from its edges and slipped one or two steps lower, where they smashed into glittering clouds of crystals, briefly enveloping the sloping side of the pyramid in an icy mist. Not until the avalanches of snow settled could Merle see what had happened to the Barque.

Its golden crescent lay on one of the upper steps, only a

little way from where Merle and Junipa had been crouching just seconds earlier. The vessel had landed on its side, close to the next step but one above them. From the air, Merle could see only one slight sign of damage to the ship: a hole that Vermithrax had torn in the upper surface of the hull.

'Put us down again, please,' Merle asked the lion. She was breathless, but at the same time so relieved that she felt new strength flooding into her.

'Too dangerous.' The lion's hot breath formed white clouds of vapour in the ice-cold air.

'Oh, come on – don't you want to know what's in the Barque?'

'Most definitely not!'

'*Mummy warriors,*' the Flowing Queen spoke up inside Merle's head, inaudible to the other two. '*A whole troop of them. And a priest whose magic was keeping the Barque airborne.*'

Merle glanced at Junipa, who was dangling from Vermithrax's other forepaw. Her lips were moving.

'Junipa?'

'What is it?' asked Vermithrax.

'I think she's waking up.'

'*Just at the crucial moment again,*' complained the Queen.

'*Why do these things always have to happen exactly when we can do without them?*'

Merle ignored the voice inside her. Whatever it might mean for them all, and whether or not it would give her one more thing to worry about, she was glad that Junipa was coming round. After all, she herself had knocked her unconscious, and the thought of it still hurt. But her friend had left her no choice.

'*Always supposing she still is your friend.*' It wasn't the first time the Flowing Queen had read Merle's thoughts. She had fallen into that bad habit some while ago.

'Of course she is!'

'*You saw her. You heard what she said to you. That's no way for a friend to behave.*'

'It's the Stone Light. Junipa can't help it.'

'*That doesn't alter the fact that she may well try to harm you.*'

Merle didn't reply. They were hovering a good ten metres above the next step of the pyramid. Vermithrax's firm grasp was beginning to hurt her.

'Let us down,' she asked him again.

'At least the pyramid seems to be stable,' the lion admitted.

'Does that mean we can take a look at the Barque?'

'I didn't say so.'

'But there's nothing moving down there. If there are really mummies inside it, then they must be –'

'*Dead?*' inquired the Queen sharply.

'Out of action.'

'*Maybe. Or maybe not.*'

'Exactly the kind of comment to come in really helpful,' said Merle caustically.

Vermithrax had come to his decision. Beating his wings gently, he brought Junipa and Merle back to the safety of solid ground – if *safety* was the word for a four-thousand-year-old pyramid standing right above a way down into Hell.

He put Merle down on one of the stone steps first. Once she was standing there she carefully took Junipa from the lion's grasp. Junipa's lips were still moving. Weren't her eyes open just a crack now? Merle thought she saw the glint of mirror-glass under their lids.

She slowly laid her friend down in the snow. She was longing to run over and look at the Barque, but she had to see to Junipa first.

'Junipa,' she whispered. 'Are you awake?'

Out of the corner of her eye she saw Vermithrax's shining body tense as his mighty sinews contracted like fists under his obsidian coat. The lion was ready to respond to any attack, and it wasn't just the Barque of the Sun he feared. Junipa's betrayal had made him feel as suspicious as the Queen did, but he didn't show it so openly.

The girl's eyelids fluttered and then, hesitantly, opened. Merle saw her own face reflected in the shards of mirror glass that filled Junipa's eye sockets. She would scarcely have known herself. It was like looking at pictures of a snowman with ice-encrusted hair and blue-white skin.

We need to get warm, she thought in alarm. We'll die out here.

'Merle,' whispered Junipa's cracked lips faintly. 'I . . . you . . . ' Then she fell silent again, coughed miserably, and clutched the hem of Merle's dress with one hand. 'It's so cold. Where . . . where are we?'

'In Egypt.' Even though she had said it herself, it sounded to Merle as absurd as if she had said: on the moon.

Junipa stared at her with her mirror-glass eyes, but the shining fragments gave no clue to her thoughts. Even back in Venice, when Arcimboldo the magic-mirror maker had set them in her eye sockets, enabling the blind girl to see, Merle had felt that the glass was cold, and that impression had never been stronger than now, in the midst of this new Ice Age.

'Egypt . . .' Junipa's voice was hoarse, but not as indifferent as it had sounded inside the pyramid when she was trying to persuade Merle to stay in Hell. A little hope stirred in Merle's heart. Had the Stone Light lost its power over Junipa out here?

A metallic clang came from the direction of the Barque, followed by a grating sound.

Vermithrax uttered a menacing growl and spun round. Once again the ground shook under his great paws.

At the side of the Barque, in the part of its hull that now gaped open at the top, a metal segment swung out and stood quivering in the air for a moment, like an insect's raised wing.

Vermithrax placed himself in front of the two girls to protect them, blocking Merle's view. She craned her neck as she tried to see between his legs.

Something was making its way out of the opening. Not a mummy warrior. Not a priest either.

'A *sphinx*,' whispered the Flowing Queen.

The creature had the torso of a man merging at the hips with a lion's lower body, a sand-coloured coat, four muscular legs, and the knife-sharp claws of a beast of prey. He was so stunned by the crash that he scarcely seemed to see Vermithrax and the girls. Blood was flowing into his pelt

11

from several lacerations, and he had one particularly deep gash in his head. He made several unsteady attempts to force his way out of the hatch before finally losing his balance, rolling over the side of the Barque's hull, and falling. He landed a step further down as heavily as a full-grown buffalo and lay there motionless, his blood sprinkled on the snow.

'Is he dead?' asked Merle.

Vermithrax waded through the snow towards the Barque and looked down on the sphinx from above. 'Looks like it.'

'Do you think there are any more of them in there?'

'I'll go and see.' He prowled closer to the Barque, crouching low, his mane bristling.

'If the Barque was only a reconnaissance vessel, what's a sphinx doing on board?' asked the Queen. *'There's usually a priest in charge of such missions.'*

Merle didn't know very much about the hierarchy of the Egyptian Empire, but even she was aware that sphinxes usually held only the most important posts. No one but the highest-ranking of the priests of Horus stood between them and the Pharaoh Amenophis.

Agile as a kitten, Vermithrax climbed the hull. Only the slight scraping of his claws on the metal betrayed his presence. But if there were really any crew members still alive inside the ship their voices would have given them away by now.

'*Why a sphinx?*' the Queen asked again.

'How should I know?'

Junipa's hand groped for Merle's. Their fingers clasped. In spite of the tension, Merle was relieved. At least for the moment, the Stone Light seemed to have lost its influence over Junipa. Or its interest in her.

Still keeping low, Vermithrax covered the last of the distance to the open hatch. He propped his gigantic forepaw on the side of the opening, thrust his head forward and looked down.

They were all expecting an attack, but none came.

Vermithrax went all round the part of the hatch that was not hidden by the open flap, examining the interior of the ship from all sides.

'I'm freezing!' Junipa's voice sounded as if her thoughts were far away, as if her mind hadn't yet worked out what had happened.

Merle drew her closer, but she was still watching Vermithrax.

'*Surely he's not going inside?*' said the Queen.

Want to bet? thought Merle.

The obsidian lion took a sudden leap. His mighty body just fitted through the opening, and when his glowing, shining outline disappeared inside the ship their surroundings were suddenly grey and colourless. Only now did Merle realise how his brightness had made the icy surface glitter all around them.

She waited for some sound, the noise of a fight, shouting and roaring, the hollow thud of bodies falling against the interior of the Barque's hull. But all remained quiet, so quiet that she began to feel really anxious about Vermithrax.

'Do you think anything's happened to him?' she asked the Queen, and saw Junipa shrug her shoulders. She had put her question out loud. Of course, Junipa didn't yet know what had happened to Merle! Before their reunion in Hell they had last seen each other in their native city of Venice, when the Flowing Queen had been no more than a legend to Merle herself. At the time it would never have entered her head to think that one day – in fact only a few hours later – the Queen would be inhabiting her own mind.

So much had happened since then. Merle wanted nothing more than to tell Junipa about her adventures and her journey through Hell, where they had hoped to get help against the Empire's superior strength. Instead, they had found only misery, danger and the Stone Light down in the depths of the earth. But they had found Junipa too. Merle longed to hear her story, to rest at last and talk to her best friend as they once used to talk, evening after evening.

A metallic clang sounded inside the Barque.

'Vermithrax?'

The lion did not answer.

Merle looked at Junipa. 'Can you stand up?'

A dark shape flitted across the mirror-glass eyes. It was a moment before Merle realised that it was only the reflection of a bird of prey flying overhead.

'I can try,' said Junipa, but her voice sounded so faint that Merle seriously doubted it.

However, Junipa struggled to her feet. Heaven knew where she found the strength. But then Merle remembered how the fragment of the Stone Light in Junipa's breast had healed her wounds at lightning speed. Junipa rose and dragged herself closer to the Barque at Merle's side.

'*Are you going to climb in after him?*' asked the Queen in alarm.

Someone has to take a look, thought Merle.

Privately, the Queen was as anxious as she was about Vermithrax, and wasn't even concealing it particularly well;

Merle sensed her uneasiness almost as clearly as if it were her own.

Just before they reached the far end of the curved hull, she looked down at the lifeless sphinx two metres below them in the snow. He had lost more blood; an irregular red star was spreading in all directions. The blood was already freezing in the cold.

A loud crash made her jump, and instantly relieved her of her fears.

Vermithrax was sitting on top of the hull again. He had taken a leap that catapulted him out of the hatch, and was looking down at the girls with his gentle lion eyes.

'Empty,' he said.

'Empty?'

'No human beings, no mummies, no priests.'

'That's impossible,' said the Queen in Merle's mind. *'The priests of Horus would never let the sphinxes go on patrol by themselves. Priests and sphinxes hate each other like poison.'*

You seem to know a lot about them, thought Merle.

'I protected Venice from the Empire and its leaders as long as I could. Are you surprised I've found out a few things?'

Vermithrax unfolded one wing and raised first Merle and then, with some hesitation, Junipa up beside him on the golden hull of the Barque. The lion pointed to the hatch. 'Climb in there. It's warmer inside; at least you won't freeze.'

He had barely finished before something gigantic and massive rose suddenly from the abyss next to the wreck, and landed on the hull behind the girls with a moist, hollow sound. Before Merle knew it, Junipa's hand had been torn from hers.

She whirled round. Before her stood the wounded sphinx, holding the girl in his gigantic paws. Junipa looked even more fragile than before, like a toy in this beast's clutches.

She did not scream, just whispered Merle's name and then fell silent.

Vermithrax was about to push Merle aside, making it easier for him to get at the sphinx on the hull of the Barque. But the creature shook his head, with difficulty, as if every movement cost him terrible pain. Blood from his head wound dripped on to Junipa's hair and froze there.

'I will tear the child to pieces,' he said ponderously, in Merle's language but with an accent that made it sound as if his tongue were swollen. Perhaps it was.

'*Don't say anything.*' There was a note of warning in the Queen's voice. '*Leave it to Vermithrax.*'

But Junipa –

'*He knows what to do.*'

Merle's gaze was fixed on Junipa's face. The girl's fear seemed to have frozen on it. Only her mirror-glass eyes remained cold and expressionless.

'Don't come any closer,' said the sphinx. 'Or she dies.'

Vermithrax's tail was swishing slowly from side to side, backwards and forwards, again and again. He shot out his claws, and there was a shrill, screeching sound as they scratched the hull.

The sphinx was in a hopeless position, for if it came to a fight he stood no chance against Vermithrax. Yet he defended himself in his own way, holding Junipa in a firm grip to use her as a shield. Her feet dangled half a metre above the hull of the ship.

Merle noticed that the sphinx was unsteady on his legs, holding his right foreleg at an angle that kept the ball of its paw from touching the snow. He was in pain, he was desperate, and that made him unpredictable.

Merle forgot the cold, the icy wind, even her fear. 'You'll be all right,' she reassured Junipa, not sure if her voice would reach her friend. Junipa looked as if she were retreating a little further into some private part of herself with every breath she drew.

Vermithrax prowled a step closer to the sphinx, who retreated, still holding his hostage. 'Stay where you are,' he said in a voice that betrayed his tension. The radiance of the obsidian lion was reflected in his eyes. He couldn't understand who or what it was standing before him: a mighty winged lion glowing like newly forged iron – the sphinx had never seen such a creature before.

This time Vermithrax obeyed, and stood still. 'What's your name, sphinx?' he growled.

'Simphater.'

'Very well, Simphater, then think carefully. If you hurt a hair of the girl's head I'll kill you. You know I can do it. So fast that you won't even feel it. Or if you make me really angry I can do it slowly.'

Simphater blinked. Blood was running into his left eye, but he didn't have a hand free to wipe it away. 'Stay where you are!'

'You said that before.'

Merle saw the muscles and sinews stretched taut in the sphinx's arms. He changed his position, grasping Junipa by both her upper arms and then holding her up in the air again.

He's going to tear her to pieces, she thought, panic-stricken. He'll just tear her apart!

'*No, he won't,*' said the Queen, but without much real conviction.

He'll kill her. The pain is driving him mad.

'*Sphinxes can bear much more pain than you humans.*'

Vermithrax was the image of endless patience. 'Simphater, you are a warrior, and I won't try to deceive you. You know I can't just let you go. Yet I have no interest in killing you. You can fly this Barque, and we want to get away from here. That's convenient for us all, don't you think?'

'Why the Barque?' asked Simphater, puzzled. 'We were fighting up there. You can fly yourself, you don't need me.'

'I don't, but the girls do. A flight through the air on my back would kill them within minutes in this cold.'

Simphater's veiled glance moved over Merle and the lion, and then swept the dazzling white of the endless snowfields. 'Did *you* people do this?'

Vermithrax raised an eyebrow. 'Do what?'

'The ice. The snow. It never snows in this desert – at least, it never did before.'

'No, we didn't do it,' said Vermithrax. 'But we know who's responsible. And he is a powerful friend.'

The sphinx blinked again. He seemed to be trying to decide whether Vermithrax was lying. Did the lion merely want to make him feel insecure? His tail lashed back and forth, and in spite of the icy cold a drop of sweat appeared on his forehead.

Merle held her breath. Suddenly Simphater nodded, almost imperceptibly, and gently put Junipa down. She realised what was happening only when her feet touched the golden surface of the Barque. Stumbling, she ran to Merle. The two of them hugged each other, but Merle did not get into cover. She wanted to look the sphinx in the eye.

Vermithrax hadn't moved. He and Simphater were staring at each other.

'You will keep your word?' asked the sphinx, sounding almost surprised.

'Certainly. If you will get us away from here.'

'And no magic tricks,' added Merle, but this time it was the Queen's voice speaking through her. 'I am familiar with sphinx magic, and I shall know if you try using it.'

Simphater stared at Merle in surprise, and seemed to be wondering if he had underestimated the girl at the lion's side.

No one was more surprised by her words than Merle herself, but she didn't attempt to forbid the Queen to speak out loud using her tongue – although she now knew that she could.

'No magic,' said the Queen once more, through Merle's mouth. And then she added a few words that were not from Merle's vocabulary or that of any other human being. They were in the language of the sphinxes, and they seemed to impress Simphater deeply. He looked suspiciously at Merle yet again and then, as his hesitation turned to respect, he lowered his head and bowed humbly.

'I will do as you wish,' he said.

Junipa's glance asked: how do you know all this? But Merle had to leave her in ignorance for the moment. This was no time for an answer.

Vermithrax, on the other hand, knew just who was speaking through Merle. He sensed the Queen's presence more strongly than any human being, and Merle had wondered more than once what link there was between the spectral being inside her and the obsidian lion.

'You get in first,' he told Simphater, pointing to the hatch.

The sphinx nodded. His paws left red prints in the snow.

Then a shrill sound rang out above the icy plain, so clear and high that Merle and Junipa put their hands over their ears. The screech echoed, vibrating, all the way to the isolated snow-covered pyramids in the distance. The icy crust cracked. Icicles shook free from the edges of the steps above and below the Barque and bored into the snow two metres down.

Merle knew that sound.

The cry of a falcon.

Simphater froze.

Above the horizon rose the shape of a mighty bird of prey, many times taller than all the pyramids, with golden plumage and wings as wide as if it meant to embrace the whole world. When it spread them, they set off a raging snowstorm.

Merle saw the masses of ice whipped up from the plain charging towards them in a white wall like a cloud. Only just before reaching the pyramid did the storm lose force and die down. The gigantic falcon opened its beak and uttered its shrill cry again, even louder this time, and now the snow all around them began to move, shaking and quivering as if in an earthquake. Junipa clung to Merle, and Merle instinctively reached for Vermithrax's long mane.

Panic-stricken, Simphater retreated with his eyes wide open, lost his balance on the smooth hull of the Barque of the Sun and slid over the edge into the depths below, more heavily this time. The next step down did not halt him. Still he tumbled down, his long legs folded. His head hit ice and stones several times, and the sphinx did not stop until he reached the foot of the pyramid many steps and many metres below. He lay there distorted at such an unnatural angle that there could be no doubt of it now: he was dead.

The falcon gave one last cry, then folded its wings in front of its body like a conjuror sweeping his cloak together with a flourish after a successful trick, hid itself behind them, and disintegrated.

Moments later the horizon was empty again, and everything was as it had been before – except for Simphater, lying lifeless in the snow far beneath them.

'Into the Barque, quick!' called Vermithrax. 'We must –'

'Get away?' asked someone above them.

A man was standing one step higher, naked in spite of the cold. For a moment Merle thought she saw fine plumage on his body, but then it faded. An illusion, perhaps. His skin had once been painted golden, but now only a few smeared strips of colour were left. A fine gold network had been let into his shaven skull. It covered the entire back of his head, like the pattern of a chessboard, and came down over his forehead almost to his eyebrows.

They all knew who he was: Seth, the high priest of Horus, greatest of the priests of Egypt, close to the Pharaoh, the second most important man in the Imperial hierarchy.

He had flown up from the underworld in the shape of a falcon after his failed attempt to assassinate Lord Light, the ruler of Hell. Vermithrax had followed the bird, and so they had all found the way out of the pyramid that brought them back to the surface.

'You're going nowhere without me,' said Seth, yet he sounded not half as terrifying as perhaps he hoped, for the sight of the icy desert had shaken him as much as the others. At least he didn't seem to feel the freezing cold, and Merle noticed that the snow beneath his feet had melted. Not for nothing was Seth considered the most powerful magician among the Pharaoh's servants.

'Into the Barque!' Vermithrax whispered to the girls. 'Hurry!'

Merle and Junipa raced for the hatch, but Seth's voice stopped them in their tracks.

'I don't want a fight. Not now. And certainly not here.'

'What do you want, then?' Merle's voice shook slightly.

Seth seemed to be thinking about it. 'Answers.' His hand indicated the great expanse of the icy plain. 'Answers to all this.'

'We know nothing about it,' said Vermithrax.

'That's not what you said just now. Or were you lying to

poor Simphater in his last moments? You know who did this. You said he was your friend.'

'We don't want to fight any more than you do, priest of Horus,' said Vermithrax. 'But we are not your slaves.' The priest was no ordinary enemy, and Vermithrax did not underestimate his opponent.

Seth smiled unpleasantly. 'You are Vermithrax, are you not? Known to the Venetians as the Traitor of Old. You left your own people, the talking stone lions, behind in Africa long ago when you came to wage war with Venice. Don't look at me in such astonishment, lion – yes, I know you. And if we're talking about slaves, I wouldn't want a creature like you as a servant. Your kind are too dangerous and too unpredictable, as we found out to our cost with the rest of your people. The Empire ground their bodies to sand in the corpse-mills of Heliopolis and scattered them on the banks of the Nile.'

Even if Merle had wanted to, she couldn't have moved. Her joints felt frozen, even her heart seemed to stand still. She stared at Vermithrax, saw the rage, hatred and despair in the glowing lava of his eyes. Ever since she had known him he had been driven by the hope of returning to his own people some day.

'You are lying, priest,' he said tonelessly.

'Possibly. Perhaps I am lying. Or then again, perhaps not.'

Vermithrax crouched, ready to spring, but the Queen cried, through Merle's mouth, 'No! If he dies we'll never get away from here alive!'

For a moment it looked as if nothing could stop Vermithrax. Even Seth took a step back. Then the lion controlled himself, although he remained in his crouching position.

'I shall discover if you are telling the truth, priest. And if so I'll find you. You and all who are responsible.'

Seth smiled again. 'Does that mean we can leave our personal feelings aside for the moment and get to the heart of our deal? You tell me what's happened in Egypt – and I will get you away from here in this Barque.'

Vermithrax was silent, but Merle said slowly, 'Agreed.'

Seth glanced at her, and then looked back at the lion. 'Do I have your word, Vermithrax?'

The obsidian lion drew the claws of one front paw over the metal of the Barque. They left behind four grooves as broad as fingers and as deep as the length of the forefinger on Merle's hand. He nodded, just once and very grimly.

Ground to sand in the corpse-mills. The words re-echoed in Merle's mind. A whole people. *Could* that happen?

'Yes,' said the Queen. '*This is the Empire. Seth is the Empire.*'

Perhaps he's lying, she thought.

'*Who knows?*'

But you don't think so?

'*Vermithrax will find out the truth some time. What I think doesn't matter.*'

Merle wanted to go to Vermithrax and put her arms around his mighty neck, comfort him, mourn with him. But the lion stood there as if frozen.

She signed to Junipa, and clambered inside the Barque behind her friend.

UNDERSEA

Serafin and Eft followed the mermaids down into the depths of the ocean. They both wore diving helmets, transparent globes tied round the neck with a leather thong. What looked like ice was really solidified water, a technological development of the Sub-Oceanic Realms which had fallen into ruin thousands of years ago. Serafin had hesitated to entrust his life to that plain globe, but Eft assured him that Merle herself had swum beneath the canals of Venice with the aid of such a helmet, when it was the only way she could escape pursuit by the Empire's allies.

Serafin had breathed in deeply a few times before putting the helmet over his head, only to find out next minute that there was no need — although the solidified water felt like glass, he could still breathe easily inside it. The globe didn't even mist up inside. Once he had overcome the first moment of doubt and rising panic, he got used to it surprisingly quickly.

He and Eft had shaken hands with all their companions, including Lalapeya the sphinx, who was still in her human form. Then they had gone down to join the mermaids in the water. Serafin's clothes were soaked, but not a drop passed the leather thong around his throat. He was convinced that the helmets were magical, or if they really were the work of some kind of ancient technology it had perished long ago, together with its masters.

He had imagined their descent into the sea-witch's realm as a fantastic journey through the deep, with breathtaking views of coral reefs, twining plants and unknown creatures, shoals of millions of fish, shimmering and brightly coloured, almost painfully beautiful.

Instead, darkness awaited them.

They left the light from the surface behind when they were only a few metres below the water. Their surroundings became first dark green, then black. He couldn't see Eft any more, or the two mermaids holding his hands and guiding him steeply down. The pressure on his body hurt but didn't seem to do him any other harm, which contradicted everything he had ever heard about deep-sea diving. It was naive, he realised, to put all that down to the influence of the helmet, but in the end he could find no other explanation.

The blackness around him was complete, like a wall; he couldn't even see his own arms. He might have been floating along disembodied. And perhaps that was it: on your way into the sea-witch's realm you left your body in the cloak-room, so to speak, as you might leave a hat and coat in the world above. It bothered him – no, to be honest, it terrified him – that he couldn't see Eft and the mermaids, although he could still feel their hands. But suppose that was just imagination? Suppose he'd really been drifting alone all this time, in an abyss of cold and darkness and heaven knew what kinds of creatures?

Don't think about it. Don't send yourself crazy. Everything's all right, it will all turn out well.

He summoned up the memory of Merle's face, her smile, her courage, the sparkle in her eyes, the brave set of her lips, her wild, unruly hair. He had to see her again, he simply had to. For that, he'd even put up with meeting a sea-witch.

Below him – in front of him? – above him? – faint lights appeared in the darkness. As they came closer, they looked like – well, like *torches*.

Soon he saw that his impression came very close to the truth. Globes were hanging in the sea, long distances apart, not rigid like his helmet but wavering and constantly changing shape: air-bubbles with little fires burning inside them.

Fire in the depths of the sea, dozens, hundreds of metres below the surface!

Now there was enough light for him to see his companions again, pale, long-haired figures, women whose hips merged into supple fish-tails. Even glimpsed behind the drifting clouds of particles and inky strands of shadow, their faces were immaculately perfect – or would have been but for the wide mouths reaching from ear to ear and full of razor-sharp teeth. But it was not the shark-like mouths of the mermaids that attracted his gaze, it was their beautiful eyes.

There were more of those air-bubbles with interior flames licking at their curves here, and soon he saw them on the seabed too. It was rocky, with extreme differences of height. The fire-bubbles bounced up and down on strange rocky ridges and needles of stone, or floated in invisible currents, while the deep crevices and gorges were lost in darkness. Soon he could see that the surfaces and even the sides of this underwater mountain range were covered with structures: the ruins of walls, buildings, streets and paths. He couldn't tell whether this place had once been above the surface, or whether its inhabitants used to live under the sea like fish, but it was certain that this city had been abandoned long ago.

If it was once part of the Sub-Oceanic Realms, that made it a little less mysterious, thought Serafin. Anyone who had lived here couldn't have been too different from ordinary people. They had needed the same things: walls to shelter them, streets to help them get about, the protection of stone and metal.

The sea-witch lived on a cliff high above this submerged, rocky landscape.

She wound her way through the darkness like a white worm, with fire-bubbles dancing round her like glow-worms, yet she was mysteriously remote from their light, as if her skin refused to reflect it. She blew out a bubble of air as big as the hold of a merchant ship, and then beckoned to Serafin and Eft with thin-fingered, slender hands. Her long hair floated around her head like a forest of waterweed, surging and swirling, never falling to her shoulders. She was as tall as a tower, even larger than the corpse of her rival that Serafin and the others had found on the surface. Her face united the beauty of the mermaids with the menace of a giant kraken.

The air-bubble floated towards Serafin and Eft. Just before it reached them the mermaids left their side, swimming away with a few agile flicks of their scaly fish-tails. Serafin tried to avoid the bubble, but it was already touching him, and then drew him inside it. Gasping, he slid down the curve of its side and came to rest at the bubble's lowest point. Only a moment later Eft arrived beside him. She was still carrying her little rucksack containing Arcimboldo's mirror-glass mask on her back; nothing and no one could part her from it. The buckles were done up so tightly that the straps cut into her shoulders.

The witch's face emerged from the darkness. She pursed her lips into a kind of pout and sucked the bubble towards her. Her gigantic features came closer and closer until they were the size of a house. Serafin tried to retreat, but his hands and feet found no holds on the slippery floor of the bubble. He could only sit and wait as they floated steadily towards the witch's mouth.

'She'll suck us up.'

'No, I don't think so.' Spellbound, Eft looked at the mighty face. It was a terrible and beautiful sight.

'Sea-witches are man-eaters,' he insisted. 'Every child knows that.'

'Carrion-eaters. There's a difference. They eat the dead, not the living.'

'And who's going to stop her finding a way around that little drawback? It wouldn't take her a moment!'

'If she wanted to kill us she could have done it on the surface. But she's just defeated another sea-witch and taken over her territory, which has probably left her in a good temper – if sea-witches can ever be called good-tempered.'

The face was only about ten metres away now. A dozen fire-bubbles floated up to flicker like a crown round the witch's head. Serafin had eyes only for her lips, which were full and dark, not a broad slit like the mermaids' mouths. White teeth flashed behind them, long and pointed as fence-posts.

The wall of the air-bubble bulged in when the witch's features touched it, her nose, mouth and eyes broke through, and were suddenly there in the dry right in front of Serafin and Eft. The witch had fitted the bubble over her face like a mask. Water ran down her grey-white skin, broad rivulets flowing down from the bridge of her nose to the corners of her mouth and her chin. She had the face of a young woman enlarged to the point of absurdity, as if seen under a microscope. Looking into her eyes meant glancing so quickly from right to left that you felt dizzy, they were so far apart.

Eft had abandoned any attempt to stand up. She sat

there, doing her best to sketch a bow. Serafin assumed that the same was expected of him, so he copied Eft.

The sea-witch looked down on them, a great wall of mouth and eyes and terrible teeth. 'I welcome you to Undersea.' Her voice was not as loud as Serafin had feared, but the stink of her breath as it came through her lips like a gust of hot, stormy wind pressed him back against the side of the bubble. Within seconds, the inside of the bubble smelled like the abattoir in the Calle Pinelli. The foul smell even got through his diving helmet. 'What brings you to my realm?'

'We're in flight,' said Eft, straight out.

'From whom?'

'You know what times we live in, lady. And who has put human beings to flight.'

The witch just nodded very slightly, but the movement made the whole air-bubble shake, and threw Serafin and Eft against each other. One of the corners of that gigantic mouth was raised in amusement. 'Ah, the Egyptians. But you're no human being.'

'No, but I live among them.'

'You have a mermaid's mouth. How could they ever accept you as one of themselves?'

'I was young when I left the water. I didn't know what I was doing.'

'Who took your fish-tail from you?'

'You must have picked up her scent on me.'

The witch nodded again, and once more Serafin and Eft were shaken around like insects caught in a jar by a child. 'I killed her. She was old and foolish, and full of evil thoughts.'

Serafin thought of the witch's corpse on the surface, and he was amazed by what the creature before them said. He could never have imagined that a sea-witch was even able to conceive of evil. Or would want to. They're carrion-eaters, Eft had said. But did that make her naturally bad? Human beings ate dead flesh too.

'I never served your rival,' Eft told the witch. 'We struck a bargain. She was rewarded for exchanging my fish-tail for legs.'

'I believe you. When she died she had no servants left. Even some of the other witches feared her.'

'Then it was good that you defeated her.'

Far below Serafin and Eft, the witch made a sweeping movement with her tree-sized hands. 'You know who once lived in this domain?'

Eft nodded. 'The peoples of the Sub-Oceanic Realms

were strong in these latitudes of Undersea.'

'There is still a great deal to be discovered here. The ruins of the Sub-Oceanic civilisation are full of riddles. But I'd have more time to look into them if I had nothing to fear from the Egyptians.'

'Why should a being like you be afraid of the Pharaoh?'

For the first time the witch allowed herself a genuine smile. 'There's no need to flatter me, mermaid-with-legs. True, I am powerful here Undersea. But what gives the Egyptians their power could endanger me as well. Yet I do not fear for myself alone. The Empire has almost exterminated the mermaids. We sea-witches were born to rule, but who are we to rule over if we have fewer and fewer subjects? One day there will be no mermaids left, and then our own hour will have come. The sea will be a dead, empty realm full of mindless fish.'

'Then hatred of the Egyptians unites us,' said Eft.

'I don't hate them. I recognise their necessity in the scheme of things. But that doesn't mean I'm ready to come to terms with them. Not with all the anger and grief they've caused me.' For a moment the witch's immense eyes were turned inwards, lost in thought and weighed down by care. However, her attention returned just as quickly to the here and now. 'What will you do if I let you two go?'

All this time Serafin had kept quiet, and he still thought it was sensible to let Eft do the talking. She was most likely to know how to deal with a being like this. 'The other humans with me,' said Eft, 'would die of thirst on the open sea, and I will not go on alone. I'd sooner die.'

'Big words,' said the witch. 'You mean them, don't you?'

Eft nodded.

'Where are you going?'

Yes, thought Serafin, where in fact *are* we going?

'To Egypt,' said Eft.

Serafin stared at her. The witch noticed. 'Your companion seems to have other ideas?' She put the question as if it was meant for Eft, but in fact she was looking at Serafin now, and she expected him to answer it.

'No,' he said uncertainly. 'Not at all.'

Eft gave him the ghost of a smile. Turning to the witch, she said, 'Our only choice is to hide or to fight. I will fight. And I am sure my friends will make the same decision once they've had a chance to think about it.'

'You plan to attack Egypt?' asked the witch mockingly. 'Just you few?'

Serafin thought of the little company waiting for them

on the surface. He supposed that Dario, Aristide and Tiziano would join them. But Lalapeya? She was a sphinx, even if she had taken human shape. She had already set herself against her people and thus against the Empire in Venice, but defeat had left her exhausted. He wasn't sure she would be ready to continue the struggle now. He wasn't sure why she would want to either.

And what did 'struggle' mean anyway? What kind of struggle could it be? The witch was right: at the most there were six of them – against all the forces of Pharaoh and the sphinx commanders combined.

The witch asked Eft the same question.

Eft smiled, but her smile had an even grimmer look than usual. 'We'll find ways to harm them. Even if they're on a small scale: a guerrilla attack here, a dead priest there. A scuttled ship, perhaps even a dead sphinx.'

'None of that will even reach Pharaoh's ears,' said the witch, 'let alone disturb him.'

'That's not the point. The action itself is what counts, not what comes of it. You of all people should understand that, lady. Didn't you speak of exploring the ruins of the Sub-Oceanic Realms? What good will that do? They will never be restored to their old glory. You'll achieve no result – it's only the will to do something. Just like us.'

'Are you speaking of an obsession?'

'Dedication is what I'd call it.'

The witch fell silent, and the more time passed the surer Serafin felt that Eft had taken the right tone with her. At the same time, he realised that the mermaid meant every word she said. That alarmed him a little, but also aroused his admiration. She was right. He'd go with her, never mind where.

'What is your name?' the witch asked at last.

Eft told her. Then she added, 'And this is Serafin, the most skilful of all the master thieves of Venice. And a friend of the mermaids.'

'You're crazy, both of you, but courageous too. I like that. You are a strong woman, Eft. A dangerous woman, to yourself and to others. Take care the balance doesn't come down too far on your side.'

It would never have entered Serafin's mind that sea-witches could be wise. There was far more behind this terrifying facade than an animal hunger for human flesh.

'Does that mean you will let us go?' Eft spoke in matter-of-fact, emotionless tones.

'Not only will I let you go, I'll help you.'

The witch's words might have impressed Serafin, but that didn't mean he liked the idea of her as a companion – far from it. However, that was not what the witch had in mind. 'My servants will take you back to your companions. Wait there for a while, and then you will see what I mean.'

And so it was settled.

The witch's face withdrew from the air-bubble and sank into the shadows. Serafin made out her bowed figure there one last time before the fire-bubbles around her were extinguished, and the titanic being was one with the darkness.

They went back the way they had come. When they came up to the surface and saw daylight overhead, Serafin sighed thankfully. Perhaps he wasn't the only human ever to have survived an audience with a sea-witch, but he was certainly one of a very few. He had learned something new in listening to her, and his idea of the world had once again become a little wider, more lively and diverse. He was grateful to her for that.

Dario and the other boys helped them out of the water and up on the drifting corpse of the old sea-witch. *Full of evil thoughts.* Serafin remembered the voice from the depths, and now it seemed a little more horrible than before to set foot on the dead flesh of the body, resting his hands on its skin as he climbed up on it.

Lalapeya was waiting for them on the crest of the lifeless fish-tail. The sphinx was not smiling, but she looked relieved. It was the first time since their flight from Venice that Serafin had seen any emotion but grief and mourning in her face.

In turn, they told the others what had happened, neither of them once interrupting the other. Even when Eft said what she had named to the witch as their destination, no one protested.

Egypt then, thought Serafin. And in an absurd, nightmarish way it seemed *right*.

An hour or two later the water began to bubble, and a mighty shape emerged from the waves.

THE HEART OF THE EMPIRE

Flying low, the Barque of the Sun followed the course of the frozen Nile. It was buffeted by wintry winds, but there no new snowfalls threatened to force it down.

Merle looked out through one of the viewing slits at the land that lay dazzling white below them. The once green banks of the Nile could scarcely be distinguished from the desert; everything was hidden under the deep snows. Only a few frozen palm groves emerged from the ice here and there, and once or twice they saw ruined huts with their roofs crushed by the weight of masses of snow.

Where are all the people? she wondered.

'Perhaps they're frozen,' said the Queen in her mind.

Only perhaps?

'If Pharaoh didn't enlist them in his mummy armies first.'

You think he killed his own people to get recruits for his army?

'You mustn't think of Pharaoh as an Egyptian. He was a devil

even in his own lifetime, over four thousand years ago, but since the priests of Horus resuscitated him there's been nothing human about him. It doesn't matter to him whether the people who lived here on the Nile were once his own. He's probably never distinguished between the Egyptians and the people of all the other countries he's conquered.'

A land without people? But who is he fighting this war for, then?

'Not for the Egyptians, that's for sure. Probably not even for himself. You mustn't forget the influence on him of the priests of Horus.'

Junipa was leaning against the side of the Barque beside Merle, with her legs drawn up and her hands around her knees. Merle knew that Junipa was watching her, sometimes openly, sometime surreptitiously, as if she expected to see some sign of the Flowing Queen, for Merle had now told her what happened to her in Venice, very briefly and in the softest whisper she could manage. As soon as the Barque took off Seth had fallen into a kind of trance; it was probably necessary if he was to steer the vessel. Merle had watched him for a while, and then decided to take this chance of telling Junipa the whole story. The girl with the mirror-glass eyes had listened, first motionless, then looking increasingly upset. But she had said nothing, and asked no questions. Now Junipa just sat there, and Merle could positively sense her friend's mind working away.

Merle's eyes strayed to Seth, who sat on a small raised platform at the front of the Barque and facing its interior. A vein stood out on his forehead and then disappeared under the gold network on his head. His eyes were closed. All the same, Merle thought she felt him putting out invisible feelers to her. Once before, on their first meeting, she had had the impression that he was looking straight into her mind – and could see who was hidden there.

She wondered whether the Queen shared her feelings, but this time there was no reply. The idea that even the Flowing Queen might fear the high priest of Horus frightened her.

Seth was steering the Barque by the power of his thoughts. The golden vessel hovered thirty metres above the pack ice of the Nile, not going very fast, for the snow-bearing cloud cover above them was still unbroken, and no ray of sun came through. The muted daylight kept the Barque airborne, but was not strong enough for it to put on any speed.

Merle had expected to see all kinds of strange apparatus inside the Barque, and some kind of instrument panel like those in the steamers that cruised the Venetian lagoon. But it contained nothing of the kind. The interior was empty, the metal walls plain. There weren't even any seats built in — the undead mummy warriors who were usually transported in the Barques needed no comfort. The airship had all the charm of a prison cell.

Vermithrax stood watching Seth closely and never took his eyes off the priest. He had folded his wings, but his claws were still out. His lava glow filled the interior of the Barque with a bright radiance that was reflected back from the metal of the walls. The golden glow burned in Merle's eyes, even penetrated her closed eyelids; she felt as if she were encased in amber.

Junipa was leaning against the wall of the Barque beside her. She had closed her eyes, but Merle knew that she could still see. Those mirror-glass eyes saw through her lids in light and dark alike, and if Professor Burbridge had been telling the truth they could even see into other worlds. That was more than Merle could imagine. More than she *wanted* to imagine.

The task of telling Seth the truth about this new Ice Age had of course fallen to Merle. Vermithrax would sooner have had his fangs pulled out than do anything to oblige his enemy the priest. So before they set out Merle had told Seth about Winter, the mysterious albino figure whose life she had saved in Hell. Winter, who said that he was the season personified, in search of his lost love Summer. She had vanished years ago, he said, and since then there had been no real summer in the world, no July heat and no stifling sunny August days. Down in Hell, Winter had seemed to be only an ordinary human being, but he had told them how he brought ice and snow to the land on the surface. He couldn't touch any living creature without freezing it instantly. Only Summer, his beloved Summer, withstood that curse and counteracted it with her burning heat. Only the two of them could lie in each other's arms. They would kill any other partners, so it was their fate to belong together always.

But now Summer was lost, and Winter was searching for her.

Professor Burbridge — or Lord Light, as he called himself now that he was ruler of Hell — must have told Winter something to bring him here to Egypt for the first time in thousands of years. In his wake, snowstorms had razed the dunes and deadly ice lay over the desert like armour plating.

There was no doubt that Winter had been here. Like Merle, he had left Hell through the interior of the stepped pyramid. But where had he gone now? North, presumably, for Seth too was steering the Barque northwards, and there was still no end to the snow.

Seth had listened to her story without once interrupting, although what was going on in his head remained his secret. But he had kept his word: he had got the Barque into the air and saved their lives. He had even succeeded in generating a dry warmth inside the airship, given off by the layer of gold on the walls.

'*He knows more about Winter than he admits,*' said the Queen.

What makes you think so? Merle asked in her mind. Her ability to talk to the Queen without making any sound had improved noticeably since they went down into Hell. She still found it easier to form the words with her lips, but now she could manage quite well without doing that if she concentrated.

'*He's the second most important man in the Empire, Pharaoh's deputy,*' said the Queen. '*If the Egyptians have anything to do with Summer's disappearance he must know about it.*'

You mean Summer is here?

'*Well, Winter is in Egypt, and he must have his reasons.*'

Merle glanced at Seth again. With his eyes closed and a relaxed expression on his face, he had lost a little of his outward menace. Yet she did not for a moment cherish any illusions: she was sure he was planning to kill them all at the end of their journey. Their lives would depend on Vermithrax, who would have to get his blow in first, for there was surely going to be a fight between the lion and the priest.

Seth's words had struck Vermithrax where he was most vulnerable, despite his strength. They had sown doubt in his mind, clouding his one gleam of hope for a better future. Vermithrax had left his people behind somewhere in Africa long ago, and it had always been his aim, the final purpose of his journey, to be reunited with them. Now his fear that Seth might have told the truth troubled him. Had the Empire really destroyed all the speaking stone lions?

Merle turned to the Flowing Queen again: Do you think it's true?

'The Empire would be capable of such a thing.'

But the lions are so strong . . .

'So were other peoples. And they were more numerous than the last of the free lions. Nonetheless, every one of them was butchered or enslaved.'

Merle looked out of the window. Who were they actually fighting for if there was no one left out there in the world?

In an absurd way, that made them like the Pharaoh: they were all fighting a battle whose real aim they had long ago forgotten.

Seth opened his eyes. 'We are nearly there.'

'Where?' asked Merle.

'At the Iron Eye.'

'What's that?' Merle had assumed that he would take them to Heliopolis, the Pharaoh's capital city. Or perhaps to Cairo or Alexandria.

'The Iron Eye is the sphinxes' fortress. They watch over Egypt from it.' His tone suggested that he felt only contempt for the sphinxes, and it occurred to Merle for the first time that Seth was not ruled solely by an absolute will to power, but had other motives too. 'The Iron Eye stands in the Nile delta. It will soon be in sight.'

Merle turned to her viewing slit again. If they were already so far north they must have flown over Cairo. Why hadn't she noticed? The snow was deep, but not deep enough to bury a city which had millions of inhabitants.

Unless someone had razed Cairo to the ground. Had the Egyptian people perhaps come together there to resist when Pharaoh and the priests of Horus seized power? The idea that such a great city and all its inhabitants could have been completely destroyed took Merle's breath away.

Junipa's voice brought her back from her thoughts. 'What are you going to do in the sphinxes' fortress?' she asked the priest.

Seth looked at Junipa expressionlessly for a moment. 'You're a clever child. No wonder they gave you those mirror-glass eyes. Your friends have probably been wondering what *they* are going to do in the Iron Eye. But you ask what sends *me* there. And that's the point, don't you think?'

Merle wasn't sure she understood what he was talking about. She cast a glance at her friend, but Junipa made no sign to show what was going on in her mind. Only when she went on did Merle realise what she was getting at – and saw that she was right.

'You don't like the sphinxes,' said Junipa. 'I can see that.'

For the fraction of a second Seth appeared surprised. But he was back in control of himself next moment. 'Perhaps.'

'You're not here because the sphinxes are your friends. You won't ask the sphinxes for help in killing us either.'

'Do you really think I'd need help with that?'

'Yes,' said Vermithrax. It was the first time he had spoken for hours. 'I certainly do.'

The two adversaries glared at each other, but neither felt like stepping up the quarrel – not here, not now.

Once again it was Junipa who defused the tense situation. Her soft, perfectly composed voice called for Seth's attention. 'You tried to kill Lord Light, and you're coming back from Hell to a country that has turned to a desert of ice. Why don't you go to Pharaoh's court first, or the temple of the priests of Horus? Why straight to the sphinxes' fortress? It seems odd to me.'

'And what does it all mean in your opinion, little mirror-glass girl?'

'A fire in your heart,' she said mysteriously.

Merle stared at Junipa before her eyes met the obsidian lion's. For a moment astonishment drove the chill from Vermithrax's gaze.

Seth put his head on one side. 'A fire?'

'Of love. Or hate.' Junipa's mirror-glass eyes shone in the lion's golden radiance. 'More likely hate.'

The priest said nothing, but thought about it.

Junipa's voice went on. 'I think a fire of vengeance. You hate the sphinxes, and you're here to destroy them.'

'*By all the gods!*' murmured the Flowing Queen in Merle's mind.

Vermithrax was still listening attentively, and his eyes went from Junipa back to Seth. 'Is that true?'

The priest of Horus ignored the lion. Not even Merle, whom he had been watching before, seemed to matter to him now. He might have been alone in the Barque with Junipa.

'You really are a remarkable creature, little mirror-glass girl.'

'My name is Junipa.'

'Junipa,' he slowly repeated. 'Very remarkable.'

'You're not the Pharaoh's right-hand man any more, are you? You lost everything when you failed to kill Lord Light down there.' Deep in thought, Junipa was twisting a strand of her ash-blonde hair between thumb and forefinger. 'I know I'm right. Sometimes I see not just the surface but the heart of things.'

Seth took a deep breath. 'Pharaoh betrayed the priests of Horus. He gave me the task of assassinating Lord Light. The sphinxes prophesied to Amenophis that someone would come from Hell and destroy him. So he wanted me to kill Lord Light – and preferably die myself at the same time. Amenophis had all my priests arrested, and he threatened to execute them if my mission did not succeed.'

'Ah,' said Vermithrax with relish, 'and you failed. Congratulations.'

Seth looked daggers at him, but did not reply. Instead, he went on, 'I am sure Amenophis already knows that Lord Light is still alive.' He lowered his eyes, and Merle almost wished she could feel sorry for him. 'My priests are dead by now. The cult of Horus no longer exists. I am the only one of us left. And the sphinxes have taken our place at Pharaoh's side. They planned it that way from the first. We were to revive Amenophis and lay the foundations of the Empire, and then the sphinxes would reap the fruits of our labours. They waited in the background until the time was ripe to bring Pharaoh over to their side. They induced him to betray us. The sphinxes have used Amenophis, and they used us too. We were manipulated without knowing it. Or no, that's not quite true. Others did warn me, but I dismissed their advice. I didn't want to admit that the sphinxes were playing a double game. Yet it always came out the same way: the Empire was to conquer the world and then the sphinxes would take over the Empire. They made us all their servants, and I was the most simple-minded of all, because I shut my eyes to the truth. And my priests had to pay for my mistake.'

'And now you're on the way to revenge yourself on the sphinxes,' said Junipa.

Seth nodded. 'That at least I can do.'

'*My heart bleeds for him,*' remarked the Queen sarcastically.

Merle ignored this. 'How are you going to destroy the sphinxes?'

Seth seemed almost a little alarmed to have spoken so freely. He, the high priest of Horus, destroyer of countless lands, butcher of whole nations, had told a couple of children and an embittered stone lion what he really thought.

'I don't know yet,' he said after a moment's thoughtful silence. 'But I shall find a way.'

Vermithrax snorted scornfully, but not as loud as he probably would have done *before* Seth's confession. He too had been surprised by the priest's frankness, even a little impressed.

Yet no one made the mistake of regarding Seth as an ally. He would sacrifice them all at the first opportunity if it gave him any kind of advantage. This was a man who had destroyed tens of thousands of lives with a wave of his hand, a man at whose brief command cities had burned down, who had ordered the graveyards of whole nations to be desecrated to make mummy warriors of the corpses.

Seth was no ally.

Seth was the Devil himself.

'*Good*,' said the Flowing Queen. '*I was just thinking he'd wind you all round his little finger with that amusing little tragic act of his!*'

Merle reached for Junipa's hand. 'What else do you know about him?' she asked, ignoring Seth's blazing glance.

The mirror-glass eyes reflected Vermithrax's golden glow so intensely that Merle's reflection burned out in them like an insect in a candle flame. 'He is a wicked man,' said Junipa, 'but the sphinxes are infinitely worse.'

Seth sketched a mock bow.

'That will look good on your tombstone,' said Vermithrax grimly.

'I shall make sure it's carved out of your obsidian flank,' retorted the priest.

Vermithrax scraped the floor of the Barque with one paw, but abstained from any further verbal fencing. He preferred fighting with his bared claws to this kind of hair-splitting.

Merle looked at Junipa for a moment with growing anxiety, and then her eyes went to the window – and the monstrous shape rising from the ice out there above the delta.

'Is *that* the Iron Eye?'

Seth did not look out; his gaze was fixed on Merle. No one needed any confirmation. They all knew the answer.

Junipa too pressed her face to the narrow pane. Frost-flowers had formed around the viewing slit, fine branching fingers groping for their reflection in her eyes.

At first it looked like a mountain, a tapering cone of ice and snow, an unnatural fold in the flat landscape, as if someone had crumpled the horizon like a piece of paper. On coming closer, Merle could make out details. The structure ahead of them was shaped like a pyramid, but with a steeper slope to its sides, and the top was flattened as if someone had cut it off with a scythe. Where the cap of the pyramid should have been a collection of towers and gables, balconies, balustrades and pillared arcades rose from the snowdrifts. Whatever was concealed inside the Iron Eye, its *real* eye was up there. To Merle, it resembled the look-out of a gigantic ship surveying the land below, perhaps the entire Empire. The colossal building itself – was it made of steel, or stone, or was it really iron? – looked to Merle utilitarian, unadorned, without any unnecessary decoration. But the structures on top of it were improbably elegant: fantastic, lavishly ornamented buildings, narrow bridges, extravagantly framed windows. If there was a place where the sphinxes really *lived*, rather than just a place where they ruled and governed, then it was here on the summit of the Iron Eye.

The fortress was tall, perhaps reaching high into the sky, but the cloud cover was as grey and heavy overhead as it had been all the way. The Iron Eye might be all-powerful, but it was not supernatural, not heavenly.

The sphinxes are far more wicked than Seth. Merle heard Junipa's words once more, a whispering echo in her mind.

The Barque circled the entire complex, describing a wide arc. Merle wasn't sure what Seth's idea was. Did he want to impress them with a final display of his magic powers? Or was he anxious to demonstrate the power of the sphinxes as shown by the fortress? Was it a warning?

He finally steered the Barque into one of the countless openings in the south side of the Eye, horizontal loopholes in the snow-covered slopes of the walls. As they came closer, Merle saw a whole squadron of Barques of the Sun inside.

A dozen reconnaissance vessels were cruising around the fortress, checking the frozen arms of the river delta. But their movements were ponderous; the cloudy sky had robbed the much-feared Barques of the Sun of their agility in the air. They were lame ducks rather than birds of prey.

'What are you going to do now?' asked Merle.

Seth closed his eyes again, concentrating on the approach flight. 'I have to land the Barque in the hangar.'

'But they'll see us there when we get out.'

'That's not my problem.'

Vermithrax took a step towards Seth. 'It easily could be.'

Once again the priest opened his eyes, but he turned them on Junipa, not the lion who was threatening him. 'I could try to land on top of the platform. The patrols will notice, but if we're lucky we'll have disappeared among the buildings by then.'

'*Why is he risking his life for us?*' asked the Queen suspiciously.

'It's some kind of trick,' Vermithrax growled.

Seth shrugged his shoulders, his eyes closed again. 'Do you have a better suggestion?'

'Get us away from here,' said the lion.

'And what about the truth you're looking for?' Seth smiled. 'Where else will you find it?'

That silenced Vermithrax. Merle and Junipa said no more either. They had the choice of being put down in the snow again, or hiding somewhere in the Iron Eye until they had all agreed on some sensible plan.

The Barque banked just outside the entrance to the hangar, rose again and spiralled upwards. Merle tried to keep her eye on the patrols, but she had a limited view from the narrow viewing slit, and she could make out only individual crescent ships in the distance. Finally she gave up. She would have to resign herself to putting her life in Seth's hands for the moment.

It took the Barque some minutes to reach its destination. Merle moved over to the other side of the airship so that she could get a better view of the buildings. A thick layer of snow lay on all the roofs, balconies and ledges, and the outer edge of the platform, which had no structures on it, was so deep in snow that Merle wondered whether they would be able to leave the Barque at all. It would be next to impossible to run from their adversaries in such snowdrifts.

Seth brought the Barque of the Sun down. It landed gently on the snow, with a crunching sound as the crust of ice broke. The first buildings were about twenty metres away from them. Merle saw high, narrow alleys through the viewing slit. Given the countless rooftops and towers they had seen from the air, this must be a positive labyrinth of passageways and paths.

Instinctively, Merle thought of Serafin and how, master thief that he was, he would have known how to move around such a maze of alleys better than any of them.

She thought how much she missed him, too.

'Out of here!' Seth's voice obliterated Serafin's face from her mind. 'Out of here, *quick*!'

Then she ran. Sometimes holding Junipa's hand, sometimes on her own, then back with Junipa again. Stumbling. Freezing. Not daring to look up for fear of seeing a Barque descending on them. Only when they reached cover behind a wall, one by one, with even Seth and Vermithrax moving together almost in harmony, did Merle dare to breathe again.

'Now what?' The lion stared at the edge of the platform, where the glittering snowfield came to an abrupt end against the grey of the cloudy abyss.

'You can go where you like.' Seth glanced sideways first at Merle and then at Junipa. The intent way he had kept looking at Junipa in the Barque had not escaped Merle's notice. Now he was doing it again out here, and she didn't like it in the least.

Junipa herself did not notice. She had put one hand flat

against the wall of the building, and now a suppressed groan rose from her throat. She jerked her arm back and stared at the palm of her hand – it was bright red, and drops of blood glistened on the ball of it.

'Iron,' said Vermithrax, as Merle bent over Junipa's hand with concern. 'The walls really *are* made of iron.'

Seth smiled to himself.

The lion snuffled at the wall, a finger's breadth away from it. 'Don't touch! It's so cold that your skin will stick to it!' Only now did he seem to realise that Junipa had already made exactly that mistake. 'Are you all right?' he asked her.

Merle was dabbing the blood off Junipa's hand with her sleeve. There wasn't much, and it had stopped flowing. Junipa had been lucky. Apart from a few places where the thin upper layer of skin had stuck to the ice-cold iron and come away, she was uninjured. It would have taken a couple of days for a normal person to be able to clench that hand into a fist again, but Junipa had a chip of the Stone Light inside her. Merle had seen with her own eyes how quickly Junipa's wounds healed.

'It'll be fine,' Merle said quietly.

Seth pushed past Merle, took Junipa's hand in his own,

whispered something and let it go again. After that the red patch faded, and the edges of the scraps of skin had closed up again.

Merle stared at her friend's hand. Why is he doing this? she wondered. Why is he helping us?

'*Not us,*' said the Flowing Queen. '*Junipa.*'

What does he want from her?

'*I don't know.*'

Merle wasn't sure whether to believe her. The Queen still had too many secrets from her, and when she really thought about it more and more riddles kept adding to them. Merle didn't even try to hide these thoughts from her invisible guest. The Queen might as well know that she didn't trust her.

'*Seth is playing a double game,*' said the Queen. Suspicion stirred in Merle's mind again. Was she trying to divert attention from herself?

The priest had turned away from the little group and was hurrying through the snow, bending low, to a door leading into one of the buildings: a tall tower with a flat roof. Its surface was covered with a bizarre frost-flower pattern. At first sight you couldn't see that the crust of ice hid shining metal.

'Wait!' Vermithrax called after the priest of Horus, but Seth acted as if he hadn't heard the lion. He stopped only just outside the door, and looked briefly back.

'I can do without a bunch of children and *animals*.' The way he emphasised the word was an open declaration of war. 'Do whatever you like, but don't keep running after me.'

Merle and Junipa exchanged glances. It was so cold out here; the wind cut like broken glass. They had to get inside the fortress, whatever Seth thought.

With two smooth strides, Vermithrax caught up with the priest and simply thrust him aside, a little more roughly than was absolutely necessary. When he saw that the door was barred he pushed it in with one blow of his paw. Merle saw that the lock was broken and the door was made of wood. Only its surface was covered with a reflecting metal alloy. Presumably the walls were constructed in the same way and were not really solid iron, as she had thought so far. In fact she wasn't sure whether ordinary iron could reflect images like this; it was probably some other metal. Real iron existed here only in the name of the fortress.

'Very discreetly done!' remarked Seth sarcastically, walking past Vermithrax and into the building. Beyond the door, a short entrance hall led to a stairway going down.

It was all silver reflections; the walls, the floor, the ceiling. In here the mirrors were not metal but silvered glass. They saw themselves reflected in the walls of the passage, clearly and without any noticeable distortion. Since the mirror glass lined both walls of the corridor, their reflections marched on into infinity, a whole army of Merles, Junipas, Seths and obsidian lions.

In this multiplication of mirror images the radiance shed by Vermithrax shone like a sun, a whole series of suns, and the brightness that had been very useful to them until now – a constant source of light entirely independent of lamps or torches – was a liability here, an alarm signal to everyone who approached them.

The steps of the stairs were broader than in a human building. The distance between them must have been meant for the four lion paws of a sphinx, and the height of the individual steps was enormous too. Only Vermithrax could manage their unusual dimensions, so he took Merle and Junipa on his back, and watched Seth with satisfaction, for the priest was soon sweating with the effort.

'Where are we going?' asked Merle.

'*I'd like to know that too,*' said the Queen.

'Down,' replied Seth, who was ahead of the others.

'Oh yes?'

'I didn't ask you to come with me.'

Vermithrax tapped his shoulder with one wing tip. 'Down where?' he asked forcefully.

The priest stopped, and for a moment such anger flashed in his eyes that Merle felt Vermithrax bracing his muscles beneath his pelt. She wasn't even sure if it was just anger raging in the priest's head; perhaps it was magic, black, evil, deadly magic.

But Seth cast no spell on them. Instead, he glared at Vermithrax for a moment longer, and then said quietly, 'It will soon be swarming with sphinxes up here. Someone is sure to have seen us landing on the platform. And I don't want to be around when they arrive. It will be easier to hide further down. Do you seriously think the sphinxes are so stupid they'll fail to see a thousand lions shining like the full moon, and presumably endowed with as few brains?' And he pointed to the endless series of reflections of Vermithrax in the stairwell all around them.

Before the obsidian lion could say anything, Seth was on his way down again. Vermithrax growled and followed him. As they leaped faster down the stairs, Merle watched herself and Junipa in the mirrors. The sight gave her a headache and made her dizzy, yet she couldn't resist the fascination of such apparent infinity.

She remembered the magic water mirror in her pocket again, and the mirror phantom that had been caught in it since the beginning of their journey. Taking out the shimmering oval, she glanced into it. Junipa was looking over her shoulder.

'So you still have it,' remarked Junipa.

'Of course.'

'Do you remember when I looked right through it?'

Merle nodded.

'And I didn't want to tell you what I saw there?'

'Will you tell me now?' asked Merle.

They both looked at the moving surface of the water mirror for a moment longer, studying their own rippling faces.

'A sphinx,' said Junipa, so quietly that Seth couldn't hear them. 'There was a sphinx on the other side. A woman with a lion's body.'

Merle lowered the mirror until its cool back was resting on her thigh. 'Seriously?'

'I don't make jokes,' said Junipa sadly. 'I haven't made jokes for a long time.'

'But why –?' Merle broke off. Until now she had thought

that the hand reaching out to her on the other side of the water mirror when she thrust her fingers into it belonged to her mother. The mother she had never known.

But – a sphinx?

'Perhaps it was some kind of warning?' she said. 'A glimpse into the future?'

'Perhaps.' Junipa didn't sound convinced. 'The sphinx was standing in a room full of yellow curtains wafting in the air. She was very beautiful. And she had dark hair, just like you.'

'What do you mean?'

Junipa hesitated. 'Nothing. At least, I don't think so.'

'You do.'

'I don't know.'

'Do you really think my mother was a sphinx?' Merle swallowed, and tried to laugh at the same time, but it was a dismal failure. 'That's just nonsense.'

'What I saw *was* a sphinx, Merle. I didn't say it was your mother. Or anyone else you'd be likely to know.'

Merle gazed in silence at the mirror that had been with her all her life. She had cherished it as the apple of her eye. Her parents had put it in the wicker basket with her when they left Merle afloat on the canals of Venice as a newborn baby, and it had been her only link with her origins, her one point of reference. But now she felt as if its reflections were a little darker, a little stranger.

'I shouldn't have said anything,' said Junipa unhappily.

'Yes, you were right to.'

'I didn't want to frighten you.'

'I'm glad to know.' But what did she really know?

Behind Merle's shoulder, Junipa shook her head. 'Perhaps it was just a random picture. We neither of us have any idea what it really means.'

Merle sighed, and was about to put the mirror away again when, once more, she thought of the phantom caught there: a milky breath flitting back and forth over the watery surface.

She gently touched the water in the mirror with her fingertips. Not far enough to break through the surface. Very, very softly.

'*There's someone around*,' said the Flowing Queen.

Silence.

'*Everywhere*,' said the Flowing Queen, and for a moment she sounded almost panic-stricken. '*Someone . . . someone here!*'

'Here?' whispered Merle.

Vermithrax noticed that something was happening on

his back and briefly bent his head without turning it, so as not to draw Seth's attention to whatever the two girls were doing.

'Hello?' whispered Merle.

A single syllable sounded in her mind, and then blurred to a whisper and a hiss.

Was that you? she asked the Queen, although she already guessed the answer.

'*No.*'

She tried again, with the same result. The voice from the mirror was too indistinct. Merle knew what the trouble was: her fingers had dipped too deep into the water. As Vermithrax climbed down the steps, it was impossible to keep them still enough to touch only the surface of the mirror very lightly – but that was what it seemed she must do to hear the phantom's voice. She was annoyed with herself for not trying before. But when? She hadn't had a quiet moment or a real chance to stop and get her breath back since her flight from Venice.

'Later,' she whispered, withdrawing her fingers and slipping the mirror back into the buttoned pocket of her dress. 'It doesn't work here,' she told Junipa. 'We're moving too much.'

'There's something wrong,' Seth suddenly said.

Vermithrax slowed down. 'What do you mean?'

'Why haven't we met anyone?'

'People say there aren't so very many sphinxes,' said Merle, shrugging. 'At least, that's what we were always told.'

'True,' said Seth. 'No more than two or three hundred. They've stopped reproducing.'

'*They never did reproduce*,' said the Queen.

How come you know so much about them? Merle asked.

'*Just old stories*.' For the first time Merle really thought she had caught the Queen out telling a lie.

Seth went on, 'But there are still enough to man their own fortress.'

'If even the Barques are being steered by sphinxes now, quite a lot must be somewhere else,' said Merle.

'Even leaving out those in Venice or at the court of Heliopolis, though, there should still be well over a hundred in the fortress. It's unusual for everything to be so deathly quiet here, of all places.'

'Maybe we should be glad of it instead of worrying,' suggested Vermithrax, whose natural inclination was to contradict everything Seth said.

The priest lowered his voice. 'Yes, maybe.'

'Anyway, there were patrols outside,' said Merle. 'So the sphinxes must be somewhere.'

Seth nodded and went on. They must have climbed about fifty metres down by now, but there was no end to the stairs. Once or twice Merle managed to cast a glance over the balustrade, but there were only more and more mirrors shining down below. It was impossible to see where the staircase ended.

And then, completely unexpectedly, they reached the foot of the stairs.

The stairwell led to a hall lined with mirrors, like everything else in this fortress. The walls were made of countless reflective surfaces, like the facets of an insect's eyes.

'I wonder who cleans all this glass,' murmured Merle, but she was only covering up the fear that she felt for their surroundings. The hall was empty and seemed to be circular, but the mirrors reflecting each other back a thousand times made it impossible to see its dimensions clearly. They might as well have been wandering in a mirrored labyrinth of narrow corridors. Vermithrax's radiance, shining back at them from all directions, didn't make matters any easier but left them permanently dazzled. Only Junipa was not disturbed by it; she looked straight through the brightness and the illusion of duplicating mirrors with her own mirror-glass eyes.

Someone roared an order.

For a moment Merle thought it was Seth. Then she saw the truth: they were surrounded.

What at first sight looked like a hundred sphinxes coming towards them from all sides, however, soon turned out to be a single one.

The dark-haired figure, like a man with a tawny lion's lower body, had broader shoulders than any of the dockers working on the quays of Venice. He carried a spear with a point like a sword blade that reflected Vermithrax's golden glow and shone like a torch.

Seth stepped forward and said something in Egyptian. Then he added, in words they could all understand, 'Do you speak the language of my . . . my friends?'

The sphinx nodded, and balanced the spear in his hands for a moment without lowering its point. His glance kept going uncertainly to Vermithrax.

'Are you Seth?' he asked the high priest of Horus in Merle's language.

'I am, and I have a right to be here. Only the Pharaoh's word overrules mine.'

The sphinx snorted. 'Pharaoh's word says we're to take

you prisoner the moment we set eyes on you. Everyone knows that you have betrayed the Empire and are fighting on the side –' he hesitated – 'on the side of our enemies.'

Seth bowed his head, but what might look to the sphinx like humility was really preparation for – well, for what? A magic spell to tear his enemy apart?

Merle was never to find out, for at that moment the sphinx's reinforcements arrived. A troop of mummy warriors appeared behind him, passing through an almost invisible gap between the mirrors. Their reflections multiplied on the walls like a chain of cut-out paper shapes pulled apart by unseen hands.

The mummies wore armour of leather and steel, but even that could not hide the fact that these undead warriors were unusually strong specimens. Their faces were ashen grey with dark rings under the eyes, but they didn't look as emaciated and half-decomposed as other mummies in the Imperial forces. Presumably they hadn't been dead for long when they were torn from their graves to serve in the Pharaoh's army.

The warriors got into position behind the sphinx. With all those reflections, it was hard to say just how many of them there really were. Merle counted four, but perhaps she was wrong and there were more of them.

75

The air above the golden network set into Seth's scalp was shimmering as it does on a very hot summer's day.

Horus magic. The thought shot through Merle's mind, and she couldn't help thinking that he could use it against her just as easily as against her enemies.

At that moment the leading mummy warrior raised his crescent sword. The sphinx looked back over his shoulder, obviously surprised by the arrival of the warriors, but also glad of their support. Then he turned back to Seth, Vermithrax, and the girls on the lion's back. He realised that the priest of Horus was not bowing to him in awe, he saw the shimmering air above Seth's head, he swung his spear round and was about to aim it at the priest –

– when he was felled from behind by a stroke of the mummy warrior's sword.

The warriors swiftly leaped on the sphinx where he lay on the floor and attacked him from all sides. When there was no life left in him, their leader slowly turned. His eyes went to Vermithrax and the girls, and then stopped to linger on Seth.

The golden network on the priest's head was glowing, and little globes of fire like balls of pure lava appeared in Seth's hands.

'No, don't,' said the mummy warrior. His voice sounded remarkably alive. 'We aren't what you think.'

Seth hesitated.

'Leave them alone, Seth,' cried Merle. She didn't expect the priest to take any notice of her, but for some reason or other he didn't throw the fiery globes.

'They're not real,' said the Queen in Merle's head.

The mummies?

'Those too. But I mean the globes. They're just an illusion. The priests of Horus have always been masters of lies and deceit. And admittedly of alchemy and raising the dead as well.'

Then can't he burn the warriors at all?

'Not by those farcical means.'

Merle took a deep breath. She saw the leading mummy warrior raise his left hand and rub his face with it. The grey colour came off and the dark rings round his eyes were smudged.

'We're no more dead than you are,' he said. 'And before we slaughter each other we might at least find out whether it wouldn't make more sense to work together.' The man spoke with a strong accent, rolling his curiously harsh 'r's.

Seth's globes of fire went out. The air above his head calmed down.

'*I think I know who they are,*' said the Queen. '*Merle, you remember what you found in the abandoned camp on the way down to Hell, don't you? Before the Lilim appeared and destroyed everything.*'

It took Merle a couple of seconds to realise what the Queen was talking about.

The chicken's claw?

'*Yes. Do you have it with you?*'

In the rucksack.

'*Tell Junipa to get it out.*'

A moment later Junipa, sitting behind her, was fumbling with the straps of the rucksack.

'Who are you?' Vermithrax asked again, taking a menacing step forward. Seth stepped aside, more cautious now, and perhaps realising that his illusions were less useful than the lion's fangs and teeth.

'Spies,' said the false mummy warrior.

Junipa fished the chicken's claw on its leather thong out of Merle's rucksack and handed it forward to her.

The mummy warrior saw it at once. It was as if Merle had waved a blazing torch at him.

'Spies from the Tsarist Empire,' he said, smiling.

PIRATES

Serafin was standing at a round porthole, watching the wonders of the seabed move past. Shoals of fish sparkled in the dim light. He saw underwater forests of strange growths, with strange things that might be animals or might be plants among them.

The submarine that had taken them aboard on the sea-witch's orders was moving through the deeps like a giant ray, accompanied by dozens of the fire-bubbles that they had already seen with the witch. The glowing globes moved along on both sides of the vessel like a swarm of comets, covering the bottom of the sea with a flickering pattern of light and dark.

Dario came and stood beside him. 'Isn't it incredible?'

Serafin felt as if he had been woken from a dream in a deep sleep. 'This ship? Yes . . . yes, I suppose it is.'

'You don't sound too enthusiastic.'

'Have you seen the crew? And that madman who calls himself the captain?'

Dario grinned. 'You still don't get it, do you?'

'Get what?'

'They're pirates.'

'Pirates?' Serafin groaned slightly. 'What makes you think that?'

'One of them told me so while you were just standing around here moping.'

'I was thinking about Merle,' said Serafin quietly. Then he frowned. 'You mean *real* pirates?'

Dario nodded, and grinned more broadly than ever. Serafin wondered why his friend seemed so pleased that they had fallen into the hands of a gang of robbers and murderers. Romantic notions of piracy, he supposed; the old tales of noble buccaneers proudly sailing the high seas, fearing no authority.

But Serafin wasn't particularly surprised. Dario's discovery certainly fitted the picture. What kind of allies should they have expected a sea-witch to have? In addition, Captain Calvino ruled his men with a rod of iron. As for the sailors themselves, you could recognise them a mile off as cut-throats: sinister figures with unkempt hair, dirty clothes and countless scars.

Great. Fantastic. Out of the frying pan into the fire.

'They pay the witch protection money in the form of corpses,' said Dario with relish.

Serafin's eyes flashed. 'And there was I thinking we'd all seen quite enough corpses.'

Dario flinched. The memory of their flight from Venice and the death of Boro was still fresh in his mind, and the remark obviously hurt him. Serafin immediately regretted his sharp retort: Dario's enthusiasm for the pirates was only a mask to hide his true feelings. In reality, he was as miserable as the rest of them about what had happened.

Serafin put a hand on his shoulder. 'Sorry.'

With difficulty, Dario managed a smile. 'My fault.'

'Tell me what else you've found out.' And in a fit of harsh self-criticism he added, 'At least you had the sense to discover more about these new friends of ours, instead of just gaping out of the window.'

Dario briefly nodded, but then his grin gave way to a look of anxiety. He came to stand next to Serafin at the porthole, and they both turned their faces to the glass.

'They keep their victims' bodies in a hold at the back of the submarine. To be honest, I'm not sure whether there are still any ships up above for pirates to rob anyway. You can bet they wouldn't venture near the Egyptian war galleys, and as far as I know there's been almost no trade at all in the Mediterranean since the war began.'

Serafin nodded. The Empire had cut off all access to the trade routes, and there were no customers left for merchants to trade with in the deserted harbour towns. Like almost everyone else, traders and the crews of their ships had ended up as slaves in the mummy factories.

Dario cast a cautious glance behind him. They were in one of the small cabins that had a maze of pipes running along their bronze-coloured walls, intricately worked in lavish decorative effects like the stucco in Venetian palaces, with the sole difference that the patterns here were made of wood and metal. Serafin wondered, not for the first time, who Captain Calvino had captured this vessel from. He had certainly not designed it himself, for he didn't seem to be a man who valued beauty. And for all the functional purpose of the submarine, someone with excellent taste and an understanding of art had obviously been at work here.

As well as the boys there were two crew members in the cabin. One sailor was pretending to be asleep in his berth, but Serafin had seen him blink and glance his way several times. The second man sat on the edge of his bunk, swinging his legs and carving the figure of a mermaid from a piece of wood: wood-shavings fell on the empty bunk below him. There were still eight bunks free, and the boys knew that there were several such cabins for the crew on board the ship. Captain Calvino had put Serafin and Dario in this one, Tiziano and Aristide in another. Eft and Lalapeya shared a double cabin at the end of the central gangway that ran right through the boat like a backbone. Their cabin was not far from the captain's.

At this time of day most of the crew members were going about their business in the labyrinthine spaces of the submarine. It was obvious that however hard they tried to look casual, the two men in their berths had been stationed here to keep watch on the passengers. No one prevented the boys from exploring the vessel as they pleased, yet they were under observation at every step they took. Captain Calvino might be a cruel and unscrupulous slave-driver, but he was no fool. And not even the sea-witch's direct orders for him to carry his passengers to Egypt and land them there unharmed could prevent him from showing openly that he disapproved of them.

In a low voice, Dario went on with his account of what he had discovered. 'The sea-witch has put this boat under her protection as long as Calvino supplies her with the flesh of corpses. They collect drowned men and shipwrecked bodies from all over the Mediterranean and take them to the witch. The man I talked to told me they've been taking the submarine down under the scenes of all the great naval battles for years, catching the dead in nets. Appetising job, don't you think? Well, that's what they do, anyway, because piracy doesn't pay these days. No one, not even that crazy Calvino, wants to fight the Egyptians. And when he isn't fishing corpses out of the water, he's running errands for the sea-witch. Like taking us to Egypt.'

'Do you know how they came by this ship?'

'Seems that Calvino won it and its crew at dice. I've no idea if that's true or not. If it is, we can assume the bastard cheated. Did you see the way he stared at Lalapeya?'

Serafin smiled. 'To be honest, I'm less worried about her than anyone.' The idea of Calvino having the sphinx brought to his cabin was irresistible: he could just imagine the stupid look on the captain's face when the sphinx took her true shape and showed a lion's claws. It would be priceless!

'Have you spoken to Tiziano and Aristide?' asked Serafin.

'You bet. They're wandering around the ship sticking their noses into what's none of their business.'

Serafin felt guiltier than ever. All the others had immediately begun exploring their new surroundings – he was the only one wasting valuable time by indulging in his gloomy thoughts. His uncertainty about Merle and what had become of her troubled him more and more the longer their journey went on. But he couldn't let that take his mind off the most important thing: getting them all out of this adventure safe and sound.

'Serafin?'

'Hm?' He blinked briefly as Dario's face took on sharper contours in front of him again.

'You're not responsible for anyone here, so don't tell yourself you are.'

'I'm not.'

'I think you are. You were our leader when we made our way into the Doge's Palace. But that's all over now. Out here we're all – well, in the same boat,' he said with a wry grin.

Serafin sighed, and then smiled slightly. 'Let's go forward to the bridge. I'd rather look Calvino in the face than sit around here not knowing if he may be giving orders to have our throats cut at this very minute.' As they went to the cabin door together, he called back to the two men on their bunks, 'Just going off for a few minutes to sabotage the engines.'

The sailor with the knife stared in surprise at his companion, who was unconvincingly faking a yawn as if he had been roused from a deep sleep at that very moment.

Serafin and Dario hurried down the gangways. They saw a similar scene everywhere: pipes and steam conduits elaborately integrated into the richly ornamented walls and ceilings, their copper now attacked by verdigris; Oriental rugs worn threadbare by heavy boots; curtains falling apart with mould and damp; chandeliers with crystal drops missing as well as whole arms that had fallen off some time in the past and were never replaced. The former magnificence of the ship had gone to rack and ruin long ago. Decorative wooden edgings had been notched or used for childish carvings, some had been broken off for use as weapons in hand-to-hand fighting. The ceilings and floors were covered with wine and rum stains. The pirates had blackened the teeth of the figures in some of the paintings on the walls and added moustaches to them.

The bridge was at the prow of the submarine, behind a double porthole looking out at the depths of the ocean like a pair of eyes. Captain Calvino, dressed in a rust-coloured frock-coat with a golden collar, was pacing up and down in front of the glass of the portholes, engaged in heated argument with someone who was hidden from Dario and Serafin by a column. Half a dozen men were busy with wheels and levers which, like most of the equipment on board, was made of bronze. One sat on a padded saddle, sweating as he worked a pair of pedals driving heaven only knows what kind of machine.

The two boys slowed down as they approached the viewing platform at the front of the bridge. Calvino did not interrupt his furious pacing for a second. As they came closer, they saw who was there with him, very obviously working him up into a white-hot rage.

Eft saw the two boys at the same moment. Her broad mermaid mouth was not, as usual, covered by a mask. The rucksack where she kept Arcimboldo's mirror-mask hung over her shoulder, very familiar to them by now, for Eft never let her precious possession out of her hands for a second.

'I know ships like this,' she said, turning back to Calvino. 'And I know how fast they can go. Much faster than you're trying to make us believe, anyway.'

'I've told you a thousand times and I'll tell you again,' roared the captain. He had a scar from his lower lip running right down to his throat, and it was scarlet with his fury. 'The Egyptians control the sea, and it's a long time since they were content to search only the surface of the water for prey. If we were to move faster we'd have to come up, and I'm not taking such a risk. The sea-witch has ordered me to take you and these children to Egypt – which is crazy enough in itself, by Davy Jones and his locker! – but she didn't say there was any great hurry about it. So perhaps you will kindly leave me to decide on our speed!'

'You're an obstinate old goat, Captain, and I'm not a bit surprised to see how badly you've neglected this marvellous ship. We can probably consider ourselves lucky to get to Egypt at all before your rubbish-heap of a boat falls to bits.'

Calvino swung round, approached Eft and stood very close to her, thrusting his scarred face out menacingly. Serafin felt sure Eft must be able to smell the remains of food clinging to his dark beard. 'You may be a woman or a fish-wife or the devil knows what, but you're not telling me how to run my ship!'

Eft remained unimpressed, although she must have seen the sword at the captain's belt. In his fury, Calvino was clutching the hilt tightly in his right hand, but he hadn't drawn the blade yet. No doubt he very soon would if Eft didn't give way. What on earth did she think she was doing?

Did it matter whether they reached Egypt today, tomorrow, or not until the day after that?

Eft assumed her sweetest smile, which in a mermaid looks about as inviting as a kraken's open arms. Her shark-like teeth glittered in the light of the gas lamps. 'You are a fool, Captain Calvino, and I'll tell you why.'

Serafin noticed the crew members on the bridge hunching their heads down between their shoulders. They probably guessed at the storm about to break over them any moment now.

But still Calvino said nothing, perhaps because he was too puzzled. No one had ever before dared speak to him in that tone. His lower lip was shaking like the body of an electric eel.

Eft was still not impressed. 'Even before the war, Captain, this ship was worth a fortune, more than you and your cutthroats could ever imagine in your wildest dreams. But today, now that there's no shipping on the seas, it's of such inconceivable value that even the treasuries of the Sub-Oceanic Realms could not have bought it.'

Now she's really gone too far, thought Serafin, but at the same time he saw Calvino frowning as he listened attentively. Eft was a little closer to her goal: she had made him curious.

'You've been on board too long, Captain,' she continued her tirade, and now the sailors too were unobtrusively paying attention. 'You've forgotten what the world above is like. You and your men are letting this ship and the wonderful works of art that it carries fall into disrepair while you travel the seven seas searching for treasures. But the greatest treasure of all is here the whole time, right under your feet, and you've nothing better to do than make it into a scrap-heap and watch your men doing a little more damage to it every day.'

Calvino's face was still hovering only a few centimetres from hers, as if frozen in space. 'The greatest treasure of all, did you say?' His voice sounded lower and better controlled than before.

'Certainly – as long as you don't let it rot away like an old plank washed up on the beach of some island.'

'Hm,' grunted Calvino. 'You think I'm . . . not very clean in my habits?'

'I think you're the filthiest fellow between here and the Arctic Circle, in every sense,' said Eft in friendly tones. 'Which makes it all the harder for me to point out your obvious *mistakes*.'

Oh, heavens above, thought Serafin.

Dario audibly drew a deep breath. 'Now she's really done it,' he whispered to his friend.

Captain Calvino was staring at Eft, eyes wide. His thumb nervously polished the pommel of his sword, while his thoughts were clearly revolving around murder, fillet of fish-wife, and a paperweight made of a mermaid's jaw.

'Captain?' Eft put her head on one side, smiling.

'What is it?' he growled. The question emerged from his throat like sulphur vapours from the crater of a volcano.

'I haven't hurt your feelings, have I?'

Two sailors were whispering together. Before they knew it, Calvino was beside them, bawling them out with such a firework display of bad language that even Serafin and Dario, both of them once street urchins in the alleys of Venice, felt themselves blushing.

'Someone ought to write it down,' said Dario.

Calvino swung round and saw the boys. For a moment it looked as if he were going to vent his anger on them too, but then he bit back the words and turned to Eft again. Dario breathed a sigh of relief.

The captain's outburst had calmed him down slightly, and now he could look Eft in the face without darting such furious glances at her. 'You are . . . outrageous.'

Eft was clearly suppressing a grin, which was probably just as well, for a mermaid's grin is not a pretty sight. 'This ship is a blot on the seascape, Captain. It stinks, it's dirty and dilapidated. If I were you – and thanks be to the Lords of the Deep that I'm not – I'd have my men at work getting it into shape as fast as they could. Every copper pipe, every picture, every rug. And then I'd lean back for a moment and enjoy knowing that I was one of the richest men in the world.'

Serafin could see the full significance of the words sinking into Calvino's mind. One of the richest men in the world. Serafin wondered if Eft really knew what she was talking about. On the other hand, you'd be a fool not to see how valuable this submarine was. In times like these it was priceless – even if, as Calvino might have overlooked in his greed, that meant *literally* priceless, for there was no one left who could have bought it.

But in any case, presumably the captain wouldn't have sold his ship at any price. It was the knowledge of its value, the sudden realisation of the riches he owned, that he liked. He had indeed been on board too long, and as so often when you see something every day, he had forgotten how precious this vessel was.

He went on looking at Eft for a moment more, then turned on his heel and barked out a string of orders to his men, who immediately passed on the captain's commands to the rest of the crew through speaking tubes running all round the submarine to its furthest corners.

Get the place cleaned up, that was the gist of it. Dust and scour, polish and remove rust, scrub the decks and clean the glass. Then, Calvino ordered, the works of art that had been stowed away over the years in one of the holds were to go back on the walls and into any glass show-cases that were still intact. And woe betide anyone who tried embellishing them with charcoal or the point of his knife!

Finally Calvino gave the mermaid a wry grin. 'What's your name?'

'Eft.'

He made her a gallant if rather exaggerated bow, but his goodwill was evident. 'Rinaldo Bonifacio Sergio Romulus Calvino,' he introduced himself. 'Welcome aboard.'

Eft thanked him, couldn't suppress her grin any more – it did seem to alarm the captain a little – shook his hand, and then at last came over to the two boys. Serafin and Dario were still standing there open-mouthed, unable to take in what had just happened.

'How did you do it?' asked Serafin quietly, as the three of them left the bridge, accompanied by the admiring glance that Calvino cast at Eft's back.

Eft winked at Serafin. 'He's only a man,' she said with satisfaction, 'and I still have a mermaid's eyes.'

Then she hurried ahead to supervise the work of cleaning up the vessel.

They reached Egypt the next day.

Nothing had prepared them for what they saw when the submarine surfaced. Ice-floes were drifting on the open sea a hundred metres from land. The closer they came to the white coastline, the more certain it appeared that winter had the desert in its grasp. No one could understand what had happened, and Calvino told his men to pray three Our Fathers to preserve them all from kobalin and sea-demons.

Serafin, Eft and the rest were as astonished as the captain and his crew, and even Lalapeya, the silent and mysterious Lalapeya, said unasked that she hadn't the faintest idea what had happened to Egypt. There was no doubt, however, that the country had never known a winter like this before. Ice-floes off the coast of the desert, she remarked, were about as usual as polar bears dancing on top of the pyramids.

Captain Calvino gave orders to measure the thickness of the ice at the water's edge. Not much more than a metre, came the report soon afterwards. Calvino growled angrily, and then conferred with Eft for a full hour on the bridge – a conversation which, like all their exchanges, entailed much shouting and angry curses, and ended with the captain giving in to the mermaid.

Soon after that, Calvino took the submarine down below the surface again, and they moved on into the Nile delta below the sheet of ice. The great river and its tributaries were not deep, and steering the ship between the ice and the river bed called for some skill in navigation. Several times they heard sand crunching under the keel, while the fin-shaped excrescences on top of the submarine's hull scraped along the sheet of ice above it. With all the noise they were making it would be a miracle, swore Calvino, a damn miracle if no one noticed them.

Most of the time they moved slowly forward at walking pace, and Serafin began to wonder where they were going anyway. The witch's orders had been to land them on the coast – now Calvino was taking them further inland of his own accord, and in conditions worse than anything any of them could have expected. Eft's influence over him was astonishing.

Much of the inside of the ship was sparkling clean by now. Sailors were at work everywhere with cloths and sponges and sandpaper, painting and varnishing, taking up old carpets and replacing them from the stocks in the over-crammed holds. Many of the items stored there had lain untouched for decades, some of them presumably since the previous owner's privateering days long before the Mummy Wars began. Even Calvino seemed surprised by what his men brought to light: artistic treasures and works of magnificent craftsmanship that he hadn't seen for a long time. Eft told Serafin she thought he was coming to realise that he had indeed lived too long in the bronze world of the submarine, forgetting how to value the beauties of the world above – which did not, however, keep him from raging like a berserker, shouting at his men, and imposing draconian punishments for any streaks of dirt and spots of rust that had been overlooked.

Serafin had a vague feeling that Eft liked the pirate captain. Not in the same way as she had revered Arcimboldo, and yet . . . yet there was something between the two of them, a ridiculous love–hate relationship that both amused and unsettled him. Was it possible for two people to come close to each other in circumstances like these? How had it happened with him and Merle? The realisation that they had spent less time together than Eft and Calvino on this short voyage weighed on his mind. He began to doubt whether Merle thought of him as often as he did of her. Was she missing him? Did he mean anything at all to her?

A fearsome crunching, grinding sound put an abrupt end to his brooding. It wasn't long before Calvino's voice came echoing down the speaking tubes, swearing profusely and telling them what had happened.

They were stuck. Stuck in the pack ice of the Nile, unable to move either forward or back. The iron fins of the submarine had eaten their way into the sheet of ice above it like saw-blades, ploughing a track several dozen metres long through the ice before they became hopelessly jammed.

Fearing the worst, Serafin hurried to the bridge, but he found Calvino and Eft standing calmly side by side at the double porthole in the prow of the ship, looking out into the waters of the Nile below the ice sheet. They had left the witch's fire-bubbles behind at the coast, but the faint light shimmering through the ice was enough for them to see the essentials. The view through the portholes made it look as if the submarine had come to a halt under the white ceiling of a dimly lit hall. Splinters of ice as thick as tree-trunks reared up in front of the glass.

In an emergency Captain Calvino acted with far more restraint than Serafin would have expected. He made sure of all the facts, consulted with Eft, and then gave orders for his men to open the top hatch of the ship so that the passengers could climb out.

What, thought Serafin, horrified, climb out? Had that been Eft's advice? Just get them landed in the middle of this desert of ice?

An hour later Eft and Lalapeya, Serafin and Dario, Tiziano and Aristide were standing ready by the hatch, wrapped in the thickest furs to be found in the holds of the pirate ship. They came, Calvino remembered, from a schooner that had run aground; he had defeated its crew at the beginning of the war. The ship had been on the way to Thule in Greenland to barter the warm clothing on board for no one remembered what. The jackets, boots and trousers didn't fit everyone, and the slender Lalapeya in particular was swamped in her garments, but they would keep them all from freezing to death. Finally they all put on shapeless fur caps and slipped their hands into warm, quilted mittens. The pirates gave them revolvers, ammunition and knives from the ship's armoury. Only Lalapeya refused to carry a weapon.

Calvino stayed behind with his men to guard the ship and try to free the fins on top of it from the ice. He suspected that would take hours, perhaps even days, and the fear of being discovered by Egyptian Barques of the Sun was clearly written on his face. Although Eft did not ask him to, he promised to wait three days for a sign of life from them before he went back out into the open sea.

Tiziano gloomily asked what they had all been wondering. 'Where are we going, anyway?'

Eft was standing under the open hatch leading outside. Its white circle framed her head like a frozen halo. Her eyes went to Lalapeya, who was looking far from happy in her voluminous fur clothing. Serafin too looked at the sphinx, and once again he asked himself what incentive she had to stay with their desperate little band. Was it really just hatred of the Empire? The loss of the dead sphinx god who had rested below the cemetery island of San Michele, and whom she had tried to protect in vain?

No, thought Serafin, there was another reason, one that she hadn't told them, and none of the rest of them could even guess at it. He felt that as clearly as if something in the sphinx's eyes were speaking to him.

'Lalapeya,' said Eft. Her words sounded a little solemn. 'I assume you have some idea where we are. Perhaps you've known all along that the first part of our journey would end here.'

Lalapeya said nothing, and hard as Serafin tried he could find no answer in her silence. She neither confirmed nor denied what Eft had said.

Eft went on. 'The sphinx fortress isn't far from here, right in the middle of the Nile delta. The mermaids have no name for it, but I think there is one. The captain knows this place, and if the onset of winter has done no worse than to cover everything with snow and ice, the fortress ought to be at the most two or three miles away.'

'The Iron Eye sees your life, sees your actions, sees your death,' recited Lalapeya, and the words sounded to Serafin like a proverb from the distant past. The sphinx had passed long ages alone in Venice, but she had not forgotten her own people's culture. 'The Iron Eye – that's the name you're looking for, Eft. And yes, I can sense other sphinxes near us, many of them in the same place. It's suicide to go there.' But the way she said it made it sound a statement of inevitable fact rather than a warning.

'Why are we going there?' asked Aristide.

Lalapeya answered instead of Eft. 'It's the heart of the Empire. If there is one point where the Empire is vulnerable, it's there.' She didn't say anything about a plan, presumably because there wasn't one. No one doubted that the sphinxes' fortress was impregnable.

Eft shrugged her shoulders, and once again Serafin remembered what she had said to the sea-witch: they had to begin somewhere if they were going to fight back against the Empire. And there could be victories on a small scale. Serafin had been unable to forget her words.

But what use was that if they all died in the process? It was like voluntarily running at a wall despite knowing that they couldn't so much as scratch it.

He was just about to express his doubts when he felt Lalapeya gently touching his hand. She leaned over to him and whispered, so quietly that none of the others noticed, 'Merle is there.'

He stared at her in astonishment.

Lalapeya smiled.

Merle, he thought, Merle is there? But he dared not ask any questions. If Dario and the others knew, they would say he had joined this expedition only because he wanted to see Merle again, not because he believed in their loftier aims.

Very well, he thought, let them do what their noble ideals tell them is right; he at least knew why he was *really* doing it, and he didn't think his motives were any less honourable than theirs. They sprang from himself, from his heart.

Almost imperceptibly, Lalapeya nodded.

Eft's voice made them both look up at the hatch. Serafin felt that he was seeing and hearing everything through a blur: their surroundings, what Eft was saying, the presence of the others. Suddenly he couldn't wait to clamber out into the open air.

Merle is there, he heard the sphinx say again and again, and the words danced in his head like moths round a candle flame.

Eft was still talking, telling them how to walk through the snow, but Serafin scarcely heard her.

Merle is there.

At last they set off.

BACK TO THE LIGHT

'I can feel it. With every step I take. Every time I breathe.'
Junipa kept her voice low so that no one but Merle could
hear her. 'It's like having something here inside, in my
breast . . . something pulling at me, as if it were working a
puppet's strings.' Her mirror-glass eyes turned to her friend
like the lamp of a lighthouse: silvery light behind glass. 'I
keep trying to resist it. But I don't know how much longer
I can hold out.'

'And you can remember everything that happened in the
pyramid?' Merle was holding Junipa's hand, stroking it
gently. They were sitting in the furthest corner of the hiding
place that the Tsarist spies had made for themselves.

Junipa swallowed. 'I know I tried to stop you. And then
we . . . we fought.' She shook her head, ashamed of herself.
'I'm so sorry.'

'You couldn't help it. That was Burbridge's fault.'

'No, it wasn't him,' said Junipa. 'It was the Stone Light.

Professor Burbridge is under its spell as much as I am, at least while he's down there. Then he's not the scientist he once was, he's just Lord Light.'

'And is it better for you up here?'

Junipa thought for a moment before she could find the right words. 'It feels weaker. Perhaps because it's stone itself, and it can't get through the rock of the earth's crust. Or not right through. But it hasn't gone. It's still with me, all the time. And sometimes it hurts.'

Merle had seen the scar on Junipa's breast after they climbed up out of Hell, the place where Burbridge had had a new heart inserted into her – a splinter of the Stone Light. That splinter now lay cold and motionless inside her rib-cage, keeping her alive the way her real heart used to, like a burning, sparkling diamond that healed her wounds very fast, and gave her strength when she was exhausted. But it was also trying to get her under its influence.

When Junipa said that it hurt, she didn't mean the scar or the pain of the operation. She meant the pressure on her to betray Merle again, her struggle with herself, torn between her own gentle nature and the icy power of the Stone Light.

And much as it upset Merle, she had to be on her guard

against her friend. It was possible that Junipa would suddenly turn on her again.

No, not Junipa, thought Merle bitterly. The Stone Light. The fallen Morning Star lying at the centre of Hell. Lucifer.

She hesitated for a moment, and then voiced an idea that she had been mulling over for some time. 'What you said in the pyramid . . .'

'About Burbridge claiming to be your grandfather?'

Merle nodded. 'Do you know if that's true?'

'He said so, anyway.'

Merle looked down. She opened the buttoned pocket of her dress and took out the water mirror, running her fingertips over the frame. Her other hand felt for the chicken's foot now dangling from a string around her neck. Deep in thought, she played with its sharp little claws.

'More soup?' asked a voice behind them.

The two girls turned. Andrei, leader of the troop of Tsarist spies, had more or less washed the grey stain off his face, and was wearing only a part of his mummy armour. He was a hard, determined man, but the presence of the girls brought out a kindness in him that seemed to surprise even his four companions.

The men were still standing on the other side of the low-built shelter around Vermithrax, their wooden soup bowls in one hand, their free hands constantly reaching out to touch the obsidian lion's shining body.

They didn't know that he had been immersed in the Stone Light, although unlike Junipa he had not fallen under its power. Merle thought that strange, but so far she hadn't noticed anything to worry her. Since he fell, the stone lion had been stronger and even a little larger than before, but apart from the lava-like glow of his body he had not changed. He was still the same old kindly Vermithrax, and now, in spite of his anxiety about his own people and his hatred of Seth, he was enjoying the attention of the marvelling Tsarists. He basked in their questions, their hesitant touch and the awe in their faces. They had all heard of the stone lions of Venice and the few that could still fly. But it was a new and fascinating idea that one of those lions could also speak like a human being, and shone as brightly as an icon in their churches at home.

Junipa refused the soup that Andrei was offering them, but Merle had a second helping. After all the days when she had had to keep herself nourished somehow on tough dried meat, this thin broth seemed delicious.

'You have nothing to fear.' Andrei had misunderstood

their reason for sitting in a corner away from the others. 'The sphinxes won't find us here. We've been camping in this place for almost six months, and so far they haven't even noticed that we're around at all.'

'Don't you think that's strange?' asked Merle.

Andrei laughed softly. 'We've wondered the same thing a thousand times. The sphinxes are an ancient people, known since the beginning of time to be wise and wily. Are they simply observing us and tolerating our presence? Are they feeding us false information? Or is it just that they don't mind we're here because we have no chance to send our discoveries home anyway?'

'I thought you had carrier pigeons?'

'We did. But how many pigeons can you keep in a place like this before someone notices? We'd used all our birds after the first few weeks, and there was no way we could get more sent here. So now we're just gathering what information we can – in our heads, nothing on paper, we don't write anything down – and soon we'll be going home, thanks be to Baba Yaga.'

He gave Merle and Junipa an encouraging smile and then went back to his companions, respecting the girls' preference for their own company.

'He's odd, don't you think?' Junipa asked.

'He's very nice,' said Merle.

'Nice too. But so . . . so understanding. Not at all what you'd expect of someone travelling half round the world in secret, a man who's been hiding in the enemy's fortress for six months.'

Merle shrugged her shoulders. 'Perhaps his mission has helped him to stay sane. He must have seen a great many terrible things.' She nodded at the other spies, her face darkening. 'So must all of them.'

Junipa's eyes wandered from the Tsarists to Seth, who was sitting close to the entrance, leaning against one of the mirror walls. He held an empty drinking cup in his bound hands. His ankles were bound as well. If Andrei had known who his prisoner really was he would probably have struck his head off without a moment's hesitation, and even though that would have suited Vermithrax, Merle thought it would be a bad idea. Not inappropriate, and certainly not undeserved, but she hoped that Seth might still be useful to them. And this time even the Flowing Queen shared her view.

'You want to try again?' asked Junipa, seeing Merle's fingertips move from the frame of her water mirror and across its surface.

Merle just nodded and closed her eyes.

Her fingers touched the lukewarm water as if they were resting on glass, without breaking through the gentle ripples. The milky phantom on the surface stroked her fingertips. Merle's eyes were still closed, but she could feel it and its rapid movement back and forth on the water.

She heard its whispers, distorted and much too far away for her to make out any words. She had to bind the phantom to her somehow, like a piece of iron attracted to a magnet.

'The word,' she whispered to Junipa. 'Can you still remember the word?'

'What word?'

'The word Arcimboldo told us when we had to catch the phantoms in the magic mirrors for him.' Back in Venice, their old master had opened the door into one of his mirrors for them. They had entered the magic mirror world and found the mirror phantoms there: beings from another world who had tried to move into this one, but were stranded in Arcimboldo's magic mirrors, just ghostly shadows. They moved through the glass labyrinths of the mirror world almost invisibly and as lightly as a breeze, but they could never go back or travel on into a physical existence. The girls had cast a spell on them with a magic word and brought them back to their master, who had let them loose into the reflections on the water of the Venetian canals.

'Mm, yes, the word,' murmured Junipa thoughtfully. 'Something beginning with "intera" or "intero".'

'Intrabilibus or something.'

'Something like that. Interabilitapetrifax.'

'*Childish nonsense*,' said the Flowing Queen crossly.

'Intrabalibuspustulence,' tried Merle.

'Interopeterusbilibix.'

'Interumpeterfixbilbulus.'

'Intorapeterusbiliris.'

Merle sighed. 'Intorapeti – wait a moment, say that again!'

'What?'

'What you just said.'

Junipa thought for a moment. 'Intorapeterusbiliris.'

Merle was jubilant. 'Almost! Now I remember: Intorabiliuspeteris.' And she spoke the word in such a loud voice that even the Tsarists and Vermithrax, talking on the other side of the room, fell silent for a moment.

'Seth is watching us,' whispered Junipa.

But Merle wasn't bothered about the priest of Horus, and she ignored Junipa's warning. Instead, she impatiently uttered the magic word for a second time, and now she suddenly felt a prickling sensation creeping from her right hand up to her elbow.

'Merle!' Junipa's voice was more urgent.

Merle blinked, and looked at the mirror. The phantom was swirling around her fingertips like a circular wisp of mist.

'*It's working*,' said the Flowing Queen. She too sounded concerned, as if she didn't quite like Merle to get in touch with the phantom.

'Hello?' asked Merle in an expressionless voice.

'Brbrlbrlbrbrl,' went the phantom.

'Hello?'

'Herrrllll . . . hello.'

Merle's heart was beating faster in her excitement. 'Can you hear me?'

The strange mumbling came again, but then: 'Of course. It was you who couldn't hear *me*.' It sounded cheeky, not in the least like a ghost.

'Is it saying something?' asked Junipa, and Merle realised that her friend couldn't hear the phantom any more than the others in the room. They had gone on with their own conversation and were paying no attention to what Merle was doing. With the possible exception of Seth. Yes, he was definitely watching her. A shudder ran down her back.

'You took your time about it,' said the phantom through her fingertips. Unlike the Flowing Queen inside her head, it still sounded far away and a little blurred, but she could understand the voice perfectly clearly now. It sounded young, and Merle felt fairly sure that it was a male voice.

'Can you help me?' she asked straight out. She didn't have time for verbal fencing just now. Andrei might summon them over to discuss the situation at any moment.

'I was wondering when you'd get around to asking that,' said the phantom, sounding stroppy.

'Well, *will* you help me?'

He sighed, like a stubborn little boy. She wondered if that was just what he had been before turning into a phantom: a boy, perhaps still a child. 'You want to know what's on the other side of your water mirror, don't you?'

'Yes.'

'Your friend was right. If a sphinx is what you call a person who's sometimes a woman and then a woman with lion's legs, then yes, she must be a sphinx.'

Merle didn't understand a word of it. 'Can you be a little clearer about it, please?'

The phantom sighed again. 'The woman on the other side of the mirror is a sphinx. And yes, she's your mother.' When Merle drew her breath in sharply, he added, 'At least, I think so. Happy now?'

'What did it say?' whispered Junipa in excitement. 'Tell me!'

Merle's heart was racing. 'He says the sphinx is my mother!'

'He says the sphinx is my mother,' the phantom mimicked her, distorting his voice. 'Do you want to know any more or don't you?'

'*You have a naughty brat in there*,' said the Flowing Queen, speaking up. The phantom didn't seem able to hear her, for he did not react.

'Yes,' said Merle in a shaking voice, 'yes, of course I want to know more. Where is she now? Can you see her?'

'No. She doesn't have a wonderful mirror like the one where you're keeping me a prisoner.'

'Keeping you a prisoner? You jumped into it of your own accord!'

'Because otherwise I'd have gone the same way as the others.'

'Did you know them?'

'They were all from my world, but the only one I knew was my uncle. He didn't want me to go with him, but I crept into his study by night and followed him through the mirror. Didn't he just look silly when he realised!' The phantom giggled. 'Well, then *I* looked silly when I found out what had happened to us.'

'*Drivel*,' said the Flowing Queen. '*Pure drivel.*'

'Let's get back to my mother, shall we?'

'Sure,' said the phantom. 'Anything you like.'

'Where is she now?'

'Last time I saw her she was sitting on a dead witch in the middle of the sea.' He said this in as matter-of-fact a tone as if he had seen her stirring a saucepan.

'The sea?' asked Merle. 'Are you sure?'

'I do *know* what the sea looks like,' he snapped back.

'Yes . . . yes, of course. But I mean what was she doing there?'

'She had one hand in the water making a magic mirror. So that she could hold your hand. Do you remember?'

Merle was dreadfully confused. 'So you can see her only when she has one hand in the water?'

'Just like you.'

'And you can hear her too?'

'I can hear you both.'

'But why can't I hear her, then?'

'We can change places any time you like,' the phantom replied snippily.

Merle thought for a moment. 'You must tell me what she says. Does she know how to talk to you?'

'She quite soon realised there was someone else in the mirror as well as her little daughter. And she was civil enough to start by asking my name.'

'Oh . . . what *is* your name, then?'

'I've forgotten.'

'But how –'

'I said she asked, I didn't say I could tell her.'

'How can you forget your own name?'

'How can you suddenly turn into a speck of dirt on a mirror? No idea. All I remember is those last few seconds in my uncle's study. Everything before that is gone. But I have a feeling it's gradually coming back to me. Sometimes I remember little things, faces, even tunes. Perhaps if you carry me around in your musty old pocket another few years I'll –'

This time she was the one who interrupted. 'Listen. I'm sorry about what happened to you, but I can't help it. No one forced you to follow your uncle. So will you help me or not?'

'Yes, yes,' he said slowly. 'Yes.'

'If you can talk to . . .' Merle hesitated. 'To my mother, then you could tell her what I say. And the other way around.'

'Kind of like interpreting, you mean?'

'Exactly.' He's got the idea now, she thought, and even the Queen sighed somewhere far inside her mind.

'I guess I could just about do that.'

'That would be very kind.'

'Will you take me out of your pocket sometimes?'

'If we get out of here safe and sound we may find some way to free you from this mirror.'

'Don't be too generous with promises you may not be able to keep,' said the Queen.

'It won't work.' Suddenly the phantom sounded downcast. 'I can't have a body in your world. Everyone said so.'

'Maybe not a body, but a bigger mirror. How about the sea?'

'Then I'd be like a sailor, wouldn't I?'

'Sort of.'

'Hm . . . I guess that would be all right.' And he began singing a song, rather out of tune, something about fifteen men on a dead man's chest. Merle thought it sounded silly.

'We'll try it,' she said quickly, to get him to shut up. 'Promise.'

'Merle?' He suddenly sounded serious . . .

'Yes?'

'Merle . . .'

Her breath was coming faster. 'What is it?'

'She's back again. Your mother, Merle . . . she's here with me.'

'What on earth does she think she's doing?' Dario shifted from foot to foot, looking sullen. The snow crunched under the soles of his boots, and Serafin thought that Dario's teeth would soon be chattering not with cold but with fury if Lalapeya didn't soon stand up and go on.

The sphinx was crouching on the bank of the frozen Nile, among great blocks of ice that had collided and cracked up, their edges grinding over and under each other. The boys had sought shelter in a dead palm grove only a few metres away. The palm fronds had long ago broken off under the weight of the snow, and only a few trunks were left leaning at a slant, sticking up like fingers from the white wilderness. The boys standing among the dead trees would make wonderful targets from the air. Eft wasn't with them; she was beside the sphinx on the bank, looking down at her with concern.

Serafin could stand it no longer. 'I'm going over to them.'

He looked up one last time at the Iron Eye that rose like a grey wall before them, unimaginably tall and monstrous. You might have thought it a mountain if it didn't rise from the icy plain so smoothly and abruptly. The twilight too did its part to hide the true nature of the fortress.

The sun was sinking somewhere behind the snow-laden clouds. At least they'd soon have no more to fear from the Barques. But there were sure to be other sentries on watch out here at the foot of the Iron Eye. Guards who could be fast and deadly even by night.

Dario muttered something as Serafin trudged away, but made no move to follow him. That was fine by Serafin. He wanted to talk to Eft and the sphinx on his own.

But when he finally looked over Lalapeya's shoulder and saw what she was doing, the words died away in his throat.

There was a hole in the ice near the bank. It looked as if a beast of prey had made it with its claws. So close to the Iron Eye, the ice sheet was much thinner than where the submarine had stuck in it. Thirty centimetres thick at the most, Serafin guessed. That must be because of the warmth radiating from the fortress. A pity they could feel hardly any of it themselves. It was certainly not so bitterly cold here, but the temperature was still far below freezing.

Lalapeya was crouching in the snow, leaning forward, and had dipped one arm into the water up to the elbow. Her hand dangled motionless in the icy cold river. The sphinx had pushed up the sleeve of her fur coat, and her bare forearm was gradually turning blue. All the same, she made no move to withdraw her hand. Only now did Serafin realise that she was whispering something to herself. Too quietly for him to make out what she was saying.

Distressed, he looked at Eft, who had come to his side. 'What's she doing?'

'Talking to someone.'

'Her hand will be frozen. She could lose it.'

'It's probably frozen already.'

'But –'

'She knows what she's doing.'

'No,' he said furiously, 'she obviously doesn't! We can't afford to drag her to the fortress with us half frozen to death.' He put out his hand to take Lalapeya's shoulder and pull her back, away from the water.

But Eft stopped him, and the hiss that suddenly emerged

from her shark-like jaws made him jump. She said, 'This is important. Really important.'

Serafin stumbled back a step or so. 'She's crazy. You've both gone crazy.' He was about to turn away and go back to the others, but once again Eft stopped him.

'Serafin,' said the mermaid imploringly, 'she's talking to Merle.'

He stared at her, bewildered. 'What do you mean?'

'The water is helping her.' Eft beckoned Serafin a little way further off, and there on the bank of the frozen Nile she told him the secret of Merle's water mirror.

Crossing his arms over his chest, he rubbed his arms vigorously under his fur coat, more from nervous excitement than the cold. 'That's the truth, is it?' he asked, frowning. 'I mean, you're really serious?'

Eft nodded.

Serafin lowered his voice. 'But what does Merle have to do with Lalapeya?'

The mermaid showed her teeth in a smile. 'Can't you work it out?'

'No, damn it, I can't!'

'She's her mother, Serafin. Lalapeya is Merle's mother.' Her terrible grin grew even broader, only her eyes were still human and wonderfully beautiful. 'Your girlfriend is a sphinx's daughter.'

Merle was concentrating hard on what the phantom said, at the same time doing her best not to dip her trembling fingers too far into the water of the mirror. She mustn't lose contact with him now, she had to hear what the sphinx – her mother – had to say to her.

'She says you must go to someone called Burbridge,' the phantom said, passing on the message.

'Burbridge?' repeated Merle.

'You're to go to him, it's the only place where you'll be safe. Safer than in the Iron Eye, anyway.'

'But we've only just escaped from Hell to get away from Burbridge! Tell her that.'

It was a little while before the phantom passed on the next answer. 'She says the two of you must meet him in his Cabinet of Mirrors. You and your friend. She will guide you there.'

'Junipa will guide me to a Cabinet of Mirrors?'

'Yes. Wait a moment, that's not all . . . yes, here we are. She will take you to him, and you'll both be safe there.'

Merle was still bewildered. 'Safe from what? The sphinxes?'

Another pause, and then: 'From the Son of the Mother,' she says. Whatever that may mean.'

Annoyed, Merle snapped, 'Would you be kind enough to *ask* her?'

While the phantom obeyed, the Flowing Queen spoke up. '*I don't know if this is a good idea, Merle. Perhaps you ought to –*'

No, thought Merle firmly. You keep out of this. This is no one's business but mine.

The phantom's voice came again. 'The Son of the Mother. Seems to be something like a name for . . . yes, for the forefather of all the sphinxes, kind of their oldest ancestor. A sort of sphinx god, I'd say. She says he's on his way here or even in the fortress already. She's not sure. And she says the sphinxes will try to bring him back to life.'

Merle jumped when the Queen uttered a strange sound. How much, she wondered yet again, do you really know?

'*The Son of the Mother,*' whispered the Queen. '*Then it's true. I sensed him, but I thought it was impossible . . . By all that's sacred, Merle, you mustn't do as she is asking. You must not leave this place.*'

You might have told me all this before, thought Merle bitterly. You should have trusted me.

The phantom went on. 'She keeps saying the same thing, Merle. Your friend is to take you to Burbridge before it's too late. The two of you are to go to his Cabinet of Mirrors and if necessary wait for him there. She says he can explain everything to you, about yourself and her and your father.'

'Ask her who my father was.'

The pause went on a long time. 'Burbridge's son,' said the phantom at last. 'Steven.'

Steven Burbridge. Her father. The strange idea startled her.

'What's *her* name?'

'Lalapeya,' said the phantom.

Merle felt her fingers begin to tremble. She bit her lip and tried to pull herself together. It was all so confusing and overwhelming. Hadn't the sphinxes been her enemies all along? Weren't they the real rulers of the Empire? If her mother was really a sphinx, then her own people had plunged the world into disaster. But Merle wasn't like them, and perhaps Lalapeya wasn't either.

'Merle,' the phantom said, interrupting her thoughts, 'your mother says only Junipa can guide you. That's very important, she says. Only Junipa has the power to use the Glass Word.'

Merle felt as dizzy as if she had been going round in

circles for hours on end. 'The Glass Word? What's that supposed to mean?'

'Just a minute.'

Time passed. Far too much time.

'Hello?' she asked at last.

'She's gone.'

'What?'

'Lalapeya has taken her hand out of the water. I can't hear her any more.'

'But that's –'

'Sorry. Not my fault.'

Merle looked up, and for the first time was aware of Junipa again. Her friend looked concerned as she sat there in front of her. 'I'm to guide you? Is that what the phantom said?'

Merle nodded, dazed as if she had woken from a nightmare. She should have been glad. Now she knew who her parents were. Yet that changed so little – nothing at all, really. It just made her even more confused. And frightened.

In a whisper, she told Junipa everything. Then she looked round, and realised that Seth had never taken his eyes off her. He gave her a chilly smile when their glances met, and she quickly looked away again.

'I know what he meant,' whispered Junipa tonelessly.

'You do?'

Junipa's breathing was shallow, her voice sounded hoarse. 'Through the mirrors, Merle. We're to go through the mirrors.' She smiled sadly. 'After all, that's what Arcimboldo gave me these eyes for, didn't he? It's not just that I can *see* with them. They're a key too, or at least part of a key. Burbridge told me all about it: why he had told Arcimboldo to find me in the orphanage and everything. I'm to look into other worlds – and I can go there too.'

'Even back to Burbridge?' whispered Merle. 'Back to Lord Light?'

Junipa's smile was more melancholy than ever, but somewhere in the bright glitter of her eyes there was something else too: a quiet, tentative triumph.

'Anywhere,' she said.

'Then why –'

'Why didn't we do it long ago? Because it isn't so easy. I need something to help me do it, the same thing Arcimboldo used to open the door in the mirror back in his workshop.'

Merle saw the scene flash over her mind's eye: Arcimboldo bending down in front of the mirror and moving his lips. Soundlessly shaping a word.

'The Glass Word,' said Junipa, as if she were letting the sound of the syllables melt on her tongue. 'I didn't know that was what it's called.'

'And you don't know what it is?'

'No,' said Junipa. 'Arcimboldo was murdered before he could tell me.'

God above, thought Serafin as Lalapeya withdrew her right hand from the water. It was grey to the wrist, almost blue, and looked waxen, hanging from the end of her arm as if it didn't belong to her body any more. Lifeless, like something that had died off.

The sphinx's features were twisted with pain, but the fiery light of her strong will still burned in those brown, doe-like eyes.

'Eft,' she said, ignoring Serafin.

Eft quickly bent forward to help Lalapeya get to her feet, but she had misunderstood: the sphinx was not asking for help.

'Merle needs . . . the Word,' she said with grim determination.

Eft shook her head. 'We must tend that hand. If we can light a fire somehow . . .'

'No.' Lalapeya looked at Eft, a plea in her eyes. 'First the Word.'

'What does she mean?' asked Serafin.

'Please!' The sphinx was begging her now.

Serafin's eyes went to Eft. 'What word?'

'The Glass Word.' Eft looked down at the ground and past Lalapeya, as if she saw something in the snow before her. But there was only her own shadow. She stared at it; she might have been asking it for advice.

'Merle and Junipa have to reach Burbridge,' said Lalapeya. 'Junipa has the *Sight*, she is a Guide. But to open the gates, the mirror-glass gates, she needs the Glass Word.' The sphinx was holding her numb right hand close to her breast with her sound left hand. Serafin himself had never had frostbite, but he had heard that it was as painful as a burn. It was astonishing that Lalapeya didn't simply collapse.

'I don't know the Word,' said Eft hesitantly.

'You don't. But he does.'

Serafin stared wide-eyed at the two women. 'He?' And then he understood. 'Arcimboldo?'

Lalapeya did not reply, but Eft nodded slowly.

'Merle has a right to the truth. I don't have the strength left . . . to tell her everything. Not here.' Lalapeya looked down at her motionless, waxen right hand. 'But the Word . . . I could tell her that.' Her gaze was pleading. 'Now, Eft!'

Eft hesitated a moment longer, and Serafin, feeling dreadfully helpless in his ignorance, wanted to take her by the shoulders and shake her. Do it, he silently begged. Do something! Help her!

Eft took a deep breath, and then she nodded. She quickly undid her rucksack and took out the mask, a perfect copy of Arcimboldo's features in silvery mirror-glass. Eft had made it after the mirror-maker's death, and Serafin had a dark suspicion that this was Arcimboldo's real face, taken from his corpse and turned into glass by some mysterious magic.

Eft handed Lalapeya the mask.

'Will he speak to me?' the sphinx asked doubtfully.

'He'll speak to anyone who puts it on.'

Serafin looked from one to the other. He dared not ask any questions that might disturb them.

Lalapeya looked at the master mirror-maker's features for a couple of seconds, then turned the mask round and examined the inside of it. Uncertainty flashed in her eyes for a moment, and then she pressed the glass to her face with her left hand. The mask clung there even when she took her hand away again. In some strange way, its interior seemed to adjust to Lalapeya's own delicate features; the glass lay over her face without overlapping it at the sides.

Serafin held his breath as he watched, almost expecting to hear the mask speak with Arcimboldo's voice. He felt revulsion at the idea, which it seemed to him would be undignified, like some ventriloquist's shabby trick.

A minute passed, and none of them moved. Even the other boys left behind in the palm grove were silent, although they couldn't see exactly what was going on. Serafin suspected that they sensed it all the same, just as he did. You could feel the magic radiating out through the ice and cold in all direction, perhaps even going down to the river and fluttering the fins of dead, frozen fish. The little hairs on the back of Serafin's hand were standing on end, and for some reason he felt slight pressure behind his eyes, as if he had a heavy cold. But the sensation went away as quickly as it had come.

Lalapeya's sound hand, fingers spread, went up to the mask and easily removed it. Her face under it was intact, not even reddened. Eft breathed a sigh of relief when the sphinx gave her back the mirror-glass mask.

'Was that all?' asked Serafin.

Eft put the mask back in her rucksack. 'You wouldn't say that if it had been on *your* face.'

Lalapeya leaned over the hole in the ice again.

'No,' whispered Serafin. But he did not hold her back. They all knew that this was the only way.

Lalapeya dipped her sound left hand in the water. Serafin thought he could feel the cold creeping up it as the blood left her forearm and its skin turned white. Sphinxes were creatures of the desert, and this icy cold must have a particularly devastating effect on her organism.

Minutes passed by again, and nothing moved. Even the frost around them held its breath, and the icy wind died down above the plain. Lalapeya's face grew paler and paler as she exposed her hand to the cold and its flesh gradually turned numb. She did not withdraw it, however, but waited patiently, feeling in the darkness under the ice for an answer to her silent question.

Then the corners of her mouth twitched in the fleeting shadow of a smile. Her lids closed as if in a deep, deep dream.

She whispered.

A tear flowed from the corner of one eye, and froze to ice.

*

'What kind of word is *that* supposed to be?' asked the phantom peevishly.

'Magic words are always tongue-twisters,' Merle explained. 'Most of them, anyway.' She spoke with as much conviction as if she had heard more than just two in her lifetime.

The phantom was still cross. 'What a word, though!' It had taken him five attempts to be sure he had spoken it correctly as Lalapeya gave it to him on the other side of the mirror.

Merle had to admit that she still couldn't keep it in her head. By comparison, she recited the binding magic for mirror phantoms as easily as a nursery rhyme.

However, Junipa nodded, and that was the main thing. 'I can say it. It's quite easy.' She spoke it out loud, and sure enough, it sounded perfect in her mouth.

She is a Guide, thought Merle, impressed, and rather upset too. But whatever being a Guide may mean – she really is one!

'Tell my mother –' she began, but the phantom interrupted her.

'She's gone again.'

'Oh.'

For the first time the phantom sounded as if he had a

little sympathy for Merle's situation. 'Don't be sad,' he said gently. 'She'll speak to you again. I'm sure she will. All this has been rather . . . well, difficult for her.'

'How do you mean, difficult?'

'You'd only worry unnecessarily if I told you.'

If the phantom intended this to reassure Merle, he achieved precisely the opposite. 'What's the matter with her? Is she ill? Or injured?' she asked urgently.

So the phantom told her what Lalapeya had done to make contact with them, something that might cost her both her hands.

Merle withdrew her fingers and let the mirror drop. For a moment she stared into space.

Now she no longer doubted that the sphinx was her mother.

'Merle?'

She looked up.

Junipa was smiling encouragingly. 'Do you want us to try it? I mean, now?'

Merle took a deep breath, and looked round for the others. The spies were still surrounding Vermithrax, listening to him telling the tale of their adventures in Hell in his sonorous voice. At any other time Merle might perhaps have felt afraid that he was talking too much –

especially as Seth was listening attentively in his corner – but at the moment she had other things on her mind.

'Could you do it, then?' she asked Junipa. 'Here?'

Junipa nodded. Merle followed the direction of her glance at the mirror-glass walls, and saw her own reflection as she crouched on the ground in distress, her hand clenched on the handle of the water mirror.

'The mirror,' she whispered, putting the water mirror in her pocket, buttoning it up and touching the ice-cold wall with her other hand. 'That's it, isn't it? That's why everything here is made of mirrors. The sphinxes have built a gateway. They want to tear down the barrier between worlds with their fortress. First they conquer this world, then they'll go on to the next one, and then another, and –' She stopped, as it became clear to her that this was the plan that the Stone Light was pursuing. What was the link? There must be some connection between the sphinxes and the Light.

'*Don't let it worry you,*' said the Flowing Queen. She had kept so quiet during the last few hours that Merle had almost forgotten her. '*Suppose you don't like the answer?*'

Merle had no time to work out what the Queen meant. Junipa had risen to her feet and was stretching out a hand imperiously.

'Come on,' she said.

Merle took her fingers.

On the other side of the room, Seth raised one eyebrow.

Andrei looked at them too. Merle smiled at him.

'*I could stop you*,' said the Queen.

'No, you couldn't,' Merle said, and knew it was the truth.

Then she went up to the wall, hand in hand with Junipa. She saw the men's reflections, saw them all turn now in surprise.

Junipa whispered the Glass Word.

They entered the mirrors and plunged, amazed, into a silver sea.

HER TRUE NAME

Mirrors upon mirrors upon mirrors. A whole world of them.

A world among the mirrors. Behind them, between them, beside them. Paths and tunnels, all made of silver. Reflections of reflections.

And in the middle of them a thousand Merles, a thousand Junipas.

'It's like travelling back through time,' said Merle.

Junipa kept hold of her hand, leading her like a child through their strange surroundings. 'How do you mean?'

'How long ago is it since Arcimboldo sent us into the mirrors to catch the phantoms?'

'I don't know. It feels to me like –'

'Like years, doesn't it?'

'It feels like forever.'

'That's what I mean,' said Merle. 'If we were to go back to Venice – and we'll do that some time, won't we? – well, if we went back to Venice I should think quite a lot of things might be different. In fact I'm sure they would. But nothing has changed here. It's just mirrors and mirrors and mirrors.'

Junipa nodded slowly. 'But no phantoms.'

'No phantoms,' Merle agreed.

'Or not here, at least.'

'Is the mirror world really a world in itself?' asked Merle.

'More like a place in the middle of all the other worlds. Or no, like a kind of shell surrounding many worlds, like space that surrounds the planets. You have to get through the shell to move on into the next world. Arcimboldo told me so, but he said it takes years to understand even a fraction of all that. Longer than a lifetime. Or many lifetimes. And Burbridge thought it was too great for the human mind to grasp. "It's not real enough," he said.'

'*Not real enough*,' the Queen repeated in Merle's mind. Did she think so too? Or did she see everything quite differently? As so often recently, the Queen was preserving her silence again.

Merle thought of Vermithrax, left behind on the other side of the mirrors. The obsidian lion must be feeling dreadfully anxious about her. We ought to have told him, she thought, we should have let him know what we were planning to do. But how could they have done that without giving the plan away to Seth and the Tsarists too?

Poor Vermithrax.

'*He knows you,*' said the Flowing Queen. '*He knows that you'll manage somehow. You'd better think about yourself, not him.*'

Merle was going to object, but the Queen added, '*Even if only for his sake. Vermithrax will never forgive himself if anything happens to you two.*'

That's a mean thing to say, thought Merle crossly. And terribly unfair.

But the Queen had returned to her brooding silence.

The girls went on through the labyrinth of mirrors, back and forth in a crazy zigzag course, and the longer they walked on the more Junipa blossomed. Where Merle expected to see a path they kept coming upon a new wall of glass, with another to the right and another to the left of it, but Junipa could always find the narrow crack between them, the loophole, the eye of the needle in this glittering, sparkling, shimmering infinity.

'The sphinxes must have been here,' said Merle.

'Do you really think so?'

'Look round you. The Iron Eye imitates it. Mirrors everywhere reflecting each other. You keep seeing yourself in yourself. The Iron Eye is a copy of this place, what you might call a reflection of the mirror world. Only much clearer, much more . . . *reasonable*. Here everything seems so random. If I turn right am I really turning right? And is left really left? Where's above and below and in front and behind?' She was going to stop, thinking that they had reached a dead end, but Junipa went ahead and drew her on, and they passed the place without coming up against any resistance. Junipa seemed to know their way as a matter of course, as if her mirror-glass eyes had picked up a trail as the nose picks up a scent. To Merle, it seemed miraculous.

She looked sideways at her friend, her glance tracing the girl's delicate profile, the curve of her milk-white skin. It lingered on the shards of mirror-glass in her eye sockets.

'What do you see?' she asked. 'I mean, *here* . . . How do you know which way to go?'

Junipa smiled. 'I just see it. I don't know how to explain. It's as if I'd been here before. When you walk through Venice you know your way without looking for landmarks or signposts. You just walk on and after a while you arrive. It seems quite natural. It's the same for me here.'

'But you *haven't* been here before.'

'Not myself, no. But maybe my eyes have.'

They said nothing for quite a long time, until Merle

spoke up again. 'Are you angry with Arcimboldo?'

'Angry?' Junipa gave a clear laugh that sounded genuine. 'How could I be angry with him? I was blind and he gave me back my sight.'

'But he did it because Lord Light told him to.'

'Yes and no. Lord Light, Burbridge . . . he told Arcimboldo to take us out of our orphanages. And the mirror-glass eyes were his idea too. But that's not the only reason why Arcimboldo did it. He wanted to help – to help both of us.'

'But for him we wouldn't be here.'

'But for him the Flowing Queen would be a prisoner of the Egyptians, or dead. Just like us and the rest of Venice. Have you ever looked at it that way?'

Merle thought that she had looked at their situation from every possible standpoint. Of course they were free now only because Arcimboldo had taken them in. But what was their freedom worth? Fundamentally, they were prisoners like all the others – even worse, they were prisoners of a fate that left them no choice except to go on along the path they had once chosen. It would have been so pleasant just to stop, sit back and tell themselves that someone else would deal with it all. But that wasn't the way things were. The responsibility was theirs alone.

She wondered whether perhaps Arcimboldo had foreseen this. And whether he had agreed to the bargain with Lord Light for that reason.

'We'll soon be there,' said Junipa.

'As quick as that?'

'You can't measure the paths here by our standards. Each of them is a short cut in its own way. That's the point of the mirror world: getting from one place to another fast.'

Merle nodded, and suddenly had the feeling that everything Junipa told her wasn't so far-fetched after all. The more fantastic the adventures on their journey had been, the less they surprised Merle. She involuntarily asked herself how long this would go on. When had her old world separated into its component parts and become a new one? Not just when the Queen had entered her mind, but that night all the same: when she first said goodbye to the old Merle and opened the door to the new one; when she and Serafin left the party and abandoned themselves to that unexpected moment; when she became a little more used to the idea that she would soon be grown up.

'There,' said Junipa. 'Ahead of us.'

Merle blinked. At first she could see nothing in the mirrors but herself, and thought caustically that that was just like her: brooding on nothing but herself, herself, herself all the time.

'*Your self-pity can be intolerable,*' said the Flowing Queen. After a moment, she added, '*Aren't you going to answer me back?*'

'No, you're right.'

Junipa took her hand more firmly and pointed to a little dot far ahead in the silvery infinity. 'There's the gate.'

'Oh yes?'

'You mean you can't see it?'

'Someone forgot to give it a handle.'

Junipa smiled. 'Trust me.'

'I've been trusting you all this time.'

Junipa stopped and turned her face to her friend. 'Merle?'

'Yes?'

'I'm glad you're here. I'm glad we're seeing this through together.'

Merle smiled. 'Now you sound quite different from back in the Iron Eye. More . . . more like yourself.'

'I can't feel the Stone Light here among the mirrors,' said Junipa. 'It's like having a normal heart. And I can see better than you, probably better than anyone. I think this is where I belong.'

And perhaps that was the truth; perhaps Arcimboldo

really had made her eyes from the glass of the mirror world. Junipa is a Guide, Lalapeya had said. And weren't guides always from the local population? The idea sent a shiver down Merle's back, but she tried hard not to show it.

'Keep tight hold of my hand,' said Junipa. In a low voice, she whispered the Glass Word, and then they took the crucial step together.

Leaving the mirror world was as unspectacular as entering it. They passed through the glass as if walking through a mild breeze, and on the other side they saw –

'Mirrors?' asked Merle, before realising that this was certainly not the place from which they had set out.

'*Mirrors?*' asked the Flowing Queen too.

'Burbridge's Cabinet of Mirrors,' said Junipa. 'Just as your mother said.'

Behind them someone cleared his throat and spoke. 'I hoped that you two would find the way.'

Merle swung round even faster than Junipa.

Professor Burbridge, Lord Light, her grandfather – three quite different identities in one and the same person. He walked towards them, but stopped a few paces away and did not come too close, as if he didn't want to make them uneasy.

'Don't be afraid,' he said. 'In here I am only myself. The

142

Light has no power over me in this Cabinet of Mirrors.' He sounded older than he had out in Hell. And he looked older too: he was more bowed now, he looked frailer.

'I'm not Lord Light in this place,' he added with a sad smile. 'Only an old fool by the name of Burbridge.'

The mirror through which they had stepped was only one of many arranged in a large circle. Most of them were still glued into the wooden frames that Arcimboldo always gave his magic mirrors when he delivered them to his customers.

All the mirrors that Arcimboldo had sold to Lord Light were on the walls here, perhaps a hundred or two hundred of them. Some lay on the floor too, like puddles of quicksilver, others were fixed flat on the ceiling.

'They keep the Stone Light away,' Burbridge explained. He was wearing a frock-coat like the one he had worn at their first meeting. His hair was untidy and he looked unkempt, as if even his old meticulous appearance had been just an illusion maintained by the Stone Light. In here, all that paled. The bags under his eyes were heavier, his eyes themselves lay deeper in their sockets. Dark veins stood out on the backs of his parchment-like hands. The liver spots of old age flecked his skin like insect shadows.

'We're alone.' He had noticed Merle examining their

143

surroundings distrustfully, fearing to see Burbridge's creatures – the Lilim. He seemed to be speaking the truth.

'My mother sent me.' Suddenly it didn't seem difficult to use that term any more. It sounded almost natural: my mother.

Surprised, Burbridge raised an eyebrow. 'Lalapeya? How I hated her at the time. And she must have hated me, no doubt of that. So now she sends you of all people here?'

'She says you could explain it all to me. The truth about me and my parents. About Lalapeya . . . and Steven.'

When they arrived, Burbridge had been standing in the middle of the room, just as if he was expecting them.

'*It's because of the mirrors,*' said the Flowing Queen. '*If the mirrors really do protect him, then he's probably safest at the centre where their reflections meet.*' Arcimboldo had once said something similar to her: 'Look in a mirror and it will look back at you. Mirrors can see!'

'*It's no coincidence,*' the Queen went on, '*that Burbridge called the capital city of Hell Axis Mundi, the axis of the world. Just as it symbolically marks the central point of Hell, this is the axis of his existence, his own centre, the place where he can still be himself, away from the influence of the Light.*' After a moment's hesitation, she added, '*Most people are searching for their centre all their lives, for the axis of their own worlds, but few are aware of it.*'

144

Burbridge took two more steps towards the girls. There was nothing menacing in itself about the way he moved.

Is *he* my axis? Merle asked in her thoughts. My centre?

The Queen laughed softly. '*He himself? Oh no. But the centre is often what we find at the end of our search. You were in search of your parents, and perhaps you are about to find them. Perhaps your family is your centre, Merle. And Burbridge is part of it, for better or worse. But some day, presumably, you will go in search of something else.*'

Then is the centre something like the happiness we're always searching for but never find?

'*It can be happiness, or it can be your downfall. Many are in search of nothing but death all their lives.*'

Well, at least they can be sure of finding that some time, thought Merle.

'*Don't laugh at the idea. Look at Burbridge! The Stone Light has been keeping him alive for decades. Don't you think he is ready to die? And if death does find him somewhere, it will be here where the Light can't reach him. At least, not yet.*'

Not yet?

'*The Light will know we're here. And it will not wait and watch idly for much longer.*'

Then we'd better get a move on.

'*Good idea.*'

Merle turned to Burbridge. 'I have to know the truth. Lalapeya says it's important.'

'For her or for you?' The old man seemed to be both amused and desperately sad.

'Will you tell me?'

His glance travelled round the never-ending circle of mirrors. Arcimboldo's legacy. 'You presumably don't know much about Lalapeya,' he said. 'Only that she is a sphinx, am I right?'

Merle nodded.

'There is a piece of the Stone Light in Lalapeya too, Merle. And in yourself, for you are her child. But I'll come to that in a minute. First the beginning, right? Always begin at the beginning . . . Many long years ago, the sphinx Lalapeya was given the task of guarding a tomb. Not just any tomb, of course, but the tomb of the ancestor of all the sphinxes. The progenitor of their line, not, as some believe, their god – although he could easily become a god if his old power is roused again. They call him the Son of the Mother. After his death thousands upon thousands of years ago, the sphinx people buried him in a place that was later to be the lagoon of Venice. At that time there was nothing there, only dismal swamps without a sign of life in them. They appointed guards to watch over his eternal sleep, a whole series of guards, and Lalapeya was the last of them. It was then, while Lalapeya was guarding him, that human beings settled in the lagoon, building first simple huts, then houses and finally, over the centuries, a whole city.'

'Venice.'

'Exactly. Sphinxes usually avoid human beings, indeed they hate them, but Lalapeya was different from the rest of her people, and she decided to let the men and women do as they wanted. She admired their strength of will and their determination to wrest a new home for themselves from that wet, inhospitable wilderness.'

An axis, thought Merle, suddenly understanding. A centre to their sad little human world. And the Queen said, *'Yes, that's it.'*

'Over the centuries, the lagoon took shape as you know it today, and Lalapeya stayed there all that time. She was living at last in a palazzo in the Cannaregio quarter. And my son Steven met her there.'

'Who was Steven's mother?'

'One of the Lilim. Not the kind you have met, of course. Not one of those uncouth brutes, and not an ordinary shapeshifter. She was what they call a succubus in the world above. One of the Lilim in the shape of a beautiful woman. And she *was* beautiful, believe me. Steven was a child who carried the inheritance of both his parents in him, mine as well as hers.'

Merle felt quite dizzy at the thought of it. Her mother was a sphinx, her father half human, half Lilim. So what was *she*?

'I often brought Steven here as a child,' Burbridge said. 'I told him about the Stone Light and what it does to us, what it makes us into. Even then, as a little boy, he rebelled against the idea. And when he grew older he left. He told no one he was going, not even me. He went by a secret path that ends near the lagoon, and he felt the influence of the Light falling away from him. He must have thought he could live as a normal man.' Burbridge lowered his voice. 'I gave up that dream myself a long, long time ago. When I was still able to make my escape I didn't want to. And now I can't. The Light won't let me go. But it was indifferent to Steven, perhaps even glad he had gone – always assuming it thinks like us human beings at all, and I have some doubts of that.

'So Steven went to Venice and stayed there. He met Lalapeya, perhaps by chance, though I'm inclined to believe that she sensed where he came from. He was a stranger in the city, like her, a stranger among your people. And for a while they lived together.'

'Why didn't they stay with each other?'

'What neither of them had thought possible happened. Lalapeya became pregnant and brought you into the world, Merle. Steven . . . well, he went away.'

'But why?'

'You'd have to know him to understand. He can't bear to be tied down, subjected to certain . . . certain constraints. I don't know how else to put it. It was the same as in Hell. He hated the Stone Light because it controls us all, and seldom lets us think our own thoughts. He felt constrained again by Lalapeya and her child, his freedom was curtailed. I think that was why he went away.'

Merle's lower lip was trembling. 'What a coward!'

Burbridge hesitated a moment before answering. 'Yes, perhaps he is. Just a coward. Or a rebel. Or a disastrous mixture of the two. But he is also my son and your father, and we shouldn't be too quick to judge him.'

That was not how Merle saw it, but she kept silent so that Burbridge would tell her the rest of the story.

'Lalapeya was in despair. She has always hated me. Steven

had told her everything, about the Light and my role in the world of the Lilim. Lalapeya blamed me for Steven's departure. In her rage and grief she wanted nothing more to do with him, or with her child, in whom she saw something of Steven.'

Junipa took Merle's hand.

'Is that why she abandoned me?' asked Merle.

Burbridge nodded. 'I think she has often regretted it. But she didn't have the power to acknowledge her daughter. She was still guarding the ancestral father, the Son of the Mother.'

Merle thought of the water mirror, and all the times she had put her hand into it and felt the touch of the fingers on its other side. Always tender, always full of warmth and friendship. What Burbridge said wasn't true: Lalapeya had acknowledged her, if in a sphinx's own mysterious way.

'Lalapeya must have known you were living in the orphanage. She probably kept track of every step you took,' Burbridge went on. 'It was harder for me. It took me years, but in the end Arcimboldo found you for me and took you into his house.' His eyes sought Junipa, and found her half hidden behind Merle. 'Like you, Junipa. If for other reasons.'

Junipa made a face. 'You turned me into a slave. So that

I could go spying on other worlds for the Stone Light.'

'Yes,' he said sadly, 'that too. That was *one* reason, but not mine, it was the Light's. I wanted something different.'

Merle's voice became icy when she understood. 'He made use of you, Junipa. Not for you but for me. He wanted you to bring me here. That was the reason, wasn't it, Professor? You had her given those eyes so that she could show me the way to this Cabinet of Mirrors.'

Burbridge nodded again, obviously with regret. 'I couldn't have you brought here by the Lilim – that would only have drawn the Light's attention to you. When you finally came to Hell of your own accord with the lion, you were in the domain of the Light. And you saw how little power I have there when the Lilim captured you. I wanted to spare you all that. Junipa was to have brought you here through the mirrors as she has today, to this Cabinet where you are safe from the Light and its influence.' He hesitated for a moment, and mopped his brow. Then he turned to Junipa. 'About your heart . . . I never planned it. The Light and not I had that done. I couldn't prevent it, for I was under its influence myself at the time. It was hard enough to resist it when I took Merle out of the House of the Heart.' He sadly shook his head, and looked at the floor. 'It would have killed me for that if it hadn't needed me. It made me lord of Hell, and the Lilim respect and fear me. Finding anyone to replace me would be difficult, and it would take a long time to build him up to what I am today.' The ghost of a bitter smile flitted over his face. 'But that has always been the Devil's fate, hasn't it? He can't just retire like a managing director or abdicate like a king. He is what he is, and for ever.'

Merle just looked at him while her thoughts went round in circles, faster and faster. She caught herself trying to give her father a face, a younger version of Burbridge without the wrinkles, without the grey in his hair and the weariness in his eyes.

'I have to be grateful for the moments when I can still be myself. But there are fewer and fewer of those, and soon I shall be only a puppet of the Light. Then I'll really have earned the name Lord Light,' he said ironically.

Did he expect her to feel sorry for him? Merle simply could not make him out. She tried to summon up hatred and contempt for all that he had done to her and Junipa, and perhaps to her father too, but she couldn't even manage that.

'I wanted to see you, Merle,' said Burbridge. 'Even when you were still a small child. And I had hoped so much the circumstances would be different. I wanted you to meet *me* first, not Lord Light. And it turned out exactly the other way around. I can't expect you to forgive me for that.'

Merle heard his words, understood what they meant, but it made no difference what he said. He was a stranger to her. Just like her father.

'What happened to Steven?' she asked.

'He passed through the mirrors.'

'Alone?'

Burbridge looked down. 'Yes.'

'But out there without a Guide, he'll become –'

'A phantom. Yes, I know. And I'm not even sure whether he didn't know it too. But I have never given up hope. If we could look into other worlds, perhaps we might find him.'

Junipa stared at him with her mirror-glass eyes. 'Was *that* what you wanted? For me to go looking for him?'

He lowered his gaze and said no more.

Slowly, Merle nodded. All at once the pieces fitted together. Junipa's mirror-glass eyes, her training with their master Arcimboldo in his mirror-making workshop: Burbridge had her future all mapped out in advance from the moment when she left her orphanage.

'But what about the offer from Hell to protect Venice from the Egyptians?' Merle asked.

'It was you I wanted to protect. And Arcimboldo, because I needed his mirrors.'

'Then all that about a drop of blood from every soul in Venice was nothing but –'

Instead of Burbridge, Junipa interrupted her. 'He wanted to save face. And keep up the idea that human beings have of Hell. He's still Lord Light. He has,' she said in a very matter-of-fact tone, 'he has obligations.'

'Is that true?' Merle asked him.

Burbridge took a deep breath and then nodded. 'You two won't be able to understand that. This struggle between me and the Light, the strength of its power . . . the way it forces its ideas on a man, changing everything that goes on inside him . . . no one can understand it.'

'*Merle.*' Ending her long silence, the Flowing Queen spoke gently but urgently. '*We must get away from here. He's right when he speaks of the Stone Light's great strength. And there are things to be done.*'

Merle thought briefly, and something else occurred to her. She turned back to the Professor. 'In the pyramid, when we were escaping from you . . . you said you knew a name. I didn't understand what you meant. Whose name?'

Burbridge came still closer, and now he could have put out his hand and touched her. But he did not venture to do so. '*Her* name, Merle. The name of the Flowing Queen.'

Is that true? she asked in her mind.

The Queen did not reply.

'What difference would it make if I knew what she's called?'

'It's not just her name,' he said. 'It's who she really is, that's the point.'

Merle scrutinised him closely. If this was some kind of trick she didn't see what he hoped to gain by it. She tried to get the Queen to explain, but she seemed to be biding her time.

'Sekhmet,' he said. 'Her name is Sekhmet.'

Merle delved into her memory. But there was nothing there, no name anything like it.

'Sekhmet?'

Burbridge smiled. 'The ancient Egyptian lion goddess.'

Is that true?

Hesitantly, the Queen said, '*Yes.*'

But –

'She's depicted as a lioness in the ruins of the ancient

temples and the tombs of the Pharaohs. Ask her, Merle! Ask her if she was a stone lioness!'

'More than that. I was a goddess, and yes, I had the body of a lioness . . . in the days when most gods still had bodies of their own and walked the world like other living creatures. And who can say whether we were really gods? Not we ourselves, anyway, but the idea pleased us, and we began believing what humans said.' She paused briefly. *'In the end we were convinced of our own almighty power. That was at the time when men began hunting us down. For copies of gods are much more easily misused for human purposes than the gods themselves. Images have no will or wishes. Statues stand for nothing but what human rulers want. That is how it's always been. The word of a god is never really anything but the word of the ruler who erects the divine statues of him.'*

Merle exchanged a glance with Junipa. Her friend couldn't hear the Queen. Merle saw her own exhausted face in those mirror-glass eyes, and she frightened herself.

How long ago was that? she asked the Queen in her mind.

'Aeons. Longer than the family trees of the Egyptians go back. Others before them worshipped me, peoples whose names are long forgotten.'

'Is she telling you the legend?' asked Burbridge. 'If not, I will. Sekhmet, the mighty, wise, omniscient Sekhmet, was impregnated by a ray of moonlight and gave birth to the first sphinx, forefather of the whole race of sphinxes.'

The Son of the Mother! That was the thought that shot through Merle's mind. She asked: why didn't you tell me?

'*Because then you wouldn't have done what you did. And what difference would it really have made? The dangers would still have been the same. But would you have faced them for an Egyptian goddess? I never lied to you, Merle. I am indeed the Flowing Queen. It was I who protected Venice from the Egyptians. As for what I was before – what part does that play in it?*'

A large one. Perhaps the main part. Because you brought me here. You know what the sphinxes are planning. You probably always did.

'*We're here to prevent it. The Son of the Mother must not rise again. And if he does, then I am the only one who can face him. For I am his mother and his lover. It was with him that I gave birth to the sphinx people.*'

With your own *son*?

'*He was the son of a ray of moonlight. That's different.*'

Oh yes?

Once again Burbridge intervened. 'Sekhmet can't help it,' he said, surprisingly coming to the Queen's aid, although he could only guess what she was saying to Merle.

'What she took for a ray of moonlight . . . well, it was really something else. A ray the Stone Light cast as it fell to earth. Did it intend to find that target? And why Sekhmet? I don't know the answer to those questions. Probably the Light foresaw that its fall would bury it deep inside the earth, and then it would be difficult for it to influence beings on the surface. So – and this is only my theory as a scientist, independent of anything else – so I think the Light impregnated the lion goddess on purpose, aiming to create its own race. A race of creatures carrying a piece of the Light inside them, possibly without knowing it. But at any rate, a race capable of being taken over by the Light at some future time to obey its orders on the surface of the earth. Just as the Lilim obey it within the earth.' He stopped, sounding tired and exhausted. Towards the end of this speech his voice had become fainter and fainter, sounding old and hoarse.

You obeyed it, Merle said to the Queen.

'*Yes.*'

Well?

The Queen seemed to hesitate, but then Merle heard the voice in her mind again. '*It was I who killed the Son of the Mother. I sensed, too late, that he had the Light in him. It was too late because the sphinx race had already been born. I could only prevent him from becoming its ruler. But as it has turned out, I was only postponing the crisis. In spite of what I did, the sphinxes have become what I always feared they would.'*

So then you went to the lagoon –

'To keep watch on him. Just like Lalapeya and those who were before her. All the same, there was one great difference: the sphinxes venerated him, and kept watch to prevent anyone from desecrating his tomb. I, on the other hand, kept watch on him to prevent his resurrection. Lalapeya was the first to guess his real nature. She had no proof of it, of course, but she sensed it when she found out that the sphinxes are behind the Egyptian Empire and regard bringing the Son of the Mother back to life as their highest aim.'

Merle understood. This was the link she had been looking for: the link between the sphinxes and the Stone Light. Pharaoh, the priests of Horus, they had all been tools in the hands of the sphinxes.

The war, the enslavement of the world, had all that not really been very important? Was it really only Venice that had been at stake – Venice, and what lay buried under it?

'The sphinxes made the priests of Horus and Pharaoh do as they wanted by holding out the prospect of world domination. But their own main aim was always the lagoon. And I was the only one who could keep them away from it.' For a moment her voice in Merle's

mind faltered, as if she were losing control over it. Then, sounding more composed, she went on, '*I have failed. But I have come to the sphinx fortress to put that right. With you, Merle.*'

Is that where you wanted to go all along?

'*No. At first I really thought we would find help in Hell. I wanted to draw the Lilim into the war against the Empire. But I never guessed how much power the Stone Light already had over Burbridge. That lost us valuable time. The Son of the Mother is already in the Iron Eye. I can feel his presence. Lalapeya couldn't prevent that either. That's why she is here.*'

What will happen if he comes back to life?

'*On the surface of the earth, he will represent the Stone Light as Burbridge does down here – only he will be incomparably more cruel and determined. He has more mastery of sphinx magic than any other being. He will have no doubts, and most certainly no Cabinet of Mirrors where he can withdraw from the influence of the Light. The Light will saturate the world as water saturates a sponge. And after that it will stop at nothing.*'

Merle's eyes went to Junipa, who was still looking at her curiously and with concern. If the Son of the Mother seized power and took control of the Empire, Junipa would fall under the spell of the Stone Light again. And so would everyone else. So would she, Merle.

Burbridge and Junipa both knew what was going on in Merle's mind. They couldn't hear her talking to the Queen, but they were watching Merle closely, noticing the expressions on her face and all her movements. Junipa was still holding Merle's hand tightly, as if she could somehow support her that way, could help her to understand and come to terms with all this new information.

The Queen's admissions had shattered Merle, but she summoned up the strength to concentrate on what mattered most: the Queen, Junipa, the Son of the Mother.

And then there was Burbridge standing opposite her and looking miserable, an old man who seemed to be in urgent need of a chair because he could hardly keep on his feet any more.

'You must go,' he said. 'The Stone Light sometimes allows me to withdraw here, but not often – and certainly not for as long as today.'

Hesitantly, Merle freed her hand from Junipa's, then came forward with a firmer step and for the first time held it out to him. He took it, and tears came to his eyes.

'What will it do?' she asked quietly. 'To you . . . Grandfather?'

'I am Lord Light. I shall still be that. It may destroy these mirrors, but that doesn't matter now. We have met, and I don't need them any more. I have told you what there was to be told . . . or at least the most important part of it. There are other things that I feel and think and –' He broke off, shook his head and began again. 'I can't withstand the Light much longer. And it will tighten its hold.' The tears were dropping from his eyes now and running down his cheeks. 'If we should ever meet again, and God preserve you from it, Merle . . . if we should ever meet again I shall finally be what you met in Hell. The man who allowed Junipa's heart to be exchanged for a heart of stone. The man who rules the Lilim like a despot. And who has sacrificed his free will to the Stone Light.'

Merle's throat felt tight. 'You could come with us.'

'I am too old,' he said, shaking his head. 'I shall die without the power of the Light.'

But that's what you want, isn't it? Merle thought. However, she did not say so out loud. The idea hurt, even though she didn't like to admit it to herself. She didn't want him to die. But nor did she want him to turn forever into what the rest of mankind had long thought him: the Devil, Satan in person.

He seemed to guess what she was thinking. 'The Light

has my soul in its grasp. I'm too weak to go to my death willingly. I've held out too long for that, I've fought it for too long. I could ask you to . . . but that would be cruel and —'

'Oh, I can't!'

'I know.' He smiled, looking strangely wise. 'Perhaps it's best that way. Every world needs its Devil, this one included. It needs the spectre of evil to understand why it's so important to defend what's good. In a way I am only doing my duty . . . even the Stone Light is doing what it must. And some time Hell will be feared again for what it has really been all through the millennia: a phantom place, people may believe in it in a way but they won't think it is real. Legends and myths and rumours transformed into ideas, very far from everyday human life.'

'But only if we manage to stop the sphinxes,' said Junipa.

'That's the condition.' Burbridge drew Merle to him and embraced her, and she returned the embrace without stopping to think about it. 'This place down here is not your story, my child. You're the heroine of the story up above. There are no heroes in Hell. Only failures. Lord Light is not your enemy. Your adversaries are up there: the sphinxes, the Son of the Mother. If you can stop them it will be a long time before the Stone Light gains any power on the surface again. If its followers there are destroyed, it will be defeated in your part of the world. And as for this one, you had better forget it again. For a few hundred years, or a few thousand. The Light and I – or I should say, Lord Light – will have too much to do in Hell to trouble with the world above.' He let go of Merle, but his eyes still dwelt on hers. 'This is your task now, and yours alone.'

'Won't the Lilim come up and attack human beings?'

'No, they've never done that. Not as an army, not to conquer their lands. There have been individual Lilim who ventured up, yes . . . but only as beasts of prey. There'll be no war between the worlds above and below.'

'But the Light will live on in Hell!'

'Powerful down here but powerless on the surface. Without its children the sphinxes, it may be thousands of years before it can venture to strike again. Until then it will be only what the church preaches – the Tempter, the Evil One, the fallen angel Lucifer – and for the human race fundamentally as harmless as a ghost rattling its chains. If it is no more than part of a religion, if it has become an empty concept again, it won't do any more harm.'

'*He's right*,' said the Flowing Queen excitedly. '*He really could be right.*'

'Go now,' said Burbridge again, with a pleading note in his voice this time. 'Before –'

'Before it's too late?' Merle forced a smile out of herself. 'I seem to have read that somewhere before.'

At that Burbridge smiled, and hugged her again. 'You see, child? It's only a story. Nothing but a story.'

He kissed her forehead, he even kissed Junipa, and then stepped back.

The girls imprinted his image on their minds for the last time: the image of Charles Burbridge, not Lord Light; the image of an old man, not the Devil he would soon be again.

They left the Hell of the Lilim through the mirrors, and returned to their own.

THE ABDUCTION

'They've gone,' said Junipa.

'What?'

'They're not in their hiding place any more.' Junipa's eyes penetrated the silvery veil of the mirror world, looking into the Iron Eye and the room where they had left their companions. 'There's no one left,' she said sadly.

'Where have they gone?'

'I don't know. I'll have to search for them.'

Merle cursed her inability to see through the mirrors herself. She could make out blurred shapes and colours, yes, but no clear images. At the moment she couldn't even see which mirror concealed the hiding place.

'There . . . there was a fight,' said Junipa. 'The sphinxes found them.'

'Oh no!'

'There are three men lying on the floor . . . three of the spies. They're dead. The others have gone.'

'What about Vermithrax?'

'I can't find him.'

'But there's no missing him!'

Junipa turned her head, and there was a note of annoyance in her voice for perhaps the first time since Merle had known her. 'Be patient for a minute, can't you? I need to concentrate.'

Merle bit her lower lip and said nothing. Her knees were trembling.

Junipa let go of her hand and looked around her, turning in all directions among the mirrors. 'The Iron Eye is so large. There are too many mirrors. They could be anywhere.'

'Then take me back to the hiding place.'

'Are you sure? It could be dangerous.'

'I want to see for myself. Otherwise it will seem so . . . so unreal.'

Junipa nodded. 'Stay beside me. Just in case we have to disappear again in a hurry.' She took Merle's hand again, whispered the Glass Word, and stepped with her through a mirror as if it were a curtain made of moonlight.

The door of the room had broken into hundreds of shards of mirror-glass. They covered the floor like scattered razorblades. The mirrors on the walls had several cracks in them too. To the right of the two girls one wall was completely destroyed, and it took them only seconds to realise that Vermithrax had fled from the sphinxes that way. The stone wall beneath the remains of the glass looked like an open mouth full of teeth with gaps in them.

'There must have been a great many sphinxes,' said Junipa thoughtfully. 'Otherwise he wouldn't have run from them. He's much stronger than they are.'

Merle was crouching down beside the three dead men. She quickly saw that there was nothing anyone could do for the Tsarists now. Andrei was not among them. Merle remembered the fifth spy, a hulking great redhead who had looked particularly grotesque in his mummy disguise. He too was missing.

'Merle!'

She looked up, first at Junipa, who had uttered that cry of alarm, then at the door.

A sphinx was racing towards her with terrifying speed. The sight of it paralysed her. But Junipa was with her, took hold of her hand, said the Word, and dragged her through the nearest mirror. Behind them they heard a scream of rage and surprise, followed by a shrill crunching sound as the massive body of the sphinx was flung against the glass by its own impetus. A crack appeared for a moment inside the mirror world, and then disappeared like a pencil line being erased from top to bottom.

Merle was out of breath. The realisation of her narrow escape from death gradually spread through her. Her heart was thudding fast and painfully.

Junipa's mirror-glass eyes were expressionless as ever, but Merle could tell how angry she was. 'I told you to stay beside me! That was a close thing!'

'I thought I might be able to help one of them.'

Junipa looked as if she were going to say something furious, but then her features softened and were as gentle as ever. 'Yes. Of course.' She gave Merle an encouraging glance. 'Sorry.'

They smiled shyly at each other, then Junipa took Merle's hand, and they went on together.

Very soon Merle had lost all sense of direction again, and had to rely on Junipa's guidance. Now and then they stopped. Junipa looked around her, almost scenting the air like a wild beast in search of prey, touched a sheet of mirror-glass once or twice, and then hurried on.

'Here!' she said at last, pointing to a mirror. It seemed to Merle that it was shining a little more brightly than the others, with a fiery, reddish-yellow light.

'There he is! That's Vermithrax!'

'Wait. Let me look.' Junipa stepped forward and placed the tip of her nose close to the glass. When she whispered the Word her breath clouded the surface. She put her face far enough through the mirror to see what was on the other side, dipping it into the white condensation on the glass as if into a jug of fresh milk. Merle, holding her hand, felt as if Junipa's fingers were getting colder the longer she stayed like that, partly in the mirror world, partly in the Iron Eye.

She whispered her friend's name.

A ripple ran through the mirror as Junipa brought her face back through it. 'They're there. All four of them.'

'Seth too?'

'Yes, he's fighting at Andrei's side.'

'Really?' That surprised her.

Junipa nodded. 'What shall we do now?'

We must go to them, Merle told herself. We must help them. We must stop the sphinxes carrying out their plan. But how? She might be the Devil's granddaughter and the daughter of a sphinx – but still she was only a fourteen-year-old girl. Any sphinx would strike her down with a single blow. And she didn't want harm to come to Junipa.

'I know what you're thinking,' said Junipa.

Merle stared past her at the mirror and the light beyond it, at the moving shapes, too distorted for her to make out what they were. She knew that Vermithrax and the others were fighting for their lives there, yet no sounds crossed the threshold of the mirror world. No clash of weapons, no shouts, no breathless gasping or groaning. The world might come to an end on the other side, and here beyond the mirrors it would still be nothing but a dazzling firework display of colours and silver.

'There's something different,' said Junipa.

'What?'

Junipa crouched down, put one hand against the glass at floor level, whispered the Word, and reached through it. When she withdrew her fingers she had clenched them into a fist. She held her hand in front of Merle's face and then opened it.

Merle stared at what she saw before her. Then she put out a finger and touched it.

'Ice,' she whispered breathlessly.

'Snow,' said Junipa. 'It's hard like that only because I compressed it.'

'But that means Winter is here! Here in the Iron Eye!'

'Can he even make it snow indoors?' Junipa frowned.

Merle had told her about Winter and his search for his lover Summer, but it was still hard for her to imagine a season which, at the same time, was a flesh and blood figure walking the mirror-glass corridors of the Eye.

Merle came to her decision. 'I want to go back there now!'

Junipa dropped the snow on the floor, where it melted to water the next moment. She sighed softly, but at last she nodded. 'Yes, we have to do something.' And after a little thought, she added, 'But don't go right through the mirror. As long as you leave an arm or a foot on the other side of it, the glass will let you in again. In an emergency we only need to jump back.'

Merle agreed, although she hardly heard what Junipa was saying. She was far too excited. Everything was going round and round in her head.

Hand in hand, they stepped through the mirror into the Iron Eye.

Dazzling brightness met them. A snowfield reflected to infinity by the walls and the ceiling. A wave of noise and fury rolled towards them, worse than anything Merle had expected. Vermithrax uttered a shattering roar as he took on two sphinxes at once. Andrei and Seth were fighting back to back. The red-haired spy lay lifeless on the floor; the blow of a crescent sword had felled him. There were several mummy warriors in this hall of mirrors, and Merle also counted three sphinxes. Another lay motionless by the door.

'Merle!' Vermithrax had seen her. He parried a sword-cut with one of his paws, and drew the claws of the other down over the sphinx's chest. Blood flowed into the snow, to be covered the next moment by the sphinx's body as he collapsed. The second sphinx hesitated before deciding to go on the attack again. When he found that the edge of his sword rebounded from the lion's shining obsidian body as if it were a wall he withdrew. Vermithrax took a couple of leaps in pursuit, but then let his adversary go.

Andrei and Seth were fighting together against the third sphinx and three mummy warriors. The undead were not much use to their commander; they kept getting in the way or stumbling as the sphinx attacked. Finally he too let out one of those furious, shrill screeches and stormed away, right across the hall and through the high gateway, beyond which a great expanse of yet more snow stretched away.

Junipa was still standing in the mirror-glass wall itself, half in this world, half in the world of mirrors. Merle had taken her advice to heart, and so far had taken care not to lose all contact with the mirror. But now, seeing the sphinxes put to flight, she was about to let go of Junipa's hand and run to Vermithrax.

Suddenly someone seized her, tore her away from Junipa and flung her to one side. With a cry, she collided with a mirror and fell on her knees. Her dress immediately soaked up ice-cold moisture.

When Merle looked up she saw Seth. He had taken Junipa's hand himself, he pushed off from the floor and hurtled through the mirror wall taking her with him. There was no splintering glass, and Merle knew why: the gate was open as long as Junipa kept in touch with the mirror. The Glass Word was still working for her and anyone who touched her. Including Seth.

'*No!*' Merle leaped up and ran through the snow to the mirror. But she already knew she would be too late.

Seth and Junipa had gone. Although she knew it was useless Merle tried to follow them, slamming her shoulder against the glass. The mirror wall creaked, but stood firm.

'No!' she shouted again as she kicked the glass and hammered her fists against it. Eyes watering, she stared into the mirror, but instead of her friend and the High Priest all she saw was herself, with wild, tangled hair, red eyes and shining cheeks. Her dress was wet with the snow, but she hardly felt the cold.

'Merle,' said Vermithrax calmly. He was suddenly there beside her.

She didn't listen to him, but went on drumming on the mirror, and then whirled round and sank to the floor with her back against the icy glass. Desperately, she rubbed her eyes, but the brightness around her dazzled her all the more. Reflected light formed blazing stars and circles, all clear outlines were blurred.

One of those indistinct shapes was Vermithrax. Another was Andrei. The stone lion had dragged him over here and laid him in the snow between them. Somewhere in the background, amid grey fountains of dust, lay the mummy warriors.

'She's gone,' said the lion.

'I can see that for myself!'

'Andrei is dying, Merle.'

'I –' She stopped short, stared at Vermithrax and then at the Tsarist lying on the ground. He reached out a hand to her, whispering something in his own language, and it was obvious that he saw not Merle herself but someone else.

Vermithrax nodded to her. 'Take his hand,' he whispered.

Merle dropped to her knees and put both her hands round Andrei's cold fingers. Her thoughts were still with Junipa, lost for the second time now, but she did her best to concentrate on the dying man. It's unreal, were the words ringing in her head, it's all so unreal.

Andrei's free hand held her shoulder so tightly that it hurt, and drew her forward. His fingers rose to her neck. As Merle was about to jerk her head back he touched the leather thong with the chicken's foot hanging from it. The sign of Baba Yaga. The emblem of his goddess.

Merle wanted to wipe the tears from her eyes, but she knew she mustn't let go of him now. Never mind what was happening around them, Andrei deserved to die in peace. Like his companions, he was a brave man; he had run the risk of abandoning his disguise for the two girls and the lion. Vermithrax could have dealt with the first sphinx on his own, but Andrei had killed him for them all the same. Perhaps because he had been glad to meet living, breathing human beings again after all those months in the Iron Eye.

Andrei clutched the chicken's foot hanging from her neck with one hand, murmuring words in Russian, perhaps a prayer, perhaps something quite different. Sometimes he spoke a word that Merle thought was the name of a woman or girl. His daughter, she suddenly thought. He had mentioned her very briefly after leading the three newcomers to the spies' hiding place. The daughter he had left behind so many thousands of kilometres away.

Then Andrei died. She had to prise his fingers loose from the pendant with her trembling hands.

Vermithrax growled quietly.

'We must leave!' he said at last, and it seemed to Merle as if those three words best described their whole journey. They had had to leave Venice first, then Axis Mundi. They were always in flight. Yet their destination seemed to be further and further away.

Vermithrax went on. 'The sphinxes will raise the alarm.'

Merle nodded, lost in thought. She crossed Andrei's hands over his breast, although she didn't know if that gesture was understood in his own country. Then she lightly stroked his cheek with the back of her hand before she rose to her feet.

Vermithrax looked at her with his huge lion's eyes. 'You are very brave. Much braver than I thought.'

She sobbed, and began crying again, but this time she soon got control over herself. 'What about Junipa?'

'We can't follow her.'

'I know *that*. But there must be something we can –'

'*We must get away from here! Fast.*' At moments like this Merle sometimes forgot that she was not alone in her mind. When the Queen suddenly spoke up she jumped, as if someone had come up behind her and was shouting in her ear. '*Vermithrax is right. We must stop them bringing the Son of the Mother back to life.*'

'I couldn't care less about the Son of the Mother,' cried Merle furiously out loud, so that Vermithrax could hear it too. He raised one startled eyebrow. 'Seth has abducted Junipa, and that matters more to me just now than any old sphinx gods and their mothers!'

She hoped she had made herself clear enough. But the Queen was not impressed. If there was one thing she was good at, it was sticking to her point. '*Your world will fall into ruin, Merle. It will founder and fall into ruin if you and I don't do something to stop it.*'

'My world has fallen into ruin already,' she said sadly. 'At the moment when we met.' She didn't mean to be sarcastic, and there was no malice in her voice. Every word was true, and honestly felt: her world – a new, unhoped-for world, but *her own* – had been Arcimboldo's workshop, with all its good and bad points, with Dario and the other brawling boys, but with Junipa and Eft too, and it was a place that had been hers. The arrival of the Queen in her life had put an end to that.

The Queen said nothing for a moment, but then, once again, she broke into the sad silence inside Merle's head, a silence like the stillness at the eye of a hurricane. *'Don't blame me. After the Egyptians attacked nothing was the same as before.'*

Merle knew perfectly well that she was holding the wrong person responsible. 'I'm sorry,' she said, but she didn't mean it. She couldn't turn into someone different, not here, not today, beside Andrei's body and in front of the mirror through which Junipa had disappeared as if swallowed up by silver jaws. She could say she was sorry; she couldn't really feel it.

'Merle,' said Vermithrax urgently, 'please! We must go!'

She swung herself up on his back. One last sad look at the mirror into which Junipa and Seth had gone, and then it was only one of many others, a facet on the intricately polished surface of a jewel.

'Where exactly are we anyway?' she asked as Vermithrax carried her through the gate of the hall, hesitated briefly in the corridor, and then turned right. The snow lay thirty or forty centimetres deep inside the building, churned up by the claws of the sphinxes and the boots of the mummy warriors.

'A good deal lower down than the room where the spies were hiding.' The obsidian lion peered intently ahead of them as he spoke. 'We were running down stairways almost all the time just now. Andrei knew the way very well. His friends probably did too. But I didn't understand what they were saying.'

'*Andrei knew,*' said the Queen. '*He knew that the Son of the Mother is in this fortress.*'

Merle passed that on to Vermithrax. He agreed. 'Seth told us so while you were gone.'

'Why did he do that?'

'Perhaps to keep our minds occupied while he worked out how to get hold of Junipa.'

Merle felt her heart sink a little further.

'Seth has nothing in his head but vengeance,' the lion added.

'*And why not?*' said the Queen. '*If that helps us to stop the Son of the Mother.*'

Merle felt like taking her by the shoulders and shaking her, but the Queen's shoulders, after all, were her own, and it would have looked very silly. 'All right,' she said after a while, 'then why not tell us what to do if we happen to bump into him?'

'*May I?*' asked the Queen with unaccustomed civility.

'Go ahead.'

The Flowing Queen immediately took over Merle's own voice, and told Vermithrax briefly who and what the Son of the Mother was, and what part she herself had played in his story.

'You are the mother of the sphinxes?' asked the astonished Vermithrax. 'Sekhmet the Great?'

'Just Sekhmet will do.'

'The lion goddess!'

'*Here we go again,*' said the Queen in Merle's mind, and this time Merle couldn't suppress a faint grin.

'Is that really true?' Vermithrax asked.

'No, I'm just making it up to keep us amused in this boring old fortress of theirs,' said the Queen through Merle's mouth.

'Forgive me.'

'No need to get all reverent about it.'

'Sekhmet is the goddess of all lions,' said Vermithrax. 'My own people included.'

'*And more than that,*' whispered the Queen to Merle,

before she went on out loud, 'If you say so. But I haven't been a goddess for a long time – if I ever was.'

Vermithrax sounded stunned. 'I don't understand.'

'Just keep acting the way you did before. No "Sekhmet the Great", no "goddess", none of that, all right?'

'Certainly,' he said humbly.

'Don't let it worry you,' said Merle, when she had her own voice back again. 'You'll get used to her.'

'*A little more humility might not hurt some,*' said the Queen sourly.

Vermithrax went down more stairs, going deeper and deeper into the fortress, and at every landing the snow lay deeper, the cold was fiercer. Merle looked into the mirrors that made its whiteness stretch to infinity, and came to a decision. 'We must find Winter.'

'*We must –*' the Queen began, but Merle interrupted her.

'We don't stand a chance on our own. But with Winter on our side . . . who knows?'

'*He won't help us. He has nothing in his head but his search for Summer.*'

'Perhaps the two things have something to do with each other?' The corners of Merle's mouth twisted in a chilly smile.

'*But the quickest way to –*'

'At this moment I'm in favour of the safest way. How about you, Vermithrax?'

'Anything the goddess says.'

'A *lion of principle*.'

Merle rolled her eyes. 'All right, who cares? Let's go and look for Winter! Keep going straight on to wherever the snow is deepest, Vermithrax.'

'*You'll freeze.*'

'Then we'll freeze together.'

'*That's what I'm trying to prevent at this moment.*'

'Very thoughtful of you.'

In the middle of a stairwell, the fourth or fifth after they had left the hall, Vermithrax stopped so abruptly that Merle fell forward into his mane, face first. It was like falling into a forest of bright underwater plants.

'What is it?'

He growled and looked around him, his eyes alert. 'There's something wrong here.'

'Are we being followed?'

'No.'

'Watched?'

'That's just it. We haven't seen any sphinxes or mummy warriors since the fight.'

'As far as I'm concerned that's fine.'

'Come on, Merle, don't pretend to be stupid. You know what I mean.'

She did know, of course, but she had been trying hard to suppress the knowledge all this time, and would have liked to go on trying a little longer. She was in the mood to quarrel, too. With the Queen, even with Vermithrax. She herself didn't really understand where her bad temper came from. It was Seth who had betrayed them and abducted Junipa. No, that was wrong! He'd abducted Junipa, yes – but had he betrayed them? He hadn't made any move to hand Merle and the others over to the sphinxes. He was still pursuing his own very personal aims, and if you looked at the facts, he had simply made use of his advantage. Junipa was to take him somewhere, that was certain, for she was the key to changing place swiftly and easily. But where had they gone? To Heliopolis? Or some other part of the Iron Eye?

'This whole wretched fortress suddenly seems deserted!' Vermithrax himself sounded annoyed. With his great nose, the size of a human head, he sniffed around the stairwell while his eyes kept exploring it. 'There must be someone around.'

'Perhaps they're busy somewhere else.' For instance, dealing with Winter, added Merle in her thoughts.

'*Or the Son of the Mother*,' said the Queen.

Merle imagined the scene: a huge hall with hundreds of sphinxes assembled in it. All of them staring devoutly at the corpse on its bier. Singing echoed through the air, quiet whispers. The words of a priest or leader. Grotesque machines and pieces of apparatus were switched on. Electric charges ran between metal globes and intricately winding spirals of steel. Liquids bubbled in glass flasks, steaming vapours poured from valves and rose to the ceiling. And all of it was reflected a dozen times over in silver walls as tall as towers.

Then she imagined a cry leaping from sphinx to sphinx like wildfire. Strident masks of triumph, open mouths, wide eyes, roars of laughter – a sound of joy, of relief, but also of barely concealed fear. Priests and scientists swarming around the Son of the Mother like flies around a piece of dead meat. A dark eyelid slowly lifting. Beneath it the black pupil of an eye, dried up and wrinkled as a prune. And in it, caught there like a curse in a dusty burial chamber, a spark of diabolical intelligence growing brighter and brighter.

'Merle?'

Vermithrax's voice.

'Merle?' More urgent now. 'Did you hear that?'

She jumped. 'Hm?'

'I asked if you'd heard that.'

'Heard what?'

'Listen hard.'

Merle tried to think what Vermithrax meant. She was having difficulty in shaking off the picture that had presented itself to her imagination: that dark and ancient eye, and the mind of the Son of the Mother awakening in it.

Now she heard it. A howl.

Once again the idea of a monstrous gathering of all the sphinxes rose in her. The whispering, the singing, the sounds of a ritual.

But the howl came from something else.

'Sounds like a storm,' said Merle.

She had hardly spoken the words before something came racing towards them from the depths of the stairwell. Vermithrax leaned far out over the handrail; Merle had to cling to his mane to keep from being flung over his head and down into the abyss.

A white wall rose from the mirror-lined chasm below.

Mist, she thought at first.

Snow!

A snowstorm that seemed to come straight from the

heart of the Arctic, a fist of ice and frost striking with unimaginable power.

Vermithrax spread his great wings high in the air and folded them over Merle like two giant hands, holding her firmly down on his back. The howl became deafening, and in the end was so loud that she scarcely perceived it as sound at all; it was a blade cutting through her auditory nerves and carving her mind apart. She felt she was freezing alive, like the dead seagull she had found one winter on the orphanage roof. The bird looked as if it had simply fallen from the sky with its wings still spread, its eyes still open. When Merle lost her balance on the smooth slope of the roof for a moment, it had slipped from her hand, and one wing broke off as if it were made of porcelain.

The storm passed by like a crowd of screaming ghosts. When it was over, and the wind in the shaft of the stairwell died down, the level of snow on the steps was almost twice as deep as it had been before.

'Was *that* Winter?' asked Vermithrax, dazed. Ice crystals sparkled in his coat, in strange contrast to the radiance of his body, which gave off no heat and did not seem able to melt the ice.

Merle sat up straight on his back, ran both hands

through her hair and pushed the wet strands back from her face. The tiny hairs in her nostrils were frozen, and for a while she found it easier to breathe through her mouth.

'I don't know,' she managed to gasp. 'But if Winter had been anywhere in that storm he would surely have seen us. He wouldn't just have run past. Or flown past. Or whatever.' As if dazed, she knocked the snow off her dress. She was frozen, and the fabric was almost frozen rigid over her knees too. 'It's about time we found Summer.'

'*We?*' asked the Queen in alarm.

Merle nodded. 'Without her we're going to freeze to death. And then it won't make any difference whether your son comes back to life or not.'

'The sphinxes,' said Vermithrax, 'they've frozen to death, is that it? That's why there are none of them left down here. The cold has killed them.'

Merle thought it couldn't be that easy, but sometimes Fate did play a trick of its own. And why couldn't it play that trick on their adversaries' side for a change?

The obsidian lion started moving again. He trudged through the deep snow, but he found the steps easily and went on with an astonishingly sure step. Even a little moisture could turn the mirror floor of the Iron Eye into a series of slides, so at the moment they had to be almost glad of the snow, for it absorbed the lion's footsteps and stopped his claws sliding away from him on the frozen glass floor.

'At least the storm was Winter's doing,' said Merle after a while. 'Although I don't think he was anywhere in it himself. But we must be on the right track here.' After a brief pause for thought, she added, 'Vermithrax, did Andrei say where they were taking the Son of the Mother?'

'If he did, he said it in Russian.'

How about you? Merle's mind turned to the Flowing Queen. Do you know where he is?

'*No.*'

Perhaps where Summer is too?

'*What makes you think –*' The Queen stopped short, and then said instead, '*You really think there's something more behind Summer's disappearance, don't you?*'

Burbridge told Winter something, thought Merle. That's why Winter is looking for her here in the Iron Eye. Suppose Summer had something to do with the power of the Empire?

'*You're thinking of the Barques of the Sun?*'

For one thing, yes. But I'm thinking of the mummies too. And everything that can't be explained except by magic. Why didn't the priests bring Pharaoh back to life a hundred years ago? Or five hundred years? Perhaps because only Summer gave them the power to do it! They call it magic, but it could really be something quite different. Machinery that we don't know, driven by a power that they somehow . . . oh, I don't know . . . that they somehow *steal* from Summer. Seth is not a powerful magician, you said so yourself. Maybe he's master of a few conjuring tricks, but genuine magic? He's a scientist, just like all the other priests of Horus. Like Burbridge too. The only ones who really know anything about magic are the sphinxes.

The Queen thought about it. *'Summer as a kind of living furnace?'*

Like the steam-driven furnaces in the factories out on the islands in the lagoon, thought Merle.

'That sounds crazy.'

As crazy as a goddess getting together with a ray of moonlight to bring a whole race of people into the world?

This time she actually felt the Queen laughing. It was quiet, suppressed laughter, but she was laughing all the same. After a while she said, *'The Sub-Oceanic Realms had machines like that. No one knows just how they were driven. They were used in war against the Lords of the Deep, the ancestors of the Lilim.'*

Merle saw the mosaic stones gradually fitting together to form a whole. It was possible that the priests of Horus had found remains of the Sub-Oceanic Realms or accounts of their civilisation, and had used those to help them revive the Pharaoh and build the Barques of the Sun. She was suddenly filled with bitter satisfaction to think that the cities of the Sub-Oceanic Realms had fallen into ruin aeons ago at the bottom of the sea. All at once the prospect of the same thing happening to the Egyptian Empire moved a good deal closer.

'There's someone coming!' Vermithrax stopped.

Merle was startled. 'Coming up from below?'

The lion's mane moved up and down: he was nodding. 'I can scent them.'

'Sphinxes?'

'At least one.'

'Can't you get closer to the handrail? Then we might be able to see them.'

'Or they might be able to see us,' said the lion, shaking his head. 'There's only one thing for it: we must fly past them.' Until now he had avoided flying downwards, since the shaft at the centre of the spiral staircase was very narrow. He was afraid of damaging his wings on the sharp edges of the steps, and a wounded Vermithrax was the last thing they could afford.

However, it looked as if they must take the risk.

They wasted no time. Merle clung on tight. Vermithrax took off, leaped over the handrail and down into the abyss. They had already ventured on a flying dive of this kind once before, during their flight from the Campanile in Venice. But this was worse. The cold cut into Merle's face and through her clothes, she couldn't wipe away the snow particles flying into her eyes, and her heart was galloping as if to hurry on ahead of her. She could hardly breathe.

They passed two spirals of the staircase, then three, four, five. At the sixth, Vermithrax braked his flight so strongly that for a moment Merle thought they were going to collide — with stone, with steel, perhaps with an invisible mirror-glass floor in the shaft of the stairwell. But then the lion turned into a horizontal position and hovered in the middle of the shaft beating his wings gently, with nothing below him or above him but the void, while in front of them —

'But this can't be —' Merle's voice died away, and she wasn't sure if she had actually spoken the words or merely thought them.

It could almost have been her own mirror image: a figure

riding on the back of a half-human creature that was climbing the stairs on four legs. A boy only a little older than Merle, with tousled hair and wearing soft furs. The creature on which he sat was a female sphinx, with her hands bandaged up to the elbow in rough and ready fashion. The four paws of her leonine lower body seemed to be uninjured, and had carried her rider safely up the stairs.

The sphinx was beautiful, more beautiful than Merle had imagined her, and not even her weary, exhausted expression could alter that. She had black hair falling smoothly over her shoulders down to the place where human and lion merged.

The boy's eyes opened wide, his lips moved, but his words were lost in the rushing sound of the lion's wings and the raging of distant snowstorms down below.

Merle whispered his name.

And Vermithrax attacked.

AMENOPHIS

Seth had stopped threatening her with his sword some time ago. There was no need for that, as they both knew. And there was a certain loss of dignity in a man like him showing a crescent blade to a girl like Junipa, half his height and very much slimmer.

Junipa felt sure that he wouldn't hurt her so long as she obeyed him. At heart, she thought, he was indifferent to her, to Merle and the others, to the whole world. Seth had built up the Empire with sweat and blood and self-sacrifice, and now he was going to tear it down again with his own hands, or at least take up a hammer to strike the first blow.

'To Venice,' he had said after thrusting her back into the mirror world. 'The Doge's Palace.' As if Junipa were a gondolier on the Grand Canal.

When she had looked at him incredulously for a moment, a spark of doubt had appeared in his eyes. Perhaps he wasn't really sure of her abilities.

But then she said, 'Yes' – just that. And she set out.

He had followed her for some time in almost total silence. Only now and then did the tip of the sword at his belt strike against the edge of a mirror, and the screeching sound it made was like an alarm call ringing through the glass labyrinth of the mirror world. But there was no one there to hear it, or if there was then no one appeared, not even the phantoms.

Junipa did not ask Seth what he was going to do. For one thing, she could guess. For another, he wouldn't have answered her anyway.

Just now, when she had stepped out of the mirror and back into the Iron Eye with Merle, she had felt the grip of the Stone Light again. A dreadful pain had flared up in her breast, just as if someone were trying to bend her ribs out from inside her like the bars of a cage. The fragment of the Stone Light inserted into her in Hell was giving her a forceful reminder of its presence. Sooner or later it would win power over her again, either immediately after she left the mirror world or perhaps only gradually, when she was beginning to feel safe. The stone in her breast was both a threat and a dark promise.

She felt better among the mirrors, the pain went away,

the pressure had disappeared. Her stone heart did not beat, but it kept her alive somehow, the Devil alone knew just how – and yes, the Devil certainly did know.

In this situation the threat presented by the priest of Horus seemed far less alarming. She could run away from Seth, or at least try to. There was no escaping the Light. At least, not in her own world. The Light might lose interest in her for a while, as it had after her escape from Hell, but it was still there. Always ready to take hold of her again, exert its influence on her and turn her against her friends.

No, it was just as well that she wasn't in the Iron Eye with Merle. She was beginning to move in the mirror world with ease. Everything in this silvered glass labyrinth seemed somehow familiar. Her eyes led her on, let her look at places that no one else could see, and that made her realise how entirely Seth had placed himself in her hands. Presumably even he didn't realise it.

To Venice, she thought. Yes, she'd take him to Venice if that was what he wanted.

There was no difference between night and day in the mirror world, any more than there was in Hell, although now and then darkness did seem to be falling or day dawning on the other side of individual mirrors. Then the glow of the silvered mirror-glass and the flickering colours would change. Their light fell on Junipa and Seth too, bathing them now in one hue and now another, from deep turquoise to milky lemon yellow. Once Junipa turned to look back at the priest, and saw fiery red spilling from one mirror over his face, emphasising his ferocious, determined expression. Then a gentle sky blue fell on him, and those harsh features softened.

There were many marvels to be seen in this world between worlds. The riddle of the colours and their effect was only one among countless mysteries.

She could not have said how much time passed before they reached their destination. They did not discuss it. It was certainly several hours. But while only moments passed behind one mirror, it could perhaps be years behind the next. Another mystery, another challenge.

Seth stopped beside her and looked at the mirror in front of them. 'Is that it?'

She wondered whether the priest was really full of nothing but fury, or whether there wasn't a little fear in his mind too, a trace of uncertainty aroused by the magnificence of their surroundings. But Seth gave away none of what he might be thinking. He hid his true self behind anger and bitterness, motivated as he was solely by his desire for revenge.

'Yes,' she said. 'Venice lies on the other side. The Pharaoh's apartments in the Doge's Palace.'

He touched the surface of the mirror with the flat of his hand, as if hoping to get through it even without Junipa and the Glass Word. Leaning forward, he breathed on it, and rubbed his breath away with the ball of his hand as if removing a speck of dirt. But if there had been such a speck there it was only the hatred in him, something that couldn't be simply wiped off.

Seth looked at his reflection for some time, as if he couldn't grasp the fact that the man in the glass was himself. Then he blinked briefly, took a deep breath, and drew his crescent sword.

'Are you ready?' asked Junipa, and saw the answer in his face. He nodded.

'I'll look into the room first,' she said. 'You'll want to know whether the Pharaoh is alone.'

To her surprise, he shook his head. 'That won't be necessary.'

'But –'

'You heard me, didn't you?'

'There could be ten sphinxes guarding the Pharaoh on the other side! Or a hundred!'

'Maybe. But I don't think so. I think they've left. The sphinxes will be on the way back to the Iron Eye, or there already. They have what they wanted. They're not interested in Venice any more.' He gave a cold laugh. 'Let alone Amenophis.'

'You think the sphinxes have let him down?'

'Just as he let down the priests of Horus.'

'What happened to them? Your priests, I mean.'

Seth seemed to be wondering briefly whether to tell her about it, then he shrugged, and shifted the weight of the sword in his hand. 'Pharaoh gave me the task of assassinating Lord Light. If I were to fail, he was going to have all the priests of Horus executed. I failed. And the priests —'

Junipa listened, and said nothing when he abruptly broke off. The treachery of the Pharaoh had hit him harder than he himself had thought possible. Nothing had united the two of them, yet Amenophis had his place deep in Seth's soul. Not as a human being; Seth was indifferent to him as an individual, even despised him. But as his creation, woken to new life by him, standing for everything that Seth had once believed in.

What he was planning now was far more than merely taking another man's life. It was the surrender of himself, his aims, all the prospects that his pact with Amenophis had opened up to him. It was a line to be drawn under his own work in the decades since he began planning and supervising the resurrection of the Pharaoh.

One way or another, it was the end.

Junipa took his forearm, whispered the Glass Word, and led him through the mirror.

Immediately the pressure in her breast was back again as the Light felt and pressed and tugged at her stone heart.

The hall beyond the mirror was empty, at least at first glance. But then she saw the divan covered with jaguar skins standing in the dim light on the other side of the room. It was night in Venice, and only a faint glow fell through the windows into this hall. Torchlight from the Piazza San Marco, she assumed. It lay softly on the pattern of the carved panels, the brush strokes of oil paintings and frescos, the crystal drops of the chandeliers.

Something moved on the divan. A dark outline against an even darker mound of furs.

No one spoke.

Junipa felt as if she were not really here at all, but

observing the scene from some distant place. As if in a dream. Yes, she thought, a long and dreadful dream, and I can't do anything but watch. I can't take action or run away, I can only watch.

Behind her, glass smashed and fell tinkling to the floor in a cascade of silver fragments. Seth had broken the mirror on the wall through which they came. No way of going back now. Junipa quickly looked around, but there was no other mirror in here, and she doubted whether she would get far enough along the palace corridors to find one.

Amenophis rose from his divan and its jaguar skins, a small, slim figure, stooping slightly when he moved, as if a terrible weight lay on his shoulders.

'Seth,' he said wearily. Junipa wondered if he was drunk. His voice sounded slurred, and very young too.

Amenophis, the reborn Pharaoh, ruler of the Empire, stepped into the faint light from the windows.

He was still a child. Only a boy, made into something he should never have been by gold paint and cosmetics. He was no more than twelve or thirteen, at least a year younger than Junipa herself. Yet he had been commanding his armies to lay the world waste for four decades.

Junipa stood perfectly still among the ruins of the mirror.

The splinters were scattered all over the dark wood of the floor. She looked as if she were hovering in a starry sky.

Seth walked past her towards the Pharaoh. If he had looked round for guards or other adversaries, he made no move to show it. He was staring straight ahead at the insignificant boy waiting for him in front of the divan.

'Have they all gone?' Seth asked.

Amenophis neither moved nor spoke.

'They've deserted you, haven't they?' There was no arrogance or gloating in Seth's tone. It was just a statement of fact. 'The sphinxes have gone. And without the priests of Horus . . . yes, what are you without us, Amenophis?'

'We are the Pharaoh,' said the boy. He was smaller than Junipa, very thin and ordinary. He sounded defiant but a little resigned too, as if he had secretly come to terms with his fate already. And Junipa realised that there was to be no spectacular final battle between the two of them. No wild clash of sword blades, no murderous fencing among fallen chairs and tables, no adversaries swinging from the chandeliers and the curtains.

This was the end, coming quietly with no noise. Like the conclusion of a severe illness, a quiet death after a long time spent bedridden.

'Were all the priests executed?' asked Seth.

'You know the answer to that.'

'You could have let them go.'

'We gave our word: if you fail they will die, we said.'

'You broke your word once before when you deceived the priests of Horus.'

'No reason to do it again.' The boy's smile gave the lie to his words as he added, 'Even we sometimes learn from our mistakes.'

'Not today.'

Amenophis took a few slow steps to the right, where a large basin of water stood near the divan. He plunged his hands into it and washed them, lost in thought. Junipa almost expected him to produce a weapon and turn on Seth with it, but Amenophis merely scrubbed his fingers clean and shook them briefly, sending drops of water flying in all directions, before turning back to the priest.

'Our armies are unimaginably great. Millions upon millions. We have the strongest men as our guards, warriors from Nubia and ancient Samarkand. But we are tired. So tired.'

'Why don't you call for those guards of yours?'

'They left when the sphinxes went. The priests were

dead, and suddenly there were only living corpses in this palace.' He let out a cackle of laughter which sounded neither genuine nor particularly amused. 'The Nubians looked at the mummies, they looked at us, and they realised that they were the only live men in this building.'

He's had the councillors murdered, thought Junipa with a shiver. The entire City Council of Venice.

'They left us a little later, in secret, of course. But we had seen, long before that, what was going on in their minds.' He shrugged his shoulders. 'The Empire is destroying itself.'

'No,' said Seth. 'You destroyed it. At the moment when you had my priests executed.'

'You never loved us.'

'I respected you. We priests of Horus were always loyal to you, and so we would still have been if you hadn't preferred the sphinxes.'

'The sphinxes are interested only in their own intrigues, that's true.'

'You're late waking up to that.'

For the first time Amenophis dropped the royal 'we' and spoke of himself in the singular. 'What can I say?' The most powerful boy in the world smiled, but his face twisted like its own reflection on the ruffled surface of the basin of water.

'I slept for four thousand years, I can sleep again. But the world won't forget me, will it? That's a kind of immortality too. No one can ever forget what I did to the world.'

'And you're proud of it?' asked Junipa. They were the first words she had spoken since she and Seth arrived. Amenophis did not condescend to answer her or even look at her. But something was suddenly clear to her: the two of them were speaking Egyptian, yet she understood what they were saying. At the same time, she knew what Arcimboldo had meant when he once told her, 'As a guide through the mirror world, you master all voices, all tongues. For what use would a guide be if he didn't know the language of the countries through which he takes others?' How could she have guessed what that was supposed to mean before? Even now it was difficult for her to take in the whole truth. Did it really mean that she understood all the languages spoken in countless worlds? *All voices, all tongues*, he had said. The words echoed through her mind, making her feel quite dizzy.

It was Amenophis who brought her out of her state of amazement. 'Immortality is better than what you and your priests gave me,' he told Seth. 'A few decades, no more. Perhaps it would have been a century. But you were already getting tired of me, weren't you? How much longer would you have tolerated me? You wanted to take my place . . . poor Seth, you were sick with envy and ambition. And who can blame you for it? It was you who solved the riddle of the Sub-Oceanic Realms. You gave the Empire its power. And now look at you! Only a bald man with a sword in his hand, a weapon that a few days ago he hadn't even seen, let alone used.'

The priest of Horus was standing with his back to Junipa, but she saw him tensing his muscles. Death seeped from every pore of his skin.

'All a delusion,' said Amenophis, 'all a masquerade. Like the gold paint on our skin.' He ran a finger over the smudged gold dust on his face and rubbed it between thumb and forefinger.

'The Empire is no delusion. It's real.'

'Is it? Who's to say it's not one of your clever deceptions? You're a master of those, Seth. Illusions. Masquerades. Conjuring tricks. Others may think they're magic, but I know the truth. As a scholar, you studied the remains of the Sub-Oceanic Realms. But the scholar has become a trickster. You know how to influence human minds by putting on a performance. Giant falcons and monsters, Seth, those are children's toys, not weapons for ruling an Empire. There at least the sphinxes were right.' The Pharaoh turned with mincing little steps, and sank back on the divan in the shadows. His weak voice hovered in the darkness like a bird beating a lame wing. 'Is all this illusion? Tell me, Seth! Did you really bring me back to life, or am I still lying in my burial chamber in the pyramid of Amun-Ka-Re? Have I really conquered the world, or is it just a dream you've staged for me? And is it true that all my loyal servants have deserted me, leaving me alone now in a palace full of mummies – although perhaps I'm a mummy myself and have never left my tomb? Tell me the truth, priest! What's illusion, what is reality?'

Seth still hadn't moved. Junipa made her way slowly along the wall, in the vague hope that she might reach the door before one of them noticed her.

'Do you really think that?' asked Seth. Junipa stopped, but he was speaking to Amenophis, not her. 'Do you really think the events of the last forty years were nothing but an illusion?'

'I know what you're capable of,' said the Pharaoh, shrugging. 'Not real magic, like the sphinxes, but you know all about illusions. Perhaps I'm really still lying on a sandstone block in my pyramid, and you're standing beside me with your hand on my forehead – or whatever else it takes to plant all these pictures in my mind. With every passing year, with every minute of the last few days my conviction has grown: none of this is *true*, Seth! I'm dreaming! My mind is caught up in a great illusion! I've played your game, I've moved the chessmen on the board and had my fun with them. Why not? There was never really anything to lose.'

Junipa reached the door and slowly pushed the huge brass handle down. And yes, the tall oak door moved! A cool gust of air came in from the corridor, blowing through her hair. But still she didn't run away. This last meeting between the Pharaoh and his creator held her in its grip with a macabre fascination. She had to know what happened next. She had to see it.

Seth began to move slowly towards the divan.

'Even my death is only an illusion,' said Amenophis. In the mouth of a twelve-year-old it sounded as improbable as if he were reciting complicated mathematical equations. Junipa made herself remember, yet again, that the Pharaoh was far older than his body made him appear. Unimaginably older.

'Only an illusion,' he whispered again as if his thoughts were somewhere else, in a place of deep silence and darkness. In a tomb at the core of a stepped pyramid.

'If that's what you think,' said Seth, raising his sword and bringing it down on the Pharaoh.

There was no resistance. Not even a cry.

Amenophis died quietly and humbly. Seth, who had given him life, was taking it back. Only a dream, the Pharaoh was perhaps thinking even as he died, only one of the high priest of Horus's conjuring tricks.

Junipa pushed the heavy door further open and slipped through the crack. Out in the corridor she took four or five steps before she became aware of the silence. Seth wasn't following her.

Unsure of herself, she stopped.

Turned, and went back.

Don't do it! something in her cried. Run away as fast as you can!

Instead, Junipa went back to the open doorway and looked into the hall once more.

Seth was lying on the floor in front of the Pharaoh's body, his face looking in her direction. His left hand was clenched into a fist, his right hand clutched the hilt of the sword. Its crescent blade was deep inside his body. He had thrust it into himself without a sound.

'He was wrong,' he said, with difficulty, spitting blood on the wooden floor. 'It's all . . . true.'

Junipa overcame her terror, reluctance and disgust. She slowly walked into the hall and went towards the divan and the two men who, only a few days ago, had been governing the destiny of the greatest, most cruel empire the world had ever seen. Now they lay before her, one dead in a sea of jaguar skins, the other dying at her feet.

'I'm sorry,' Seth whispered faintly, 'about the mirror – that was stupid.'

Junipa knelt down beside him and tried to find words. She wondered if she ought to say something to ease his pain and disappointment. But perhaps that was what he had just done already: he *had* eased his pain. He had killed the master he himself had made, he had done away with child and father at the same time.

It's as well this way, she thought, feeling the idea floating away from her like a feather. Like a last illusion.

In silence, she put out her forefinger and stroked the lines of the golden network set into Seth's scalp. It felt cool to the touch and not at all magical. Just like metal pressed into the flesh with terrible pain. It was exactly what it looked like: a net of gold in a place where no such thing belonged.

Like all of us, she thought sadly.

'Don't go . . . through the palace. There are mummy warriors everywhere. And no one left to . . . to control them.'

'What will they do?'

'I . . . don't know. Perhaps nothing. Or . . .' He stopped speaking, started again. 'Don't go. Too dangerous.'

'I have to find a mirror.'

Seth tried to nod, but he couldn't manage it. Instead he reached out a shaking finger. Junipa looked the way he was pointing, and saw what he meant.

Yes, she thought. It might work.

'Good luck,' gasped Seth.

Junipa met his gaze. 'Luck? When you've destroyed everything?'

Seth couldn't answer any more. His eyes were clouding over, his lids fluttered one last time. Then a slight quiver ran through his body, and he stopped breathing.

Wearily, Junipa went over to the great basin of water beside the divan. It was large enough. Junipa bent low, put her mouth close to it and whispered the Glass Word. Then she clambered up on the marble basin, swung her legs over the edge, and let herself drop into her own reflection.

The stone in her breast dragged her down.

THE SPHINXES SPLINTER

It hadn't been easy. Very far indeed from easy. But somehow Merle had managed to stop Vermithrax before he could leap over the handrail with a roar and tear the sphinx and the boy to pieces.

Now, much later, the obsidian lion stood at the foot of the snow-covered stairway looking at Lalapeya. The sphinx put her head back, closed her eyes, and seemed to be scenting the air as Vermithrax sometimes did, but in her it looked less like the action of a beast of prey. Even that she does with grace and beauty, thought Merle.

'That way,' she said, and Vermithrax nodded. He had come to the same conclusion.

Exactly *what* the two of them had scented Merle didn't know. Only after a while did she realise that they had picked up the scent of snow as many animals do, knowing by instinct when to escape an imminent cold spell or store provisions in their burrows.

Some time had passed since they all met on the spiral staircase. Time in which Merle had adjusted to the idea that the sphinx beside her really was her mother, and it was really Serafin sitting on Vermithrax's back behind her, with his hands round her waist to hold her firmly.

Once the obsidian lion had realised that the sphinx on the stairs was not an enemy, he had put Merle down on the steps. She and Serafin had fallen into one another's arms, and just stood there for a long time, saying nothing, clasping each other. Merle had a feeling that he had almost kissed her, but then his lips merely brushed her hair, and all she could think was that it was days since she last washed it. That was really crazy! Here they all were, caught in this terrifying sphinx fortress, and she was thinking about washing her hair! Was that what being in love did to you? And *was* being in love to blame for the lump in her throat and the fluttering in her stomach?

Serafin bent close to her ear. 'I've missed you,' he whispered. Her pulse raced. She was sure he must be able to hear the hammering in her ears, the rushing of her blood all through her body. Or if not that, then he could certainly feel the trembling in her legs, in fact the way she was trembling all over.

She said that she'd missed him too, and suddenly thought it sounded dull and ordinary, because he'd said it to her first. Then she just chattered away, saying all kinds of things which thank goodness she couldn't remember two minutes later, because she had probably been just stammering at random. She felt stupid and childish, yet she didn't even know why.

And then there was Lalapeya.

That was a very different kind of reunion from her meeting with Serafin, particularly because it wasn't really a reunion at all, at least from Merle's point of view. She couldn't remember her mother, either her voice or what she had looked like. All she knew of her was her hands, from the hours when they had held hands together inside the water mirror. But Lalapeya's hands were bandaged now, and Merle couldn't touch them to make sure they were the hands that she had always known.

Not that she seriously *needed* to make sure. She knew that Lalapeya was her mother, had known it at the moment when she saw the sphinx on the stairway even before she recognised Serafin on her back. The simplest thing would be to put it down to their appearance, to a similarity about the eyes, faces of the same shape, their long dark hair. But far more than that immediately bound Merle to Lalapeya. The sphinx had the perfection that Merle sometimes lent herself in her thoughts, the kind of beauty she'd like to have too, and perhaps might one day when she was grown up. But she was still only fourteen, and changes would come over her face before it became the determined, unchanging countenance of her older self. The face that she now saw before her above the slender shoulders of a sphinx.

She couldn't hug Lalapeya for fear of touching her injuries, and she wasn't sure if it would be right at their first meeting anyway. So they made do with words, in a conversation that they both conducted with some reserve, but with barely concealed joy too. In spite of her pain Lalapeya was radiant – there was no mistaking the fact that she was genuinely happy. And probably also relieved that Merle wasn't resentful for what had happened to her as a baby.

All this time the Flowing Queen said not a word. She just kept quiet, as if she were no longer a part of Merle. As if her mind were already involved in her fight with the Son of the Mother, and she had switched off from her present surroundings entirely, even at a moment like this. Once Merle thought: she's planning something. Then she told herself that the Queen presumably knew better than any of them exactly what they faced. And who could blame her if she didn't feel like talking?

It was Vermithrax who reminded them that they must go on their way, and Merle carefully explained their plan to Lalapeya and Serafin. So much had happened since any of them last met that she soon realised she must confine herself to the bare essentials. Even so, she more than once met with incredulous looks, and it was some time before she finally reached Winter's part in the whole story: who he was, what he was looking for, and why *they* were looking for *him*.

As they set out together on the downward climb, Serafin in his own turn told Merle and Vermithrax how they had come here. When he said that Eft, Dario and the others were in the Iron Eye too, Merle could hardly believe it. Dario, of all people! Her arch-enemy from the mirror-making workshop. And he had been Serafin's enemy even more than hers; if the two of them were friends now, then a great deal must indeed have happened. She was longing to hear the details.

'Eft is injured,' said Serafin. He told Merle that their party had had to fight a sphinx guard at the foot of the fortress. Eft had broken a leg, while Dario and Aristide had suffered some nasty cuts. None of their lives was in danger, but when they all tried climbing one of the flights of steps in the lower part of the Eye together, the others had to give up. Tiziano had stayed with them so that the wounded members of the party wouldn't be entirely on their own, while Lalapeya and Serafin continued with the climb. 'I didn't want to leave them behind,' he finished, 'but what else were we to do?'

'We could have gone back to the submarine together,' said Lalapeya, 'but then it would all have been for nothing. So Serafin and I decided to go on by ourselves.'

'Where are the others now?' asked Merle.

'In a library close to one of the entrances,' said Serafin. 'There are huge libraries down there, incredibly large.'

Merle looked at him with disbelief. So far she had seen nothing but mirrors in the Iron Eye. Halls, rooms, chambers, all lined with mirrors. The idea of one or even several large libraries didn't fit the picture she had formed of the fortress, and she said so out loud.

Lalapeya looked back over her shoulder. 'The sphinxes may seem to you like a people of warriors and conquerors. That's the only way you have known them, in Venice with the Pharaoh and here. But sphinxes are far more than that.

They are scholars. There are many wise members of the race, and once they gave the world great philosophers, storytellers and playwrights. There were theatrical arenas in the old desert cities where we gathered not just to watch performances but for discussion too. Not all sphinxes settled their arguments with weapons then. I can remember the great speeches, the scholarly debates and lectures – all at a time when human beings were more like animals than the sphinxes are today. There were great minds among us, and as for our artists . . . the old songs and lyric poetry of the sphinxes have a beauty that is foreign to mankind.'

'*She speaks the truth,*' said the Flowing Queen suddenly. '*In a way, at least. Although the human beings of those days were not quite as simple and primitive as she claims.*'

No, of course not, thought Merle caustically, or I don't suppose they'd have made a goddess out of you.

'*That wasn't by my own choosing,*' said the Queen. '*It's a peculiarity of humans not to ask permission first when they want to worship someone. And I fear it's a peculiarity of gods to get used to being worshipped.*'

For a good two hundred metres they had been following a broad corridor with a high vaulted ceiling, almost a kind of roofed street, although larger and more imposing, when

Vermithrax nodded his head to indicate what lay ahead. 'There! Do you see that?'

Merle blinked as she looked at the dazzling white of the snow-covered surface. The mirrors on both sides of the corridor stretched it out into a snowy plain. The light was too bright for her to see anything in the distance. Nor did Serafin or even Lalapeya see what Vermithrax had spotted with a big cat's keen eyes.

'Sphinxes,' he said. 'But they're not moving.'

'Guards?' asked Lalapeya.

'Maybe. But I don't think that's going to make any difference now.'

The sphinx glanced at him in surprise, while Merle gently tickled him behind his ear. 'What do you mean?' she asked.

He purred briefly, perhaps because he really enjoyed her touch or perhaps just to please her. Then he said, 'They're white.'

'White?' repeated Serafin, puzzled.

'Frozen to ice.'

Merle could sense the strain that Serafin was under. He didn't like sitting on the lion's back doing nothing, just waiting. He was longing to go into action again himself. She knew just how he felt; it wasn't in her own nature to be simply a victim of events either. Perhaps she had let herself drift too much since she met the Queen, doing what was expected of her and not what she really wanted. At the same time she had to recognise that she had never had a choice: her way had been marked out for her in advance, and even at the few places where the path forked, leaving it had never been an option. Not for the first time, she felt like a puppet with everyone else pulling the strings. Or even worse, like a *child*. And that was something she had never really been. There was no time for it in the orphanage.

They went on, and soon Merle and the others could see what Vermithrax had meant. Like a forest of statues, shapes emerged from the ever-present white, at first barely visible, then a little more distinct, finally as clear as cut glass. And that was what the sphinxes most resembled: glass. Ice.

There were over a dozen of them, frozen in many attitudes of fear and retreat. Some had tried to escape the touch of Winter by running away; others had tried to fight, but the expressions on their faces bore witness to the courage of despair or often downright panic. Weapons had slid from some of their hands; crescent swords lay half-buried in the snow. One sphinx still held his gun, but when Serafin was going to lean over from Vermithrax's back and reach for it, Merle let out a warning cry. 'No, don't! Your hands would stick to it in this cold.'

A question escaped Lalapeya. 'What happened here?'

'Winter passed by,' said Merle. 'Everything he touches freezes to ice. He told me so. Every living creature, with a single exception – Summer. That's why he's looking for her. That's why they love each other.'

A crunch met her ears. Beside them, cracks were spreading through a sphinx's icy body, and a moment later it collapsed into sharp-edged fragments with a resounding roar. Only its four lion's legs still stood there, stuck in the snow like a waymark that someone had left behind.

For a moment no one moved, as if they had frozen to ice themselves. None of them knew what had made the sphinx explode – until Serafin, cursing quietly, pointed to a small bolt stuck in one of the icy fragments.

'Someone's shooting at us!'

Merle quickly glanced down the corridor, and it wasn't long before she saw the sphinx standing under an arched gateway and taking aim at them for a second time. Before any of them could react, he fired his weapon. Lalapeya let out a cry as the shot grazed her shoulder and crashed into a frozen sphinx behind her. Crunching and splintering, the icy sphinx broke apart.

More sphinxes appeared behind the marksman, but only a few of them were armed. Several held small hammers and chisels, along with glass containers and bags.

They're going to investigate their dead, thought Merle. They'll knock small pieces off the bodies to analyse them, hoping to find some weak point in us that way.

Unfortunately the scientists were accompanied by several warriors, who didn't look at all like the intellectual beings Lalapeya had described just now. They were tall and muscular, with broad leonine bodies and wide human shoulders.

Vermithrax took advantage of his wings by rising into the air with his riders. Lalapeya was left on the ground, but the obsidian lion had no intention of abandoning her. From the air, he swooped on the first of his adversaries standing in the arched gateway, knocked the firearm with the bolts out of his hands, and struck the sphinx's skull with his hind paws as he flew past. The sphinx was dead before his legs gave way beneath him and he sank into the snow.

The other warriors reacted fast and efficiently, thrusting the sphinx scientists back under the arch where they were safe from attack by the lion in the air. One leaped forward and faced Vermithrax with his sword raised aloft, while another tried to get at the gun – obviously their only firearm – where it lay in the snow.

Vermithrax raced past the first sphinx and didn't even flinch when a sword blade sent sparks flying from his obsidian body; the shock of the blow knocked the weapon out of the sphinx's hand. The lion pounced on the second sphinx, seized his arms, carried him high up in the air, and then flung him against the mirror wall like a rag doll. The glass could not stand up to the impact. The lifeless sphinx fell to the floor in a hail of silver splinters and didn't move again.

One of the scientists had taken his chance to leap out of the cover of the archway and retrieve the gun. He was unused to handling weapons; his first shot passed Vermithrax a metre wide of him and left a crack in the vaulted ceiling.

Meanwhile, Lalapeya had been running behind the frozen statues towards the only possible way of escape: a low corridor leading into the broad mirror-lined street about thirty metres further on. If she had followed the street itself she would have presented a perfect target, so her only option was the corridor, although its lower half was blocked by a snowdrift the height of a man. She plunged into it as if into a hill of flour: powdery whiteness exploded in all directions and then she was out of sight.

Vermithrax swooped in a looping flight close to the ceiling. Merle, who was used to such manoeuvres, shouted to Serafin to hold on to her. He tightened his grasp with rigid, ice-cold fingers, while she herself did her best to clutch the shining lion's mane. Serafin was slender and wiry, but he was still considerably heavier than the feather-weight Junipa. Merle wasn't sure how long she could hold on. Her fingers, numb with frost, had lost strength, and she could hardly feel any of her limbs. The thick mane protected her hands from the icy draught, but that wasn't much comfort in view of their situation. It was only a matter of time before they both fell off the lion's back. Down below, they would either break all their bones or be impaled on the bodies of the frozen sphinxes.

'Did you notice how many sphinxes there are there?' yelled Serafin into her ear, making himself heard above the wind and the sound of the beating wings.

'Too many, anyway.'

'But not enough, right?'

'What do you mean?'

'*I know what he's thinking,*' said the Queen, '*and he's correct.*'

Serafin leaned even closer to Merle, which even here and now was pleasant, and put his lips so close to her ear that they touched her hair. The tingling in her stomach increased, and not just because Vermithrax was flying down to attack the sphinxes again. 'Too few of them!' shouted Serafin. 'This is their fortress, the safest place they have. What happened down there is destroying their world. And then they just send out that handful of warriors and scientists?' Merle felt him shaking his head, close to the nape of her neck. 'It doesn't make sense.'

'Unless they can't spare any more,' she said. 'For the same reason as you were able to walk into the fortress so easily.'

'It wasn't *easy*,' he protested.

Merle thought of those who had been left behind with injuries, but stuck to her point. 'In normal circumstances there'd have been several dozen guards waiting for you, not just one. Do you think the sphinxes leave the Iron Eye almost unguarded?'

Flying past a sphinx warrior, Vermithrax killed him as easily as he might have picked a flower from its stem. His adversaries' crescent swords struck sparks from his stone underbelly again, but the tiny splinters they knocked off his body did not weaken him.

'There are too few of them,' said Serafin. 'That's what I mean. Too few guards, and now too few to investigate the disaster that happened down there. Unless –'

'Unless,' said Merle, 'this isn't the only part of the Eye where something of the kind has happened!' Of course. Winter was searching for Summer all over the fortress, just as he had searched the whole of Hell. If he followed his path through the world as chaotically as this, no wonder the seasons were so unreliable these days: sometimes there was still frost in April, sometimes there wasn't, and you could never tell in advance what the weather would be like next week.

The sphinxes must have come from all over the world to witness the resurrection of the Son of the Mother,' said the Queen. *'None of them will want to miss that.'*

And Winter fell on them like a stormy wind, thought Merle, imagining vast halls full of sphinxes frozen to ice and looking like the workshops of some deranged sculptor.

'That's how it could have been.'

Then that's why Burbridge told Winter about this place, thought Merle. He intended Winter to come here as his revenge on the sphinxes.

'What about the Stone Light?'

Burbridge must somehow have managed to get Winter into the Cabinet of Mirrors.

'It certainly looks like it.'

It's not the first time this has happened, am I right?

'You're right. But last time it may not have been Winter. It's possible that Summer freed herself then, or someone or something else helped her.'

The downfall of the Sub-Oceanic Realms!

'And the Mayas. The Incas. Atlantis.'

Merle did not know any of those names, but the mere sound of them sent a shiver down her spine. While Vermithrax left the sphinxes and flew towards the corridor down which Lalapeya had disappeared, she told Serafin what she suspected, as well as she could with the wind blowing against them. He agreed with her.

They ducked their heads when Vermithrax flew through the low arch of the opening, sent the rest of the snowdrift whirling in all directions, and finally landed on all fours. The corridor was too narrow for him to fly far along it. And in addition Lalapeya was waiting for them, her face full of concern. She glanced at Merle, saw that she was uninjured, and then turned to Vermithrax. 'How many of them are there?'

'Four still left. At least. Perhaps a few more.'

'It ought to have been a whole sphinx army.'

'It ought indeed.'

Merle suppressed a smile when she realised that they were all thinking the same thing. Easily as Vermithrax had defeated the sphinxes, Winter had done a lot of the work for him in advance.

The lion and the sphinx raced down the corridor side by side, while their opponents appeared at the mouth of the tunnel behind them. The scientists had stayed behind; two warriors took up the pursuit. An alarm signal sounded several times back in the mirror-lined street. The sphinx scientists were blowing horns to summon reinforcements from inside the vast fortress of the Iron Eye.

'Do you know your way around this place?' Vermithrax asked the sphinx.

'No, the Iron Eye hadn't been built yet when I left to keep watch over the lagoon. The sphinxes have always been a people of deserts and deep caverns. All this,' she said, shaking her head with a look of resignation, 'all this is nothing like what I used to know.'

Although the corridor was as cold as everywhere else in the Iron Eye, once they had gone a few steps the covering of snow was thinner, and then it disappeared entirely. Bitter winds blew towards them, but brought no more ice. Nonetheless, the mirror floor was already slippery with frozen moisture, and neither Vermithrax nor Lalapeya could move as fast as they would like. The obsidian lion could have turned to face their pursuers, and would very probably have defeated them, but he feared that the two sphinxes would soon be followed by a larger number of adversaries, and while he was fighting he couldn't protect Merle and Serafin from attack at the same time.

Another corridor joined theirs, and they saw more sphinxes coming down it from the right. After a quick glance at them, Vermithrax hurried straight on. There was no way the sphinxes could fail to see the shining light of his body. Hiding was out of the question, and there were hardly any doors anyway, just open archways leading to wide halls and endless rooms in this imitation of the real mirror world.

They crossed open canals with frozen surfaces, going over filigree bridges that looked fragile but did not even quiver as the obsidian lion's great weight thundered over them. They passed through a hilly landscape of shards of mirror-glass, with slopes as high as a house made of sharp silvery fragments and splinters, and then went down flights of steps again, more and yet more flights of steps.

And then they were stumbling through deep snow once more, wetter and heavier snow this time, so deep that Vermithrax sank into it up to his belly and Lalapeya was hopelessly stuck after she had taken a few steps. The obsidian lion pushed masses of snow aside with his wings, but it soon turned out that he was not doing her much good that way.

'Vermithrax,' called Lalapeya, 'can you carry a third rider?'

'Two or three more if there's room. But that won't help us much.'

'It might.' And even as she spoke a change came over her.

Merle watched, open-mouthed and wide-eyed, while Serafin reassuringly took her hand. 'Don't worry,' he whispered, 'she does that quite often.'

Around Lalapeya, yellow fountains of sand seemed to be rising from the footsteps in which her lion's legs were stuck. They swiftly enveloped her before she appeared to dissolve herself in them, as if her whole body were exploding in an eruption of desert sands. The tiny particles came together again just as quickly and Lalapeya emerged, unchanged above the hips but human below them, with long slender legs that were bare in spite of the cold. The fur jacket that the pirates had given her came down to her thighs, but her knees and lower legs were unprotected in the snow.

Serafin let go of Merle and leaned back slightly. 'Up here, quick!' he called.

Lalapeya fought her way through the snow, and Merle and Serafin hauled her up to sit between them on the lion's back. The sphinx couldn't use her injured arms, and if she had stood barefoot in the snow much longer her legs would have suffered too. Serafin moved as close to her as possible, put his arms round her to hold Merle's waist as well, and shouted, 'Ready to go!'

Vermithrax rose from the floor, shaking the snow from his paws. Now he was flying over the ice only a few metres below the mirror-glass roof. The walls were hardly wide enough apart for him to spread his huge wings, but somehow he managed not to brush them with his wing-tips as he carried his riders safely over the snow. Their pursuers were left behind trying to trudge through the deep snow in their own turn. After a few steps they had to give up.

With a roar of triumph, Vermithrax shot out of the round opening at the end of the tunnel and into a far higher hall where it was still snowing. The snow fell in large, thick flakes from grey mists that hung below the ceiling, looking like genuine wintry clouds. Snowflakes in their thousands immediately clung to Vermithrax and his riders, stinging their eyes. The reflection of the lion's body was like bright mists of light. But visibility was restricted to a few metres.

'I can't see anything!' Vermithrax was lurching as he flew, and once sneezed so violently that Merle was afraid they would all be thrown off his back. Whatever else his dip in the Stone Light had done, it hadn't made him immune to the common cold. The obsidian lion was having trouble in maintaining his height. He was as good as blind in the flurries of falling snow, and the wet flakes weighed heavily on his wings. 'I'll have to come down,' he called at last, but by then they had all realised that it was inevitable.

They sank lower and lower down with the snowflakes, but the floor that they expected to meet did not materialise. What they had taken for a great hall was really a huge shaft, an abyss.

'Ahead there!' shouted Merle through the shower of snowflakes. Snow got into her mouth. 'The bridge!'

A narrow mirror-glass bridge stretched like a guitar string over the infinite void. It was hardly more than a metre wide, and had no parapet. Both ends were hidden somewhere in the snow flurries.

Vermithrax flew to it and came down, trusting implicitly to the sphinxes' mastery of architecture. There was a slight quiver, but no sign that the structure would give way under his weight. Clogged masses of snow came loose from both sides of the bridge along a length of five or six metres, and fell into the greyish white depths.

Vermithrax shook his wings until they were free of the clumped ice that had hindered him in his flight. Serafin tried to pull the skirts of his coat far enough forward to cover Lalapeya's bare thighs, but she pushed them away.

'Put me down. I can walk by myself here. Vermithrax won't be able to fly in this snow anyway.'

'The bridge is too narrow,' said Serafin. 'If you climb off Vermithrax sideways you'll fall straight into the abyss.'

'What about behind him?'

Serafin and Merle looked over their shoulders at the same moment. The sight of the sheer drop on both sides of the bridge was terrifying. As a master thief, Serafin had climbed the rooftops of Venice for years without giving more than a passing thought to the danger of a fall. But this was something else. If he slipped on the wet, slushy snow nothing could save him, neither luck nor skill.

'I'll try,' he said.

'No!' protested Merle. 'Don't talk such nonsense.'

He looked past Lalapeya at her. 'Her legs will freeze if she doesn't change back. She *has* to get down to do that.'

Merle's eyes flashed at him. As if she didn't know! All the same, she was terrified for him and Lalapeya. The idea that the sphinx really was her mother seemed almost more absurd and incredible after her transformation just now.

'Be careful,' said Lalapeya, as Serafin slowly slid backwards.

'*Courageous*,' commented the Flowing Queen drily.

'Keep still!' Serafin called to Vermithrax. There was grim determination in his voice. Merle held her breath.

'Don't worry,' replied the lion, and indeed he didn't move a millimetre. Even his heartbeat, which Merle could distinctly feel against her calves most of the time, seemed to stop.

With infinite care, Serafin slid back over Vermithrax's hips. As he did so his hands grasped the lion's tail, which gave him additional stability when the soles of his boots sank into the snow. For a moment he swayed slightly, casting anxious glances down into the abyss to left and right. Finally he signed to Lalapeya to follow him. His footing on the bridge was so insecure that his boots seemed to be swimming in slush. Too sudden a movement, and he would slide over the edge, taking a huge mass of snow with him.

He let go of the lion's tail to leave room for Lalapeya. She nimbly slipped backwards and off the lion, while Merle turned her head, anxiously watching what was going on behind her.

'*They'll do it*,' said the Queen.

All very well for you to talk, thought Merle.

'Take one more step back,' the sphinx told Serafin. 'But cautiously.'

With the utmost caution he moved back, taking care not even to think about the depths below him any more.

'Good,' said Lalapeya. 'Now sit down on the ground. Support yourself on your hands.'

He did it. Master thief or no master thief, he felt sick and dizzy. Only when he was sitting more or less safely in the snow did he breathe more easily.

Lalapeya transformed herself into a pillar of rising sand which swiftly became flesh, hair and bones again. Once the sphinx was standing there in her lion's form, she told Serafin to get on her back. He obeyed, and the pallor left his features. It was some slight reassurance to think that Lalapeya and Vermithrax both had four legs, giving them a steady footing up here. They could thank their wild-cat inheritance that the pull of the abyss had no power over them. Fear of heights was entirely foreign to Lalapeya and the winged lion Vermithrax alike, and it was impossible for them to make any clumsy or unnecessary movement.

A shudder of relief passed through Merle when Serafin was safe on Lalapeya's back at last. For a moment she had even forgotten the cold, which she was finding harder and harder to bear. Only now did she feel the biting chill of the frost again, the icy weight of snow, and the whistling blast of the high-altitude winds.

'Now what?' asked Vermithrax.

'We go on over the bridge,' suggested Merle. 'Unless anyone has a better idea?'

They moved forward on eight lion's paws, uncertain of what they might find beyond the dense, driving snow. But after only a few steps Vermithrax stopped again. At the same moment Merle saw the obstacle in their way.

A figure was crouching on the narrow bridge ahead of them. A man sat there cross-legged.

His long hair was pure white, his skin very pale, as if someone had shaped the motionless figure out of snow. The man had thrown his head back, and his closed eyes were directed upwards. His bony hands were clasped round his knees, and the dark blue veins on them stood out clearly.

'He's meditating,' said Lalapeya in surprise.

'No,' replied Merle softly. 'He's searching.'

Winter bowed his head and looked wearily at them.

THE ONLY WAY

It looked almost as if he had been expecting them.

'Merle,' he said, and he sounded neither glad nor sorry. 'She's here. Summer is here.'

'I know.'

Vermithrax was within two paces of him. 'Don't come any closer,' said Winter. 'You would all freeze to ice if you touched me.'

'You killed the sphinxes,' said Merle.

'Yes.'

'How many are there left?'

'I don't know. Not enough to withstand me.'

'Do you know where they're hiding Summer?'

He nodded, and pointed to the abyss below.

'Down there?' Merle wished she didn't always have to work so hard to worm every word out of him.

Another nod. Only now did she notice that the dense snow was not falling on him. No ice crystals caught in his hair, no snowflakes clung to his white clothing. Even his breath didn't emerge from his lips as vapour. It was as if Winter himself were not part of the season that he personified.

'I have come as far as this,' he said, 'but now I lack the power to take the last step.'

'I don't understand.'

'Summer must be being held captive at the bottom of this shaft. There is no other way in. I've looked everywhere.'

'So?'

Winter smiled slightly, looking very vulnerable. 'How am I going to get down there? Jump?'

She had assumed, as a matter of course, that a being like Winter could fly if he had to. But apparently not. He had plunged Egypt and the Iron Eye into a new Ice Age, but he was unable to reach the bottom of this shaft.

'How long have you been sitting here?'

Winter sighed. 'Far too long.'

'*He's a snivelling coward,*' said the Flowing Queen scornfully. '*All his noise and the havoc he wreaks make no difference to that.*'

Don't be so unfair, thought Merle.

'*Huh! A snivelling coward!*' If the Queen had had a nose of her own, she would probably have been looking down it.

'How long do you think he can have been here? He left Hell only just before we did.'

He's . . . well, sensitive. He exaggerates.

'Sensitive? He's a liar! If he got from the pyramid to the delta here so quickly, and then managed to wander round the Eye freezing hundreds of sphinxes to death . . . that's quick work, wouldn't you say?'

Merle glanced back over her shoulder at Serafin and Lalapeya. They both looked impatient, but also unsure of the strange creature who was blocking their way over the bridge.

She turned back to Winter. 'Are you sure you can't fly?'

'Not down there. I ride the icy winds and driving snow, but that means nothing here.'

'Why not?'

Winter heaved a deep sigh, while the Queen groaned with dramatic impatience. 'I'll explain it to you, Merle,' he said. 'And your friends too if they'd like to listen.'

Serafin growled something that sounded like, 'What choice do we have?'

'Summer is at the bottom of this shaft. Her power, the heat of her sun if you like, normally rises up through it. Anyone who approached the bottom of the abyss would be instantly burnt to a cinder.'

Merle nervously shifted her weight, looking down from Vermithrax's back into the depths. All she saw was greyish-white chaos. And she was freezing cold. It was getting worse and worse.

'My presence here in the shaft breaks the flow of heat,' he went on. 'Ice and fire meet somewhere down there, halfway between her and me. The snow suddenly melts in mid-air, cold turns to heat. Sometimes storms rage and thunder rolls when we meet. I could have myself carried down by the icy winds, but Summer is a prisoner, and has no control over her heat. She is weakened, unable to cool herself down as usual when we meet. The winds would turn to a mild breeze down there, the ice would melt, and I myself . . . well, think of a snowflake falling on a hot stove-plate.' He buried his bony face in his hands. 'Now do you understand?'

Merle nodded uncomfortably.

'Then you will understand the full hopelessness of my situation,' he announced, with a dramatic gesture.

'*I don't believe this!*' said the Queen venomously. '*This fellow has just exterminated almost the whole of a race, and now he sits here complaining!*'

You might show a little more sympathy.

'*I can't stand him.*'

I bet you weren't everyone's favourite god.

'*Ask him if he's ever heard of the word dignity.*'

I most certainly will not.

'*I could do it for you.*'

Don't you dare!

Serafin interrupted them. 'What now, Merle? We can't stand here forever.'

No, of course not, she thought, shivering.

Vermithrax spoke up. 'I have an idea.'

They all waited in suspense, and only the Queen murmured crossly, '*Whatever his idea is, it had better work quickly. We don't have any time left. The Son of the Mother is waking.*'

'I could fly down and try to set Summer free,' said Vermithrax. 'I am made of stone. Heat and cold can't harm me . . . at least, I think not. And I survived being submerged in the Stone Light, so I shall probably survive here too. Once Summer is free I can carry Winter down to her. Or her up to him.'

Merle buried her fingers even deeper in his mane. 'That's out of the question!'

'It's the only way.'

Merle felt the Queen trying to take over her voice, and forced her violently back. For the last time, she snapped at the Queen in her mind, will you please let it alone?

'*Vermithrax will put everything at risk if he does that! We won't get far without him.*'

You mean if he doesn't do what you say, isn't that so?

'*That's not the point.*'

Oh yes, it is, thought Merle. That's exactly the point. You've been exploiting him just as you exploited me. You knew from the first that we'd end up here with no other option left to us. You've always taken us exactly where you wanted us to be. 'And that's that!' She had spoken the last words out loud. The others all heard her and looked at her in surprise. She had gone red, and the heat that rose to her face felt almost pleasant in the icy air.

'She doesn't want me to do it,' Vermithrax deduced.

Merle grimly shook her head. 'What she wants doesn't matter at the moment.'

The lion turned to Winter. 'What will happen when Summer is set free?'

The albino made a dramatic gesture with both hands, indicating the entire Iron Eye. 'What has always happened. All this will lose its power. Just as it did before.'

Merle pricked up her ears. 'When the Sub-Oceanic Realms fell?' She was guessing, but she hit the mark.

Winter nodded. 'They were not alone in what they tried to do, but theirs was the most spectacular failure.' He thought briefly. 'How can I explain? They tap her power, the power of the sun – perhaps that's the best way to describe it. They don't realise that they are only harming themselves. They know about the mistakes made by the ancients, but they repeat them again and again. They are so terribly weak, though they think themselves infinitely strong.' Winter shook his head. 'The fools! They can't win, one way or another. They will destroy themselves sooner or later, even if we don't set Summer free.'

'But what do they want?' asked Serafin. 'Why are they doing all these things?'

It was Lalapeya who answered him. 'They use Summer to drive their ships, factories and machinery with her energy. That was how they brought the Pharaoh to power and conquered the world. Yet this world was really just a simple exercise for them to practise on, only a toy. What they are really after is something else.'

'All the mirrors,' whispered Merle.

'Their plan is to use the Iron Eye to break down the barriers between worlds. They intend to move from world to world with their fortress, conducting a campaign of conquest never before seen on such a scale.'

'But for that they'll need magic,' growled Vermithrax. 'More magic than an ordinary sphinx can master.'

'The Son of the Mother,' said Merle, as coming events ran through her mind like the play of light and shadow in a magic lantern show. '*He* is the key to everything, isn't he? When he wakes, the Stone Light will rule. And it will move the Iron Eye through the mirror world with him, breaking down the gateways to other worlds.' She imagined the vast fortress appearing inside the labyrinth of the mirror world, destroying thousands upon thousands of mirror gates. The chaos in the worlds beyond them would be indescribable. And the sphinxes, like a race of pirates, would travel through those gates under the leadership of the Light, spreading death and destruction just as they had done in this world of their own. Once again, they wouldn't get their own hands dirty, they would find tools like the priests of Horus and Amenophis and raise them to power. Others would do their work for them while they sat in their fortress, biding their time. A people of scholars and poets, Lalapeya had said. And it was true: the sphinxes *were* artists, scholars and philosophers, but the price of their life of art and argument was a high one. A price to be paid by whole worlds.

'Merle,' said Vermithrax firmly, 'go to your mother.'

She still hesitated, although she sensed that his mind was made up. 'You must promise me to come back.'

Vermithrax purred like a kitten. 'Of course I will.'

'Promise!'

'I promise you.'

It was poor comfort, perhaps no more than empty words. Still, she felt a little better.

'*Don't fool yourself*,' said the Queen, caustically. '*You human beings have always been wonderful at that.*'

Merle wondered why the Queen was being so insufferable. Perhaps because Vermithrax's plan was better than her own. He intended to set Summer free, thus robbing the last sphinxes of their power, and preventing the Son of the Mother from coming back to life.

And what about the Queen's own plan? Why wasn't she telling them about it? Where was the snag? For Merle had realised a long time ago that she *had* a plan.

'*I'm afraid for him.*' The Queen's tone had abruptly changed: no sarcasm now, no cutting irony, but genuine concern. '*I want to speak to him – if you will allow me.*'

'Yes,' said Merle. 'Of course.' The Queen was playing on her feelings like someone playing the piano, and knew exactly which key to strike when. Merle saw through her, but there was nothing she could do about it.

'Vermithrax,' said the Queen, in Merle's voice, 'I am here.'

Serafin and Lalapeya stared at Merle, and she had to remind herself that although the two of them knew her story, this was the first time they had actually heard the Queen *speak* through her mouth. Vermithrax had pricked up his ears too.

'There's something I have to tell you.'

Vermithrax looked uncertainly at Winter, who had risen to his feet and was standing on the bridge, legs planted wide apart, not swaying or even blinking. 'Now, Queen? Can't it wait?'

'No. Listen to me.' He listened, and so did the others. Even Winter put his head on one side, as if he were concentrating on the words that passed Merle's lips but were not her own. 'I am Sekhmet, mother of the sphinxes,' the Queen went on, 'as you know.'

To Lalapeya and Serafin at least, however, it was a surprise. Lalapeya was about to say something, but the Queen interrupted her. 'Not now. Vermithrax is right, we must hurry. What I have to say concerns him closely. When I had borne the Son of the Mother, and then with him bore the race of sphinxes, I soon understood what had happened: the Stone Light had deceived me. And made use of me. I brought obedient servants into the world for him. Once I had realised what that meant I decided to do something. I could not kill all the sphinxes and undo what had been done – but I could prevent the Son of the Mother from making them his slaves. I fought him, mother against son, and in the end I overcame him. I was the only one with the power to do it. I killed him, and the sphinxes buried him in the lagoon.' She paused, hesitated, and then went on. 'You all know what happened then. But it is not the end of my story, and it's important for you to hear it. You above all, Vermithrax.'

The lion nodded with deliberation, as if he already guessed what was coming.

'I knew that I could not guard the lagoon on my own, and so I took stone and made the statues that human beings erected in my honour, the first stone lions. I made them of magic and my own heart's blood, and I would say that because of that – like and yet not like the sphinxes – they are my children too, would you not agree?'

Unable to look Merle and the Queen in the eyes, sitting there on his back, the lion bowed his head. 'Great Sekhmet,' he whispered humbly.

'None of that,' snapped the Queen. 'I don't want worship! I just want you to know the truth about the origin of your people. No one now remembers how and when the stone lions came to the lagoon, so I am telling you. The lagoon is their birthplace, for after the Son of the Mother was buried there I made you to guard him. I would watch over him myself, but I needed helpers to be my arms and legs and hands and claws. So I made the first of your people, and when I was sure they could perform their task I gave up my own body and became the Flowing Queen. I could not live any longer as a goddess with the shame of what I had done, nor did I want to. I united with the water. In one way that was the right decision, but in another it was a mistake, for it meant that I had given up control of the stone lions. My servants were strong creatures but too trusting, and they threw in their lot with human beings.' She paused briefly, before going on in a bitter voice. 'You know what happened then. How humans betrayed the lions and robbed them of their wings; the flight of those who had escaped that crime; and finally the unsuccessful attack on Venice led by you yourself, Vermithrax, to right the wrong that was done to your ancestors.'

The obsidian lion said nothing. He had listened with his

head bowed. He and his kind were the children of Sekhmet. The stone guards of the Son of the Mother.

'Then it is right that I'm here now,' he said at last, raising his head with new determination. 'Perhaps I can atone for the mistake my ancestors made. They failed to keep watch on the Son of the Mother.'

'As I failed too,' said Lalapeya.

'And I myself,' said the Queen through Merle's mouth.

'But now fate has given me a chance,' growled Vermithrax. 'And all of us, perhaps. We failed in the past, but today we have an opportunity to stop the Son of the Mother. And I'm no lion if we don't succeed.' He uttered a warlike roar. 'Get off now, Merle.'

She obeyed, moving very slowly, very cautiously, until Lalapeya took her in her injured arms and drew her close. But Vermithrax went over to Winter. The pale figure touched his nose, tickling him under the chin. Vermithrax purred. He had been right. The frost had no effect on his stone body.

'Good luck,' said Merle quietly. Serafin leaned down from the back of the sphinx and placed one hand on her shoulder. 'Don't worry,' he whispered. 'He'll make it.'

Winter nodded to Vermithrax one last time, and then the

lion roared a battle cry and with one bound leaped into the depths below. A few metres down his wings stabilised his flight, and a moment or so later he was only a bright outline behind curtains of ice and snow. Finally he disappeared entirely, extinguished like a candle flame drowning in melted wax.

'*He'll do it*,' whispered the Queen.

Suppose he doesn't, thought Merle, what will become of us then?

Lalapeya clasped her daughter even closer in her arms, despite her bandaged hands. Merle turned to her, and looked into her eyes from very close.

And so they stood there for a long time, and no one spoke a word.

Vermithrax felt it. He felt the Stone Light in him, yet he knew it could not harm him. When he had been immersed in the Light down below the domed roof of Axis Mundi, he had been able to feel it. Nothing tangible, no clear sensation, but he had known there was something in him that protected him from the Light, and at the same time was uniting itself with him. Now he realised that it was the inheritance of Sekhmet, primeval mother of all stone lions and sphinxes, the Flowing Queen herself. She had been touched by the rays of the Stone Light, and something of that contact had passed into the lions too. When he had fallen into the Light, it had recognised itself in him and spared him. More: it had made him stronger than ever before. Unintentionally, perhaps, but that made no difference now.

He was Vermithrax, the greatest and mightiest among the lions of the lagoon. And he was here to do what he had been born for. If he died in the attempt, that would only bring his life full circle to its close. And if Seth had been telling the truth he was the last of his race anyway, the last of the lions who could both speak and fly. The last free lion of his kind.

Beating his wings strongly, he dropped to the depths, flew down with the snowflakes, overtook them, shot through them like a comet falling into the abyss. Soon he thought they were smaller and damper, not the fluffy flakes further up in the shaft but slushy, and then they became drops of moisture. Snow was turning to rain. As heat rose the water evaporated too, and he came to a zone of pleasant warmth, then heat, finally roaring fire. The air around him quivered and boiled, but he breathed it as easily as the icy air of the heights above, and his lungs, shining like everything else about him, sucked the oxygen out of it and kept him alive.

He was right. The Light that had made him strong preserved him from heat and cold alike.

Soon it was so hot that even stone would have melted to glass, but his obsidian body withstood the heat. The distant walls of the shaft could not be made out any more; whatever material they were made from, it was not of this world. Magic mirrors, perhaps, like the rest of the Iron Eye. Or pure magic. He did not understand these things, nor did they interest him. He just wanted to carry out the task he had set himself. He wanted to set Summer free. Overcome the sphinxes. Stop the Son of the Mother.

Then he saw her.

At first he didn't even realise that the floor of the shaft was already below him. It might have been a lake of fire, with even more glowing light than heat in it. But it was a pure, natural light, not like the Stone Light spinning its webs of malice and war in Hell. This was the light that gave warmth, the light in whose rays Vermithrax's own lion people had basked on the rocky plateaux of Africa.

The light of Summer.

There she lay, stretched out in a lake of blazing, gleaming

light, borne up on the heat of the air, floating above the ground like a fruit waiting to be picked.

There were no guards, no chains. Both would have been consumed by the heat instantly. Sphinx magic, nothing else, had put her into a trance and held her here.

Gently beating his wings, Vermithrax stopped in the air above the hovering figure of Summer and looked down at her for a moment. She was as like Winter as a sister, tall and thin, almost bony. She did not look healthy in any human sense, but that might be in her nature. Her hair was fiery. Flames blazed behind her eyelids too, yellow and red as burning coals. Her lips were silken as flower petals, her skin pale, her fingernails crescents of pure fire.

She isn't in control of her heat, Winter had said, and indeed the fire was licking out of her body, which seemed to be flickering and blurring like a wax figure in the heat of August.

Vermithrax watched her for a moment longer, then put out his left forepaw and touched her very, very gently on the thigh.

His heartbeat calmed down.

He knew how burning hot she was, yet he did not *feel* her heat.

The Light, he thought again. The Stone Light protects

me. I ought to be thankful to it and to that devil Burbridge.

He withdrew his paw, waited while he took another two or three breaths, and then began flying in a close loop around Summer's hovering body, into the blazing fountain of her fiery hair, passing through it and under it. Her locks radiated like an exploding firework frozen for ever in time. Once, twice he circled around her, until he was sure that he had cut the invisible bonds of magic holding her there. Then he carefully hovered beside her and tried to raise her from her invisible bed of heat.

She lay light as a feather between his forepaws, coming away from her hovering position with only slight resistance, as if he had used a magnet to pull out a nail. At the same moment the brightness around her was muted, the quivering air grew paler, outlines looked sharper. The heat was perceptibly less now, he could actually see that. No one, no sphinx would ever have thought it possible that any living creature could come down here and reach her. The Stone Light, the power *behind* the power of the sphinxes, had cheated itself of victory.

Vermithrax slowly rose again, clasping Summer's thin body in a firm grasp. She looked undernourished, a little like Merle's friend Junipa. But with Summer that was not a sign of too little to eat, or even illness. Who could say what a season of the year ought to look like, her skin, her hair? If Winter set the standard for a healthy specimen of his kind, then there was probably nothing the matter with Summer's body.

Her mind was something else, though.

Although Vermithrax had cut through the bonds of sphinx magic, Summer still did not seem to be coming back to consciousness. She hung in his embrace like a doll, not moving. He wondered whether at least her eyelids were fluttering, as the lids of unconscious human beings often do when they are gradually coming round. But Summer was not a human being. During the steep upward flight it was difficult for him to raise her far enough to see her face anyway.

They were flying in an aura of warmth. The snow around them melted and finally disappeared entirely as they came closer to the narrow bridge crossing the void at a dizzy height, where Winter and the others were waiting for them. The powers of the two seasons cancelled each other out now that Summer was no longer directing all her strength outwards. Vermithrax assumed that this was a sign of her cure: her body was using energy for itself again, turning its power inward, trying to heal itself.

They had almost reached the thin bridge over the mirror-glass abyss when Summer moved in Vermithrax's paws. She groaned slightly. Life was gradually returning to her.

He flew even faster now, turned around the bridge in a triumphant pirouette, and dropped Summer into Winter's outstretched arms. As the two embraced – he stormily, she barely conscious, still just a shadow of herself – the obsidian lion came down and settled gently in front of Lalapeya.

The sphinx let go of Merle, and Vermithrax was glad when the girl fell on his neck with a happy cry, buried her face in his glowing mane and wept with relief. The boy on the sphinx's back was grinning broadly. Vermithrax winked at him, feeling extraordinarily human.

Summer was reviving by the second in Winter's embrace. When she opened her eyes they were the colour of sun-baked desert sand. The flames in her hair went out. Her slender hands joined behind Winter's back, and she uttered a soft sob. 'It's happened again,' she whispered. Now she was weeping openly and without shame. Winter's closeness supported her.

Vermithrax looked at Merle, who had moved away from him again. But it was Serafin who asked the question in everyone's mind. 'So was that really all?'

For a moment there was silence. No snow was falling now, and the wintry winds around them had almost entirely died down. They stood still above the abyss, its floor deep beneath them shining like a silver lake.

'No,' said Merle, and once again it was the Flowing Queen who spoke through her. 'That was very far from all.'

'But –' Serafin was interrupted when Merle shook her head, and the Queen said, 'It happened just now, at this very moment. The sphinxes have used the last of Summer's energy to achieve their aim.'

'The Son of the Mother?' asked Vermithrax unhappily.

'Yes,' said the Queen through Merle's mouth. 'The Son of the Mother has been roused to life. I can sense him not far from here. And now there is only one who can be a match for him.'

As once before, in the past.

Mother against son. Son against mother.

'Sekhmet,' said Merle, trembling, but mistress of her own voice again. 'Only Sekhmet herself can stop her son now. But for that –' She hesitated, and searched in a daze for words that she really knew already, for the Queen had told her. 'She says that for that she needs her old body back.'

THE SON OF THE MOTHER

It began when a Barque of the Sun fell from the sky somewhere above the Mediterranean. The vessel dropped like a dead bird hit by the shot of a hunter in his hide. Its golden crescent spun down in a narrow spiral, and the sphinx on board could do nothing to prevent its fall. The Barque came down in the sea, sending up a foaming fountain. Salt water poured in on all sides through the loopholes and any joints not welded entirely watertight. Seconds later the ship had disappeared.

Elsewhere, similar scenes were going on above land. Barques of the Sun full of mummy warriors fell from the clouds and shattered to pieces on bare rock, devastated countryside, in the tree-tops of dense forests. Many fell over cities, often in the middle of burnt-out fields of rubble, sometimes on the roofs of buildings both inhabited and uninhabited. Some sank in swamps and wide marshes, others were swallowed up by jungles or desert dunes. High in mountain ranges, they scraped past steep slopes and were wrecked on rocky ledges.

Where human beings witnessed these incidents they broke into rejoicing, never guessing that the cause of it all was a girl and her motley band of companions in distant Egypt. Others suppressed their joy for fear of the mummy warriors guarding them – until they saw that a change was coming over their guards too.

All over the world, mummies collapsed into dust and dry bones, the blotched flesh of corpses and clattering armour. In some places it took only seconds for whole nations to be suddenly freed from their oppressors; in others it was hours before the last mummy warrior was only a motionless corpse.

Sphinxes tried to keep the workers in the mummy factories under control, but there were too few of them. Most had long ago set out for the Iron Eye. There were no priests of Horus left to halt the landslide either; Amenophis himself had murdered them. And as for the human servants of the Empire, they were too few in number and not strong enough to offer any serious resistance to the uprisings.

The Egyptian Empire, built up over decades, fell into ruin within a few hours.

On the borders of the free Tsarist Empire, it was not long before the defenders on their walls and palisades, in their trenches and on the towers of lonely fortresses in the tundra discovered the truth. They dared to sally out, their sallies became campaigns – campaigns against an enemy that was suddenly not a real adversary any more, against crumbling mummy bodies and Barques of the Sun that had crashed and fallen to pieces.

In many places mighty Gatherers, the dreaded flagships of the Empire, dropped from the clouds. Some fell in dismal and deserted country, a handful of them over cities. A few took hundreds of slaves to their death with them. Then they too were gone, at a single blow of Fate.

Here and there a few sphinxes tried desperately to keep their airships in the sky, bringing all their sphinx magic to bear. But their attempts were useless. Those who crawled out of the smoking, distorted steel wrecks alive were killed by their human slaves. Only a very few found shelter in forests and caves, with no hope of ever being able to emerge safely into the light of day again.

The world changed. Not gradually, not hesitantly. The change was like a thunder-clap coming out of a clear sky, a flash of lightning in the darkest night. What had been suppressed and destroyed for decades broke through the rubble and ashes like a flower, put out shoots, stretched and grew, blossomed to show resistance and new strength.

And while life re-awakened on all the continents of earth, the snow covering the Egyptian desert began to thaw.

Winter had stayed with Summer on the edge of the abyss, where the bridge led to a wall of steel reflecting like a mirror. Summer was still too weak to help Merle and the others in their fight. But not even in full possession of their powers would she or Winter have stood a chance against the Son of the Mother.

Merle was clinging to Vermithrax's mane with both hands. The obsidian lion carried her at great speed through the arched corridors, the halls and stairways of the Iron Eye. Around them water ran down the walls, snowdrifts and icicles melted into streams and lakes. Serafin was sitting behind Merle, while Lalapeya followed them at a fast gallop down the mirror-lined corridors.

'Is she sure they've kept her body somewhere in the fortress?' Serafin called into Merle's ear.

'That's what she said.'

'And does she know where?'

'She says she can sense it – after all, it was once a part of her.'

The Queen spoke up again. *'This ill-bred boy is talking about me as if I weren't here at all.'*

Well, you aren't, retorted Merle. Or not as far as he's concerned. How much further is it?

'We'll soon see.'

That's not fair.

'I don't know any more than you do. The presence of my former body fills all the lower levels of the fortress, like the presence of the Son of the Mother. They must both be somewhere very close.'

Things were approaching their end – *an* end, anyway. Merle had to admit that it had all become too overwhelming for her some time ago. So much had happened since Seth abducted Junipa in the hall of mirrors that she no longer felt able to arrange it in any kind of order. Only Serafin and the presence of Vermithrax and Lalapeya gave her a vague sense of security. She wished that Winter had stayed with them too. But he refused to leave Summer, and had relapsed into his own non-humanity again. The seasons would endure, whatever became of the world that they covered again and again with ice and heat and autumn leaves. Vermithrax had risked his life for Summer, but no one had thanked him. Merle was furious with Winter. They could have done with his help now – whatever the Queen was planning.

You do have a plan, don't you? she asked in her mind, but as usual with awkward questions the Queen gave no reply.

On their way they passed crystallised sphinxes frozen to milky ice when Winter touched them on his wanderings through the fortress. Water dripped to the mirror floors from their rigid bodies. Merle could not shake off the feeling that they had been moving for hours through a gigantic mausoleum full of mirrors reflecting images back to them.

The same thoughts were going through Serafin's head. 'It's odd,' he said, as they passed one group of frozen sphinx bodies. 'They're our enemies, but to see them like this . . . I don't know . . .'

Merle knew what he was trying to say. 'It feels somehow wrong, you mean?'

He nodded. 'Perhaps because it's always wrong for so many living creatures simply to *stop* being alive.' After a brief hesitation, he added, 'Never mind what they did.'

Merle was silent for a moment, thinking over what he had said. She came to a distressing conclusion. 'I'm not sorry for them. I mean, I'm trying . . . but it doesn't work. I simply am not sorry for them. Too much has happened for that. They have millions of human lives to answer for.' She had almost said 'billions', but her tongue shrank from putting the truth into words.

The frozen sphinx bodies rushed past them like a procession, bizarre arcades of icy corpses. White puddles had already formed round many of them. The thaw brought about by the reunion between Summer and Winter was beginning to reach the lower levels too.

All this time Lalapeya had kept silent. Merle couldn't shake off the feeling that her mother was watching her, as if to form a picture of her daughter that went beyond her mere appearance. As if her eyes were exploring Merle's mind and heart too. She was probably listening to every word Merle said.

'*Now I know!*' the Queen suddenly burst out. '*I know why the Son of the Mother's body and mine overlap as they do. Why it's so difficult to tell them apart.*'

Yes?

'*They're both here!*'

In the fortress? But we've known that for a long time.

'*Silly girl! In the same place. A hall.*' There was a short silence, and then, '*Straight ahead of us!*'

Merle was going to give the others a warning, but it

came of its own accord. All at once Vermithrax stopped. An outline sharp as a knife emerged from the panorama of mirrors and ice, a horizontal line – the edge of a broad balustrade. And beyond it, once again – another abyss.

The lion slowly made his way forwards with Lalapeya beside him.

'What is it?' whispered Serafin.

Merle could only guess at the answer: they had come to the heart of the Iron Eye, the temple of the lion goddess.

Sekhmet's sanctuary. The vault of the Flowing Queen.

Merle and Serafin leaped down from Vermithrax's back and knelt to look at the drop beyond the balustrade. Serafin's hand closed over Merle's. She gave him a smile and held his fingers in a firm grasp. Warmth crept up her arm, electrifying her. It was with reluctance that she looked away from him and down into the abyss.

On the opposite side of the hall – for a hall it was, although no human work of architecture, no throne-room or cathedral could compare with its proportions – stood the gigantic statue of a lioness, taller than the Basilica of San Marco in Venice. It was carved of stone and showed the bared fangs of a beast of prey, every one of them as long as a tree. Its expression was dark and spiteful, its eyes sunk in deep shadow. On each of its claws, also carved of rock, was the likeness of an impaled human being, carried as casually as dirt between its paws.

The statue was reflected many times in the mirror walls of the hall, reflected back again and again, so that it looked as if not one statue of Sekhmet stood there but a full dozen or more.

Was *that* you? Merle couldn't help asking.

'*Sekhmet*,' protested the Queen sadly. '*Not I.*'

But you're the same person!

'*We were once.*' Her tone was bitter. '*But I was never the way the sphinxes depict me. When I was still called Sekhmet they worshipped me as a goddess -- though not as that thing there!*' There was revulsion in her voice now. '*They seem to have made me into a demon since those days. Look at the dead bodies impaled on its claws. I never killed human beings. But they say so because it suits their plans. "Sekhmet did it," they tell themselves, "so we can do it too." It's the same with all gods who can't defend themselves any more – their worshippers make them in their own image. After a while no one asks about the truth.*'

'This must be the lowest point of the Iron Eye,' said Serafin. 'And look – down there.'

Streams of water were now splashing and gurgling into

the hall from all the ways into the mighty mirrored dome, some of them only narrow trickles, some broad torrents.

Lalapeya cautiously leaned a little further forward and looked down at the abyss. 'All this will be flooded soon, once the snow has thawed right out on the upper levels.'

Vermithrax still couldn't take his eyes off the towering statue. 'Is *that* her body?'

Although the same thought had occurred to Merle at first, now she knew better. 'No, only a statue.'

'Where's her real body, then?'

'*Over there,*' said the Queen in Merle's head. '*Look to the right, past the forepaws of the statue. Do you see that low platform? And do you see what's lying on it?*'

Merle peered hard, trying to make something out. It was a long way off. The floor of the hall lay far below them, the balustrade ran along the wall in the upper third of the building. Whatever the Queen meant, they would only be able to reach it with Vermithrax's help.

Merle saw the platform just as she was about to give up. And she saw the body lying on it too. Stretched on its side with all four paws pointing in her direction. A big cat. A lioness. She was no larger than an ordinary animal; on the contrary, she seemed to Merle far more delicate, almost fragile. She was grey on the surface as if covered with dust – or turned to stone.

Merle pointed out her discovery to the others.

'She's made of stone,' growled Vermithrax. It sounded as if he felt slightly flattered.

'I wasn't always,' said the Queen in Merle's voice, so that everyone could hear her. 'When I left that body it was flesh and blood. It must have petrified over all these thousands of years. I didn't know.'

'It could have been the touch of the Stone Light,' said Lalapeya thoughtfully.

'Yes,' agreed the Queen. 'That's possible.'

Serafin was still holding Merle's hand. He looked from her to the slender body of the lioness down below and then back again. Water from the melted snow and ice was streaming into the temple hall on all sides now. It seemed to them as if it were gurgling a little louder, more violently, more angrily every moment. Not all the openings in the walls were on floor level; some, like the one leading to this balustrade, were dozens of metres higher up, and the water was cascading from them with enormous force into the depths below. On the ledge where they now stood the ice was thawing, surrounding them all with slush and shallow puddles of water. Here and there it was already trickling over the edge and down to the floor.

'*We'll have to get down there.*' The Queen sounded gloomy and apprehensive. Once again, Merle realised that she was hiding something from her. The last part of the truth. And probably the most unpleasant part too.

Come on, she demanded in her thoughts, tell me, what is it?

The Queen hesitated. '*All in good time.*'

No! Now!

The moment of hesitation was drawn out into a stubborn silence.

What's going on, for goodness' sake? Merle tried to sound as imperious as possible – not so easy when you're only forming the words in your head, not with your mouth.

'*We can't rethink everything now.*'

No one's suggesting we should.

'*Please, Merle. This is hard enough anyway.*'

Merle was going to answer back when Serafin suddenly tugged at her hand.

'Merle!'

Nerves on edge, she spun round. 'What is it?'

'There's something wrong down there!'

'Something very wrong.' Vermithrax agreed.

Lalapeya said nothing. She was rigid with shock.

Merle followed the others' eyes and looked down into the depths below.

At first everything looked the same. The gigantic statue of the demonic goddess Sekhmet; beside it, much smaller, her motionless body on the platform; and all around them the water flowing out of the halls and corridors of the Iron Eye and covering the floor.

No newcomers. Not a sphinx anywhere.

But the reflections! The mirror images of the mighty statue had begun to move. At a quick glance it might seem to be because of the curtains of water pouring down the walls, shifting and distorting those reflections. Then a soft trembling and quivering turned to a noise as loud as thunder. Gigantic limbs were tensing and stretching. A titanic body was rousing itself from slumber.

Merle felt as if she were falling kilometres deep into an abyss of silver. Everything went round in circles for a moment, going faster and faster. Her dizziness made her feel sick. Only gradually did the truth emerge from her whirling impressions.

Some of the reflections were really those of the statue,

and they stood as still as ever. But others showed a creature that had nothing in common with the statue of the goddess except its size and part of its leonine body.

Serafin's hand clasped Merle's fingers. He had seen this creature before, when the magic of the Gatherer airship raised it from the ruins of the cemetery island of San Michele.

The Son of the Mother – the greatest of all sphinxes, ugly and deformed like a distorted image of all his worshippers – had been here in the temple all the time. The companions had seen him against the wall, but from a distance they had taken him for one of the countless reflections.

Now they knew better.

'Get down!' whispered Lalapeya sharply. 'He hasn't noticed us yet!'

They all obeyed her. Merle's joints felt as if they had frozen to ice. The obsidian hairs of Vermithrax's mane were standing on end, and he had shot out all his claws ready for the last, the greatest of all battles.

Perhaps the shortest too.

What looked beautiful and almost perfect in the sphinxes seemed, in the Son of the Mother, to have shifted into a wrong perspective, was all on edge, distorted. The sphinx god measured several dozen metres from his muscular human chest to his lion's lower body. His hands had grotesque, gnarled fingers, and far too many of them. Almost like the bodies of spiders, they were large enough to crush Merle and her companions with a single blow. His claws were yellow and could not be retracted. At every step, they punched rows of metre-deep craters in the mirror floor of the dome. The four lion's legs and two human arms were too long and had too many joints, bent and stretched by cords of muscle that lay curiously askew under his skin and pelt, as if the Son of the Mother had far more of them than any other sphinx.

And then there was his face.

His eyes were too small for the size of it, and shone with the same brilliance as the Stone Light. His cheekbones were unnaturally prominent, and his nostrils were huge and cavernous. His brow was like a steep slope covered with furrows and scars, the legacy of long-forgotten battles. The teeth behind his scaly lips were a rampart of stalactites and stalagmites, the entrance to a stinking grotto now breathing out vapours that emerged and took shape as purple clouds. Only his hair was silky and shining: full, long, and deep black in colour.

Merle knew they were all thinking just the same: there's

no point in it now. Nothing and no one could stand up to such a creature. Certainly not the delicate lioness lying lifeless on her altar far down below.

'*I'd almost forgotten how dangerous he is,*' said the Queen, tonelessly.

Great, thought Merle bitterly. Exactly what I wanted to hear.

'*Oh, I can defeat him,*' the Queen made haste to reply. '*I've done it before.*'

That was rather a long time ago.

'*I suppose you're right there.*'

The Queen seemed to have lost some of the optimism she had shown over the last few hours when it came to her battle with the Son of the Mother. She was daunted, whether she would admit it or not. And deep inside her Merle sensed a fear that was not her own. The Flowing Queen was afraid.

'What's he planning to do?' asked Vermithrax in a dry voice.

The Son of the Mother was prowling up and down in front of the grotesque statue of Sekhmet, sometimes fast, sometimes more slowly, like a hunter circling his prey. His eyes were bent on the tiny body at the feet of the statue, the lioness's petrified corpse. It seemed to trouble him far more than the great masses of water that would soon flood this mirrored dome.

'He doesn't know what to do,' whispered Lalapeya. She was resting her bandaged hands on the balustrade. They must still be hurting her, but she didn't show it. 'See how nervous he is. He knows he must make up his mind, but he dares not take that last step.'

'What last step?' asked Vermithrax.

'Destroying his mother's body,' said Serafin. 'That's what he's here for. He wants to do away with Sekhmet once and for all, so that what happened to him in the past can never be done again.'

'*Yes*,' said the Flowing Queen to Merle. '*We must hurry.*'

Merle nodded. 'Vermithrax, you'll have to take me down there.'

The obsidian lion raised one bushy eyebrow. 'Past him?'

'We don't have any choice, do we?'

The Flowing Queen had not yet said a word to explain just how she was going to move from Merle's body back into her own. But now a thought came into Merle's mind, sudden as an unexpected flash of inspiration: this, obviously, was the Queen's final secret. A secret that she had been keeping from Merle all this time.

Very well, thought Merle, here we go. Tell me.

She had the impression that, as never before, the Queen was struggling to find words. As she hesitated, time was spun out to an intolerable length.

Oh, come on!

'*When I leave you, Merle . . .*' She broke off, faltering.

Yes, then what?

'*When I leave your body you will die.*'

Merle was silent. She thought nothing. Said nothing. All at once there was only emptiness inside her.

'*Merle, please . . .*' Another and even longer hesitation. '*If there were any other way, any kind of . . .*'

It was as if her consciousness had been swept clean. No thoughts. Not even memories, nothing she could mourn for. No regrets for what she had never done, no unfulfilled wishes. Nothing.

'*I'm sorry.*'

I consent, said Merle in her mind.

'*What?*'

I consent.

'*Is that all you have to say?*'

What did you expect? Did you think I'd scream and rage and put up a fight?

A moment's silence, and then: *'I don't know what I expected.'*

Perhaps I guessed it.

'No, you did not.'

Perhaps I did, all the same.

'I . . . oh, this is hard!'

Explain. Why can't I go on living when you leave me?

'That's not it. It's not because of my move from one body to another. It's because . . .'

Yes?

'I could leave your body without doing you any harm. Passing from one living creature to another is no problem. But Sekhmet's body is dead, do you understand? It has no life of its own any more. And so –'

So you must take some with you.

'Yes, that's more or less it.'

You want to use my life force to revive the stone corpse down there.

'There's no other way. I am sorry.'

You knew all the time, didn't you?

Silence.

Didn't you?

'Yes.'

Serafin pressed her hand again. 'What are you two

talking about?' There was anxiety in his eyes.

'Nothing.' Merle thought that sounded hollow, empty. 'It's all right.'

At that moment the Queen took over her voice, and before Merle could prevent it, she said, 'The others have a right to know. Let them decide.'

'Decide what?' Serafin straightened up, looking wary.

Lalapeya came closer too. 'What do you mean?' she asked.

Merle concentrated desperately, trying to suppress the Queen's voice as she had done before in Hell. But this time she couldn't do it. She could only listen as the Queen told the others, through her own mouth, what would happen. Must happen.

'No,' whispered Serafin. 'It can't be!'

'There must be some other way,' growled Vermithrax, and it sounded almost like a threat.

Lalapeya came over to Merle and embraced her. She was about to say something, was already opening her lips, when a clear, girlish voice spoke behind all their backs.

'You can't seriously mean that!'

Merle looked up, unable to believe her eyes. 'Junipa!'

She left Lalapeya and Serafin, made her way back from the balustrade as fast as she could, wading through snow and water, and finally reached Junipa and took her in her arms.

'Are you all right? Are you hurt? What happened?' For a few moments the Flowing Queen's words and her own fate were forgotten. She couldn't let go of Junipa, she had to keep staring at her as if she were a ghost that had materialised out of nothing before her eyes. 'Where's Seth? What did he do to you?'

Junipa smiled faintly, but it seemed as if her smile was to hide a sharp pain. The hold of the Stone Light on her. Its invisible talon reaching out for her heart.

Down in the great hall the Son of the Mother was still pacing up and down, never resting. He was too deep in his angry thoughts to notice what was going on up behind the balustrade. And he still hesitated to destroy his mother's petrified body. His heavy breathing and growling echoed back from the walls, and the crunch and crack of the mirror-glass floor beneath his claws was like the sound of ice floes splintering as they crashed together.

Vermithrax had his eye on the huge beast, but at the same time he kept glancing at the two girls. Serafin too stepped slowly back from the drop where the mirror wall ended, joined the others, gave Junipa a quick hug, smiled encouragingly and then turned to the companions who had appeared behind her, four of them. The whole group had stepped out of one of the mirror-glass walls where the last of the frost patterns were gradually melting.

Serafin greeted Dario, Tiziano and Aristide. Arcimboldo's two apprentices were supporting Eft, who had a makeshift wooden splint strapped to her right leg; it looked like an outsize splinter of wood cut from a bookshelf with a knife. Eft's lipless mermaid mouth was tightly compressed. She was in pain, but did not complain.

Over Junipa's shoulder, Merle gave the mermaid a warm smile. For a moment their surroundings were forgotten, replaced by something else, a scene from the past, her journey with Eft in a gondola along a tunnel black as night. *You have been touched by the Flowing Queen,* Eft had said then. *You are special.*

Merle shook off the remembered image and turned back to Junipa. 'What happened to Seth? I've been so worried about you!'

Junipa's gaze darkened. 'We were in Venice, Seth and I. We saw the Pharaoh.'

'The Pharaoh –'

Junipa nodded. 'Amenophis is dead. And the Empire is collapsing.'

'Did Seth –'

'Kill him? Yes. And then he killed himself, but he allowed me to go.'

The Queen stirred in Merle's thoughts. *'The sphinxes let Amenophis down in the end. Just like them! They used the Empire to revive the Son of the Mother, and now they want to move on. They won't be content with this one world.'*

Junipa took Merle's shoulders. 'Just now – you didn't mean that, did you? What you said . . . or what *she* said. Whichever of you it was.'

Merle shook off her friend's hands. Her eyes avoided Junipa's mirror-glass gaze, moved from her to the others. She felt as if she had been driven into a corner from which there was no escape.

'The sphinxes have no power to leave our world without the Son of the Mother,' she said, turning to Junipa again, but still trying not to meet her eyes directly. 'And if there is only one way to defeat him . . . I have no choice, Junipa. None of us here has any choice.'

Junipa shook her head in desperation. 'That's not you speaking!'

'The Queen wanted you all to hear the truth so that you can decide for me. But I'm the one speaking now, and I won't let anyone else make that decision. It's my business, mine alone, not yours.'

'No!' Junipa went up to her and grasped her hand. 'Let me do it, Merle. Tell her she can pass into me first.'

'That's nonsense!'

'No, it's not.' Junipa's expression was firm and decided. 'The Stone Light will gain power over me again before long. I can feel it, Merle. It's groping around, tugging at me. I don't have much time left.'

'Then go through the mirrors into another world where the Light can't touch you.'

'I won't let you die. Look at me. My eyes aren't human. My heart isn't human. I'm a joke, Merle. A dreadful, bad joke.' She looked at Serafin, who was listening carefully to every word she said. 'You'll still have him, Merle. You'll have something worth living for. But what about me? If you die I'll have no one any more.'

'That's not true,' said Eft.

Merle went over to Junipa and took her in her arms, clasping her friend close. 'Look around you, Junipa. They're all your friends. None of them will let you down.'

Serafin stood there, his thoughts going back and forth. There must be some other possibility. There *must* be.

'You heard what she said.' Dario spoke up. 'The Pharaoh is dead. That's all that matters. The Empire is as good as overthrown. And if the sphinxes really want to get away from here, well, all the better for us. Why should other worlds have an easier time than ours? We've survived, haven't we? Others will survive too. They're not our business. Or yours either, Merle.'

She gave him a sad smile. Dario and she had never got on with each other, but it touched her now to find that even he was trying to make her change her mind. Serafin had done the right thing when he made up the quarrel between them; Dario was not bad at heart. Even if he didn't understand — couldn't understand — what she had to do.

'*We have no time left,*' said the Flowing Queen. '*The Son of the Mother will soon overcome any reluctance he feels and destroy my body. And then it will be too late.*'

Merle let go of Junipa. 'I must go now.'

'No!' Junipa's mirror-glass eyes filled with tears. And Merle had thought that Junipa couldn't cry any more.

She put her hand into the pocket of her dress and took out the magic water mirror. Turning, she handed it to Lalapeya. 'Here. I think this is yours. The phantom in it — promise me to let him out if you get safely away from here.'

Lalapeya took the mirror without looking at it. Her eyes were fixed on her daughter. 'Don't do it, Merle.'

Merle hugged her. 'Goodbye.' Her voice faltered as tears threatened, but she was soon back in control of herself again. 'I always knew you were there somewhere.'

Lalapeya's face was pale and frozen. She couldn't believe that having only just been reunited with her daughter she was to lose her again so soon. 'It's your decision, Merle.' She smiled faintly. 'That's the mistake all parents make, don't they? They won't accept that their children can make decisions of their own. But it looks as if you're leaving me no choice about that.'

Merle blinked back her tears and embraced her mother for the last time. Then she went over to Eft and the others, said goodbye to them too, avoided Junipa's unhappy glance again, and last of all went up to Serafin.

In the background, the Son of the Mother was growling and pawing the ground down below in the mirrored dome. His raging sounded ever angrier, ever more impatient.

Serafin took Merle in his arms and kissed her forehead. 'I don't want you to do this.'

She smiled. 'I know.'

'But that doesn't make any difference, does it?'

'No . . . no, I think not.'

'We never ought to have gone into that house back in Venice, you and I. Then none of this would have happened.'

Merle felt the warmth of him close to her. 'If we hadn't saved the Queen from the Egyptians . . . who knows what would have happened? Perhaps everything would be much worse now.'

'But we would have had each other.'

'Yes.' She smiled, the corners of her mouth fluttering slightly like butterfly wings. 'That would have been good.'

'I don't care about the rest of the world.'

Merle shook her head. 'Yes, you do, and you know it. Even Dario didn't seriously mean what he said a moment ago. Perhaps now, yes, perhaps tomorrow too. But some time or other he'll think differently. So will you. The pain will get less. It always does.'

'Let me do it,' he said urgently. 'If it's possible for the Queen to pass into me then she can take my life force to revive her former body.'

'Why should I say yes to you when I said no to Junipa?'

'Because . . . because then you could be there for Junipa. She's your friend, isn't she?'

She smiled, and nudged his nose with hers. 'Good try!'

Then she brushed his lips with a kiss, very quickly, and stepped away from him.

'*What he says is true, Merle,*' said the Queen despondently. '*I could pass into his body, and –*'

No, thought Merle, and turned to Vermithrax. 'Time to go.'

The lion's huge obsidian eyes were glittering. 'I will obey you. To the last. But I want you to know that this is not my own wish.'

'You don't have to obey me, Vermithrax. I'm just a girl. That's why you'll see it's what I have to do, won't you? You know I'm right.' Vermithrax too had once been prepared to sacrifice himself for his people. If anyone could understand her, he could.

Sadly, he bowed his head and said no more. Merle climbed on his back and bent forward to get a glimpse of the abyss below the edge of the drop. She saw the Son of the Mother slowly striding towards the statue. He was approaching Sekhmet's lifeless body on its bier, scraping the ground harder than ever with his claws. Under the surface of the water, the mirror floor broke into star-shaped patterns of silvered glass.

Merle looked back at the others for the last time as the

lion went over to the balustrade, spreading his wings.

Weeping, Junipa stared up at her. She looked as if she would run forward to hold Vermithrax back any minute now. Merle smiled at her friend and gently shook her head. 'Don't do it,' she whispered.

Eft raised herself, with difficulty, supported by the two boys and ignoring her broken leg. To think that she, who had come into the world without legs at all, should now be unable to do anything because of a broken leg bone was perhaps the worst irony of fate.

The boys too were watching Merle in dismay. Dario was gritting his teeth as if he could crush iron with them. Tiziano blinked, unsuccessfully trying to keep back the single tear running down his cheek.

Lalapeya looked strangely blurred, as if her body were caught in its change between sphinx and human form. She never took her eyes off her daughter, and for the first time Merle truly felt that Lalapeya was not a stranger any more, not just a distant hand in the depths of her water mirror. She was her mother. They had found each other at last.

Vermithrax reached the balustrade. He flexed his wings, making them rise and fall twice in quick succession as if he had to be sure they would obey him.

Even he is just trying to postpone it, thought Merle, moved. Dear Vermithrax.

'*It's time,*' said the Queen, alarm in her voice. '*He's going to destroy my body.*'

Vermithrax's forepaws took off from the floor.

A cry rang out behind him. Someone called Merle's name.

Down below, the Son of the Mother noticed the movement out of the corner of his dark eye. He swung round and saw the obsidian lion on the balustrade. A primeval roar issued from his jaws, shaking the mirror-glass walls and making the water on the floor bubble and foam.

Serafin was running after Vermithrax. Just as the lion was about to soar into the air, Serafin took off too, landed with the palms of both hands flat on Vermithrax's body, somehow got hold of his coat and scrambled up on to the lion's back. All at once he was sitting there behind Merle, swaying. 'I'm coming too! Never mind where – I'm coming too!'

The Son of the Mother roared even louder when Vermithrax dived steeply down towards him, despite the second rider on his back. It was too late to turn back now that the great beast had seen them. They could only get it over and done with as quickly as possible. Somehow or other.

'You're crazy!' Merle shouted back over her shoulder as they dropped through the air.

'Then that makes two of us, right?' shouted Serafin in her ear, although he could hardly make himself heard against the sound of the wind rushing towards them and the roar of the churning water. The world was foundering amidst noise and storms and shimmering silver.

Vermithrax raced down towards the mighty skull of the Son of the Mother. The lion was small as an insect by comparison, yet he was still an impressive sight, bathed in the lava glow of the Stone Light and roaring with determination and furious energy.

High above them the others pressed close to the balustrade, looking down into the abyss. Their faces had taken on the colour of the ice that was thawing into water around them. It made no difference now whether the Son of the Mother saw them or not. Whatever happened, there was nothing they could do to influence the course of events.

The gigantic sphinx took a step back from his mother's statue, turned right round and reached his open jaws towards Vermithrax. His screech made the heart of the Iron Eye shake. The tall mirrored dome trembled to its foundations. The water on the floor foamed and broke wildly. The monster's movements were surprisingly fast, considering his size, and anyone could see that he would be even more dangerous once he had recovered all his old skills. He had lain asleep in the depths of the lagoon for thousands of years; at the height of his powers he would probably have killed Vermithrax with a single blow.

The obsidian lion avoided those multi-jointed fingers and swooped towards one of the walls, coming so close that Merle could see herself and Serafin in its mirrored surface. They grew larger and larger and finally shot past, a spot of bright colour, when Vermithrax swerved just before reaching the wall and flew down again. The sphinx raged and roared. He was trying to snatch them out of the air like an annoying gnat, but he kept grasping nothing. Vermithrax's manoeuvres in flight took Merle and Serafin's breath away, but they kept deceiving the Son of the Mother.

The lower they flew the more dangerous it was. Here the creature was trying to catch them not only with his fingers but with his mighty lion's paws. Once Vermithrax had no choice but to fly between his towering legs. They only just escaped those long claws. The Son of the Mother hit and kicked out at them, jets of water sprayed and spurted round them from his pelt, and the monster's angry cries hurt their ears.

Vermithrax came out and up again on the other side of that great body, close enough to the stone statue of Sekhmet to fly down in its shadow and get behind it with his riders, safe from their enemy's long nails and razor-sharp claws.

'Let me get off,' shouted Merle into Vermithrax's ear. 'I can do it on foot. You distract his attention.'

Vermithrax obeyed, and settled on the floor in the shelter of the statue. Merle slipped off his back into the melted snow and ice, and Serafin jumped down after her. The swirling waters were bitterly cold and reached up to their thighs. For a moment both of them held their breath.

There was no time for any more goodbyes. Great blows were already shaking the mighty statue. The Son of the Mother had finally abandoned all respect for Sekhmet, and was doing his best to push the statue over from its other side. Merle wondered if he guessed what she was going to do.

'*Of course he does,*' said the Flowing Queen. '*He can sense my presence as I can sense his. But he hasn't been back in the world of the living long enough. His feelings confuse him. He can't put them in order yet. All the same, he can feel the danger, and soon he'll be his old self again. Don't let the show he's putting on now deceive you. He's no stupid colossus, far from it. His intelligence is sharp. When he stops acting like an angry newborn baby, he'll be really dangerous.'*

Vermithrax rose in the air with one last sad look at Merle. Then he shot round the flank of the statue and made for the Son of the Mother in a swift zigzag flight, more audacious than ever now, ready to sacrifice himself so that Merle could reach her destination unhindered.

Looking around, she saw the altar and Sekhmet's petrified body about thirty metres away, right beside the statue. They'd be exposed to the attacks of the Son of the Mother there. But if her plan worked out, Vermithrax's own daring attacks would distract him from both Sekhmet and herself.

Serafin was wading through the water beside her as she made her way past the statue's stone paws. 'Please, Merle – let me do it.'

She didn't look at him. 'Do you think I came this far to change my mind now?'

He held her back by her shoulder, and reluctantly she stopped after one last look at Vermithrax, who was cleverly luring the Son of the Mother another way. 'It's not worth it,' he said sadly. 'All this . . . it's not worth dying for.'

'Stop it,' she replied, shaking her head. 'We don't have time for any of that now.'

Serafin looked up at Vermithrax and the colossal sphinx. Merle could see what was going on inside him. His sense of impotence was written all over his face. She knew exactly what that felt like.

'Ask the Queen,' Serafin tried one last time. 'She can't want you to die. Tell her she can have me instead.'

'*It would be possible*,' said the Queen tentatively.

'No!' Merle made a gesture as if to ward off any further contradiction. 'That's enough. Stop it, both of you.'

She tore herself away and turned towards the petrified body of Sekhmet, wading through the water as fast as she could go. Serafin followed her again. Both of them now ignored the fact that the Son of the Mother had only to turn round to see them. They were staking everything on a single throw.

Merle was first to reach the platform, and quickly climbed the few steps up to it. Once again she was amazed by the delicacy of Sekhmet's body: an ordinary lioness, bearing hardly any similarity to the demonic goddess that the sculptor who created the statue had made of her. She wondered who he was: who had been allowed to enter this dome and set eyes on the real Sekhmet? Surely only a small circle of initiates, a few sphinx priests, the mightiest of their magicians.

What must I do? she asked in her mind.

'*Touch her.*' The Queen hesitated again for a moment. '*I will do the rest.*'

Merle closed her eyes and placed the palm of her hand between the stone ears of the lion goddess. At that same moment, however, Serafin took hold of her forearm, and for an instant she thought he was trying to stop her, by force if necessary. But he did not.

Instead he pulled her round, took her in his arms and kissed her.

Merle did not struggle. She had never kissed a boy before, not this way, and when she opened her lips, and the tips of their tongues met, it was like being somewhere else with him, in a place that might be as dangerous as this but was not so final, not so cold. A place where there was hope even for the desperate.

She opened her eyes, saw him looking at her, and returned his gaze, looking deep within him.

And knew the truth.

'No!' She pushed him away, shocked and confused. Unable to believe what had just happened.

Queen? her mind howled. Sekhmet?

There was no answer.

Serafin smiled sadly as he bent his head and took her place on the platform.

'No!' she cried again. 'It can't be true – the two of you – you didn't . . .'

'He is a brave boy,' said the Flowing Queen, in Serafin's voice. Speaking through *his* mouth, *his* lips. 'I will not let you die, Merle. His was a very courageous offer. And in the end the decision was mine to make.'

Serafin placed one hand between the ears of the petrified body.

Merle ran to tear him away, but Serafin only shook his head. 'No,' he whispered.

'But . . . but you . . .' Her words faded. He had kissed her, giving the Flowing Queen the chance to pass into his body. He had really done it.

She felt her knees give way. She sank down on the top step of the altar, only a little way above the water.

'The change has weakened you,' said the Queen and Serafin together. 'You will sleep for a while. Now you must rest.'

She tried to struggle up again and fling herself on Serafin once more, begging him not to do it. But her body would no longer obey her. It was as if when the Queen left it, so did the strength that had kept Merle on her feet for days on end, almost without food or sleep. Now exhaustion swept over her like an insidious illness, leaving her not the ghost of a chance.

Reality slipped away from her, shifted, blurred. Her voice failed, her limbs could no longer support her weight.

She saw Serafin in front of the altar, closing his eyes.

Saw Vermithrax circling like a firefly around the skull of the furious Son of the Mother.

Saw her friends far above behind the balustrade, small as pinheads, a necklace of dark beads.

Serafin too blurred before her eyes. Everything around her was dissolving. And then his face was suddenly near hers, very pale, his eyes closed.

Her spirit cried out in infinite pain and grief, but no sound came through her lips.

A grey shape flashed over them, bounding forward light as a feather, a prowling lioness of grey stone. Water lapped. Ripples broke against her cheek.

Sekhmet, she thought.

Serafin.

It was the end of the world inside her, and perhaps around her too.

The Son of the Mother. Sekhmet, she thought. And again and again, Serafin.

She must sleep. Just sleep. This wasn't her battle any more.

Hands reached out to her, coming up out of the silver mirror that was the surface of the water. Slender, girlish hands, followed by others. Figures in the water everywhere.

Serafin was dead. She knew it, didn't want to believe it, but knew it all the same.

The roars of the Son of the Mother echoed all around them.

'Merle,' whispered Junipa, drawing her through with her into the mirror world.

Darkness. Then silver.

No more roaring.

'Merle.' Junipa was still whispering.

Merle wanted to speak, to ask a question, but her lips only quivered and her voice was a croak.

'Yes,' said Junipa gently. 'It's all over.'

THE SNOW THAWS

They had lifted her up on Vermithrax's back. Someone was sitting behind her, holding her firmly. Serafin? No, not Serafin. It must be Eft. Eft couldn't walk with her broken leg.

Junipa led them through the mirror world. She went first, followed by Vermithrax, who was keeping the two riders on his back in place with his folded wings. His heart was racing, his breath came short with exhaustion. Merle had an idea that he was limping, but she felt too weak herself to be able to say for certain. Wearily, she looked back over her shoulder. Lalapeya in her sphinx shape was following the lion, while Dario, Tiziano and Aristide brought up the rear.

Something was lying across Lalapeya's back, a long bundle. Merle couldn't quite make it out. Everything was blurred, her surroundings felt dream-like. Something she would never have thought possible had happened: she missed that other voice inside her, someone to encourage her or argue with her, someone to talk to her and give her the feeling that her mind was not as feeble now as her body. Someone who asked questions, kept her awake and was constantly challenging her.

Now she had no one but herself.

She didn't even have Serafin.

At that moment she knew what Lalapeya was carrying on her back. It wasn't a bundle.

A body. Serafin's corpse.

She thought of his last kiss.

Only much later did Merle realise that their progress through the silvery labyrinth of the mirror world was a flight. Those who could walk at all walked fast – led by Junipa, who gained strength and determination in this place where she was free of the Stone Light again.

As if in a trance, Merle thought back to the day when she and Junipa had first entered the mirror world. Arcimboldo had opened the gate so that they could catch the phantoms infesting his mirrors. Junipa had not been sure of herself, had felt afraid. There was no trace of that now. She moved through the secret mirror world as if she belonged here, as if she had never known anything else.

Around them a mirror here and there sometimes went out, like a window showing dark at night. The glass of some mirrors cracked, a cold, strong draught blew in, tugging at anyone who hurried past. In some of the corridors a black shadow seemed to be devouring the walls as mirror after mirror darkened. Some of them broke when Vermithrax prowled by, and tiny fragments fell on the companions like splinters of starlight.

The longer they went on their way, however, the fewer mirrors cracked. Their memory of the gaping holes left by extinguished mirrors faded, and soon there was no sign of the devastation they had left behind. Pure silver gleamed all around, flickering in the light of the places and the worlds beyond it. Junipa slowed down, and so did the whole group with her.

Merle tried to sit up straight, but immediately fell forward into Vermithrax's mane again. She felt Eft's hand on her waist behind her, holding her firmly. Merle heard voices: Junipa, Vermithrax, Eft. But she couldn't make out what they were saying. At first they had still sounded alarmed, agitated, almost panic-stricken. Now they were talking more calmly. Then they said less and less, until at last they were all going along in silence.

Merle wanted to look round once more at Lalapeya, at Serafin, but Eft wouldn't let her. Or was it just her own weakness that prevented her?

She felt her mind darkening again, images blurred, the sound of her companions' footsteps was muted, further away. When someone spoke to her she couldn't understand the words.

Was it just as well?

She didn't even know the answer to that.

They buried Serafin in a place that had once been desert.

Now water from the melting snow drenched the great expanses of sand, dunes flowed away like mud, and the tawny yellow, rocky ravines became river beds. How long would it go on? No one knew. It was certain, however, that the desert would change, like the whole country.

Egypt would be fertile, said Lalapeya. For those who had resisted the Pharaoh and survived his reign of terror, this was the chance of a new beginning.

Serafin's grave was on a rocky hilltop where sand and water had merged to make firm if marshy ground. Once the sun shone again and the moisture evaporated, he would be as safe here as if he were cast in a glass mould. The hill overlooked the desert, and had a view for many kilometres in all directions. From this vantage point you could look down on the blue-green ribbon of the Nile, still the source of all life in Egypt, and someone, perhaps Lalapeya, said it was right for Serafin to set out on his last journey from this place.

Merle scarcely listened, although there were many words that day as they said goodbye to Serafin. Everyone who had seen his sacrifice said something. Even Captain Calvino, who had hardly known Serafin, made a short speech. The pirate submarine was moored by the banks of the Nile, safely tied up near a palm grove, or what the frost had left of it.

Merle was the last to go up to the grave, a hollow dug by Vermithrax in the mud with his claws. She crouched down and spent a long time looking at the cloths in which they had wrapped Serafin. Very quietly, still feeling dazed, she said her goodbyes, or at least tried to.

Her true farewell, however, would take months, perhaps years, as she knew.

Soon after that, she followed the others to the boat.

Merle had thought she would not feel the need to come back again later that evening, by herself, after the grave was filled in with sand and earth, but after all she did.

She came on her own. She hadn't even told Junipa what she was going to do, although of course her friend guessed. They probably all knew.

'Hello, Merle,' said Sekhmet, the Flowing Queen, perhaps the last of the ancient gods. She was waiting for Merle beside the grave, a dark four-footed shape, very slender, very graceful. Almost unreal, had it not been for the lion scent of her around the hill. You could pick it up from far away.

'I knew you'd come here,' said Merle. 'Sooner or later.'

The lion goddess nodded her furry head. Merle had difficulty reconciling those brown cat's eyes with the voice she had heard inside her for so long. But in the end she succeeded, and then she thought they suited each other. The same teasing, even quarrelsome expression. But eyes full of friendship and sympathy too.

'There are no happy endings, are there?' asked Merle, downcast.

'No, never. Except in fairy tales, and often not even there. And if there are, they're usually made up.' No doubt about it, this was the Flowing Queen speaking, never mind in what body and under what name.

'What happened?' asked Merle. 'After you were yourself again, I mean.'

'Didn't the others tell you?'

Merle shook her head. 'Junipa took us all through the mirrors to safety. You . . . you and your son were still fighting.'

A breeze blew over the nocturnal desert and into the goddess's fur. In the moonlight, Merle hadn't noticed the difference – everything here was grey, icy grey – but now she saw that Sekhmet's body was not stone any longer. Serafin's life force had made it what it had once been again: an unusually slender, almost delicate lioness of flesh and blood and fur. She didn't look like a goddess. But perhaps that made her all the more divine.

'We fought,' said Sekhmet in a husky voice. She sounded sad, perhaps not just for Serafin's sake. 'We fought for a long, long time. And then I killed him.'

'Is that all?'

'What difference do the details make?'

'He was so big. And you're so small.'

'I ate his heart.'

'Oh,' said Merle. She couldn't think of anything else to say.

'The Son of the Mother,' Sekhmet began, but then she interrupted herself and began again. '*My* son was huge and very strong and perhaps even cunning – but he was never really a god. The sphinxes worshipped him as one, and his magic would have been strong enough to carry their fortress through the mirror world. But he was eaten up by greed and hatred, and a rage whose reason he himself had long ago forgotten.' She sadly shook her leonine head. 'I'm not even sure if he really recognised me. He underestimated me. I opened his flank and ate my way through his entrails. Just as I did before.' Sekhmet sighed, as if she were sorry for what had happened. 'That time I left him his heart. Not again. He is dead, and dead he will remain.'

Merle let a moment pass before she asked, 'And the sphinxes?'

'Those your friend left alive have scattered to the four winds. But there weren't many of them. They saw what I did and they fear me. I don't know what they will do. Hide, presumably. A few will try to reach the Stone Light, their forefather. But they are no danger now, not today.'

'What about the Iron Eye?'

'Destroyed.' Sekhmet saw the surprise on Merle's face and purred gently. 'Not by me. I assume it couldn't stand up to the heat and cold let loose in it.'

'Heat and cold,' repeated Merle, bemused.

'Your two friends did not stand by idle.'

'Winter and Summer?'

Sekhmet growled her agreement. 'They crushed its mirrors between the elements. All that is left is a mountain of silver dust, and the Nile will carry it away to the sea over the years.' She put her head on one side. 'Would you like to see it? I can take you there.'

Merle thought about it for a second or so, and then shook her head. 'I don't want any more to do with the place.'

'What will you do now?'

Merle's eyes went once more to the unassuming grave mound. 'Everyone's talking about the future. Eft wants to stay with the pirates –' she smiled briefly, 'or with their captain, depending on who you believe. That way she can live in the sea even if she isn't a real mermaid any more. And Dario, Aristide and Tiziano . . . well, they want to be pirates too.' Now she genuinely had to laugh. 'Pirates, can you imagine it? They're still children!'

'And so you should be too. A little bit, anyway.'

Merle's eyes met those of the lion goddess, and for a moment she felt in perfect harmony with her, completely understood. Perhaps they were still two parts of one and the same creature in some way; perhaps that would never really be over, whatever happened. 'I haven't been a child any more since . . .' Merle sought for the right words, but then she simply said, 'Since the day I drank you.'

Sekhmet made a lion sound that might be laughter. 'And you really believed I would taste of raspberries!'

'You lied to me.'

'Just telling a story.'

'A *tall* story.'

'A little tall, perhaps.'

Merle went up to Sekhmet and put both arms round her furry lion's neck. She felt the warm, rough, big cat's tongue licking her behind the ear, full of love and affection.

'What will *you* do now?' Merle was trying to keep back the tears, but she choked on them, and they both had to laugh again.

'I shall go north,' said the lioness, 'and then east.'

'You're going to look for Baba Yaga.'

Against Merle's shoulder, Sekhmet nodded. 'I want to find out who she is. What she is. She protected the Tsarist Empire all those years.'

'As you protected Venice.'

'She was more successful than I was. All the same – we might have much in common. And if not . . . well, it's at least something that I can do.' Sekhmet looked into Merle's eyes again. 'But you didn't answer my question. What will you do yourself?'

'Junipa and I are going back to Venice. Eft and Calvino will take us, but we can't stay there long.'

Sekhmet's eyes narrowed to slits. 'Junipa's heart?'

'The Stone Light is too powerful. At least in this world.'

'Then you're going with her? Through the mirrors?'

'Yes, I think so.'

The lion goddess licked her right across the face, and then she touched Merle's hand gently with the rough ball of one paw. 'Goodbye, Merle, and good luck. Wherever you may go.'

'Goodbye. And . . . and I'll miss you. Even if you really annoyed me sometimes.'

The lioness purred quietly into Merle's ear, leaped over Serafin's grave, bowed her head once more to the dead boy beneath the sand, then turned away and disappeared into the night without a sound.

A gust of wind swept her tracks away.

Vermithrax left them next morning.

'I am going to look for my own people, never mind what Seth said.'

It hurt Merle to see him go. This was the third parting within a few hours: first from Serafin, then from the Queen, now from Vermithrax. She didn't want him to leave her. Not Vermithrax too. But at the same time she knew that what she did or wanted made no difference. Weren't they all looking for something new to do, another purpose?

'They're still alive somewhere,' said Vermithrax. 'Flying, talking lions like me. I know they are. And I'll find them.'

'In the south?'

'More likely in the south than anywhere else.'

'Yes, I think so too,' said Lalapeya, who was standing beside her daughter. 'They've probably found shelter there.' Lalapeya wore her human form like a dress, Merle thought. When she saw her mother like that it seemed to her a little like a disguise. She was the most beautiful woman Merle had ever seen, but she was always rather more sphinx than human, even in her woman's body. Merle wasn't sure if anyone but her felt that.

She turned back to Vermithrax. 'Good luck, and I hope we meet again.'

'We will.' He leaned forward and rubbed his gigantic nose against her forehead. For a moment she was dazzled by the bright light shining from him.

Junipa came up to him too and patted his neck. 'Goodbye, Vermithrax.'

'We'll see each other again some day, little Junipa. And look after your heart.'

'I will.'

'And Merle.'

'I'll look after her too.' The two girls exchanged a glance, and smiled. Then they both flung their arms around Vermithrax's neck and didn't let go until he growled, 'Hey there!' and shook himself as if he had fleas in his coat.

He turned, spread the stone plumage of his wings, and rose from the ground. His long tail whipped up sand; the ground had been gradually drying out now that the sun stood in the sky again.

They watched him go until he was only a shining dot in the infinite blue of the heavens, a shooting star in broad daylight.

'Do you think he'll really find them?' asked Junipa quietly.

Merle did not reply, but felt Lalapeya's bandaged hand laid on her shoulder, and then they went back together to the boat, where Eft was waiting for them.

The crew had polished up the submarine until it shone. Golden pipes and door handles sparkled brightly, any glass doors still in the hold had been rehung, and a pirate who was better with paint and a brush than his sword (said Calvino) had set about restoring one of the ruined frescos. He planned to restore all the paintings in the ship one by one. The captain had given him an extra ration of rum, for he claimed to paint better when he was tipsy, which induced the other pirates to volunteer as his assistants. Some of them had set up a workshop, and there was much hammering, polishing and planing of wood all over the ship. Others discovered their culinary gifts and held a magnificent banquet in Merle's honour. She was grateful, and ate with a hearty appetite, but in her thoughts she was still elsewhere, with Serafin, now lying alone on his rocky hilltop and perhaps dreaming of the desert. Or of her.

Eft sat beside Captain Calvino, with Arcimboldo's mirror mask lying on the table in front of her, and sometimes, depending how strongly the gas flames in their copper holders flickered, dancing on the silver of its cheeks, they made it look as if his features were moving and he was talking or smiling.

Now and then Eft leaned forward and seemed to whisper something to him, but perhaps that was an illusion too, and she was really reaching for a dish or pouring wine into her goblet. But then what was it that suddenly made her laugh, even when neither Calvino nor anyone else had said anything? And why wouldn't she let the mask be stored with the other treasures down in the hold?

By the end of the meal she had wrung a promise out of Calvino to have the silver face fixed on the bridge, above the look-out window, where it could keep an eye on everything. That way, Calvino prophesied, it would probably be better informed than he was himself. Eft patted his hand and gave him a sharkish smile.

'All we need is for her to flutter her eyelashes,' Junipa whispered in Merle's ear. Next moment both girls were spluttering with laughter as Eft gave the captain a look of wide-eyed innocence that broke the tough old sea-dog's resistance once and for all.

'I don't think we need to worry about those two any more,' said Merle, while Lalapeya, who was sitting with the girls in her human form, laughed. Even that, like everything she did or said, seemed a little mysterious.

After the banquet Junipa went back into the mirror world through a full-length mirror in their cabin. That was the only way she could keep the Stone Light from gaining in strength and influencing her. She could of course have taken

Merle and herself back to Venice through the mirrors, but they were both making the most of what time they had left to spend with Eft and the others. And there was something that Merle was still bent on doing too.

Somewhere in the Mediterranean, halfway between the continents, Calvino brought the ship up to the surface at her request. Merle and her mother climbed out of the hatch on top of the hull, crossed the tangle of magnificent gold and copper ornamentation to reach the bows, and from there looked out over the endless sea. The surface was moving nearby: fish, perhaps, or mermaids. They had already met several mermaids, for now that the galleys of the Empire were drifting without steersmen on the open sea the mermaids had come out of hiding, and were sinking warships wherever they found them.

Merle unbuttoned the pocket of her dress and took out the water mirror. Tentatively, she touched the surface with her fingertips and spoke the magic word. The pale vapour of the mirror phantom surrounded her skin the next moment.

'I will keep my promise now,' she said.

The milky ripples under her fingers quivered. 'Has the time come?' asked the phantom.

'Yes.'

'The sea, then?'

Merle nodded. 'The biggest mirror in the world.'

Lalapeya placed a bandaged hand softly on her shoulder. 'You must give it to me.'

Merle left her fingers inside the oval frame for a little longer. 'Thank you,' she said after a brief moment of thought. 'You may not know it, but without your help –'

'Yes, yes,' said the phantom. 'As if anyone could have doubted it.'

'You can't wait, can you?'

'I can feel others around. Others like me. The sea is full of them.'

'Really?'

'Yes.' He was sounding more and more excited. 'They're everywhere.'

'One more question.'

'Hm?'

'The world you come from . . . does it have a name?'

He thought for a moment. 'A name? No. Everyone just calls it "the world". Nobody knows there's more than one of them.'

'It's the same here.'

Behind them, Calvino put his head out of the hatch. 'Are you nearly finished?'

'Just a minute,' Merle called back. Turning to the mirror, she said, 'Good luck out there.'

'Same to you.'

She withdrew her fingers, and the phantom began rotating in an agitated spiral, fast as a whirlpool. Lalapeya ceremoniously took the mirror in her bandaged hands and closed her eyes. Raising the oval to her mouth, she breathed on it. Then she murmured a series of words that Merle didn't understand. The sphinx opened her eyes again and flung the mirror out to sea. It flew through the air in a glittering curve. Just before it hit the surface the water spilled out of its frame, an explosion of silvery beads that merged with the waves next moment. The mirror dropped into the sea and sank.

'Has he –'

With a nod, Lalapeya indicated the waves splashing against the hull of the ship. What Merle had thought at first was white sea-spray turned out to be something swift and ghostly, moving in a number of erratic patterns before, in farewell, it formed into a shape like a waving hand and then scurried away faster than lightning, moving in zigzags through the waves, away to freedom.

LA SERENISSIMA

Venice on a bright sunny morning. Venice liberated.

Seagulls called above the wrecks of galleys that lay half submerged off the banks of the lagoon, like the skeletons of strange ocean creatures made of wood and gold and iron. Men of the City Guard were posted on most of them to protect the wrecks from looters. It would be days yet before the work of clearing up the city itself was far enough advanced for people to turn their attention to the valuable shipwrecked vessels in the sea.

Above an islet to the north-east of the lagoon, far from the main island, a dark column stood out against the sky. Black smoke rose from the fires burning there day and night. Ferries carried the fallen mummy warriors over and laid them on pyres, their final resting place. A favouring wind carried the ashes out to sea.

Guards flew on their rounds above the roofs and towers of the city, riding mute stone lions with wings spread wide. The men kept a careful eye on what was happening in the streets, making sure that no mummy remained undiscovered even in the most remote back yards and gardens. From the sky, they called down loud commands to the clearance squads, the repairing teams and the soldiers on the ground. Down there, all distinctions were ignored: all the Venetians, whether uniformed men or labourers, fishermen or merchants, were busy clearing the streets, removing the remains of mummy warriors from buildings and squares and tearing down the occasional barricades, soot-blackened evidence of what little resistance had been offered to the Empire.

The broad mouth of the Canal Grande, Venice's main waterway, was as busy as it used to be only on feast days. Dozens of boats and gondolas raced around on the water like ants at the foot of their anthill, transporting their cargos and passengers this way and that. There were shouts and cries everywhere, and sometimes a voice was even raised in song again at last in the prow of a polished gondola.

Merle, Junipa and Lalapeya stood on the bank near the mouth of the canal, on the harbour wall of the Zattere quay. They were waving to the rowing boat that had brought them ashore. Tiziano and Aristide were at the oars, while Dario and Eft waved with arms outstretched. The sea breeze tore the words from their lips. The submarine was lying far out beyond the ring of wrecked galleys, but none of the three turned away until the little dinghy had entirely vanished from sight. Even then they still stood looking out over the water where their friends had disappeared.

'Will you come a little way with me?' asked Lalapeya at last.

Merle looked at Junipa. 'How are you feeling?'

The pale girl put a hand to the scar on her breast and nodded. 'I don't feel anything at the moment. It's as if the Stone Light has gone away for the time being. Perhaps to recover from the defeat of the sphinxes.'

Lalapeya, whose delicate woman's form was wrapped in a sand-coloured dress from the stores on the pirate vessel, led them down a passageway and on through the tangle of streets and squares. 'The Light will probably lie low for a while. Well, it has all the time in the world.'

They crossed narrow bridges, passed through secluded courtyards, and boarded a ferry going up the Canal Grande. Merle was amazed to see how fast the work of clearing up was getting on. It would take more than a few days to remove the marks of thirty years under siege, but all signs of the Empire's power had already been obliterated. Merle wondered what had happened to the Pharaoh's body. It had probably been thrown on a pyre along with the mummies.

On their way, a young woman water-carrier told them that the City Council had taken up the business of government again. Many of the councillors, including the traitors, had been executed by the Pharaoh, and now their successors were trying to restore the government's credibility. It was said that they had already taken the advice of the Flowing Queen, who had returned to the lagoon when the Empire fell; all the City Council's decisions were apparently hers, they were doing as she wanted in everything and would not for the world anger her. So it was in the interests of the population to obey all the Council's orders and not question the rule of the councillors. The young woman was beaming with confidence. As long as the Flowing Queen watched over Venice, she said, she feared nothing. The Queen and the councillors would make sure everything was put right.

Merle, Junipa and Lalapeya nodded politely, thanked her for her information, and quickly went on their way towards the sphinx's palazzo. None of them had the heart to tell the young woman the truth about the Queen; indeed, what would be the point? No one would have believed them. No one would *want* to believe them.

In the palazzo, they found most of the boys whom Serafin had left behind when he and his small band set off to attack the Pharaoh. When Lalapeya appeared in the doorway they broke into loud rejoicings. There was nothing for it but to let them go on living here – provided they made themselves useful working in this quarter of the city and kept the halls and corridors of the palazzo clean. Merle thought their company would do Lalapeya good; she wouldn't feel so lonely inside those thick old walls.

That evening they ate together in the great hall, and Merle and Junipa realised that it was their last meal in this world for a long time to come. They felt both sad and excited.

It was long after dark when Lalapeya led them to her own apartments through a labyrinth of hanging silk curtains, and showed them a wall with a tall mirror on it. The silvered glass sparkled like the purest crystal. Its frame was a wooden circle carved with all the fabulous beings of the Orient, a dance from the *Thousand and One Nights*.

'Another farewell,' said Lalapeya, as the girls stood before her with their rucksacks full of provisions and bottles of water. 'The last, I hope.'

Merle was going to say something, but her mother gently laid a finger on her lips. 'No,' she whispered, shaking her head. 'You know where you can find me whenever you want. I shall not leave this place. I am the guardian of the lagoon. And if human beings do not need me now, perhaps the mermaids may.'

Merle gave her a long look. 'You built them their graveyard, didn't you?'

The sphinx nodded. 'It lies under this palazzo. Someone must look after it. And perhaps I can teach the boys out there to respect the mermaids, even make friends with them. I think that would be a good start.' She smiled. 'In addition . . . it will soon be summer. Venice is beautiful when the sun shines.'

'Summer!' cried Merle. 'Of course! What's become of her and Winter?'

'What's become of them?' Lalapeya laughed. 'Those two will never change. They'll go on through the world as they have since the beginning of time, undisturbed by the fate of humanity. And now and then they will meet each other and act as if they themselves were human and in love.'

'Aren't they, then?' asked Junipa. 'In love?'

'Perhaps they are. Of necessity or because they have

no other choice. Even they are not entirely free.'

Junipa was still thinking this over, but Lalapeya was already turning to Merle, asking a question that had been on the tip of her tongue for far too long. Merle herself had been waiting for it for days.

'You want to find him, don't you? Steven, I mean. Your father.'

'Yes, perhaps,' said Merle. 'If he's still alive.'

'Oh, that's certain,' said the sphinx with conviction. 'Somewhere beyond the mirrors. You don't inherit your tenacity and stamina only from me, Merle, you get it from your father too. From him in particular.'

'We can look for him anywhere we like,' said Junipa, and her mirror-glass eyes flashed with determination. 'In all the worlds.'

Lalapeya gently stroked Junipa's cheek with the back of her hand. 'Yes, so you can. You'll look after Merle, won't you? She broods too much when she's alone. She gets that from her mother.'

'I won't be alone.' Merle smiled at Junipa. 'Neither of us will be.' And then she hugged and kissed Lalapeya, saying a last goodbye. Junipa touched the surface of the mirror and whispered the Glass Word.

Merle followed her through the silver wall, out into the labyrinth of the mirror world where there was so much to see, to explore, to find. Her father. That other Venice – the one she had seen in the reflections on the canals. And again, who knew, perhaps another Merle, another Junipa.

Another Serafin.

But Lalapeya stood there for a long time after the two had gone and the ripples on the mirror had died down again. Only then did she turn, parting the silk curtains with her bandaged hands, and walked through her house, which was full of life again at last.

From down in the kitchen an aroma of cinnamon and honey drifted up, and through the walls she could hear the sounds of the city, awakening to the future. Mingling with them, too distant to be caught by any human ear, came the soft singing of mermaids somewhere out at sea, far from any island; beyond the mermaids' song she could hear the cry of the sea-witch; the sound of a flower springing up in the desert sand; the wing-beats of a mighty lion prince.

And also, perhaps, very faint and far away, the voices of two girls just stepping into a new, strange world.

EGMONT PRESS: ETHICAL PUBLISHING

Egmont Press is about turning writers into successful authors and children into passionate readers – producing books that enrich and entertain. As a responsible children's publisher, we go even further, considering the world in which our consumers are growing up.

Safety First
Naturally, all of our books meet legal safety requirements. But we go further than this; every book with play value is tested to the highest standards – if it fails, it's back to the drawing-board.

Made Fairly
We are working to ensure that the workers involved in our supply chain – the people that make our books – are treated with fairness and respect.

Responsible Forestry
We are committed to ensuring all our papers come from environmentally and socially responsible forest sources.

For more information, please visit our website at
www.egmont.co.uk/ethicalpublishing